# Also By Cathryn Grant

*Cathryn Grant*

# THE WOMAN IN THE BEDROOM

*An Alexandra Mallory Novel*

**D2C Perspectives**

# 1

*Sydney, Australia*

The first settlement of Anglo Saxons on the continent of Australia consisted of fifteen-hundred convicted murderers, kidnappers, thieves, and their keepers. Twenty percent of these convicts were women. The British prisoners had relative freedom, working to establish a colony rather than being locked in cells, but their confinement was for life because there was no way back home.

The British had arrived in Australia, liked what they saw, and made it their own, as they did with so many other land masses they found appealing and felt entitled to acquire without payment of any kind. They quickly hit upon the idea of shipping some of their law-breaking population down there. Since a trip from England down the Atlantic Ocean, around the tip of Africa, brushing past the Southern Ocean, and across the Indian Ocean to Australia, meant remaining at sea for a brutal eight months, that was considered punishment enough. Convicts were sentenced to live out their lives in a place crawling with horrific spiders — the giant huntsman with a leg span of six inches and several who are capable of inflicting death. These are accompanied by crocodiles, venomous snakes, and jellyfish hovering just off the shore, ready to brush a tentacle against your skin and end your life within hours.

People tend to focus on the charming kangaroos with

adorable Joeys peeking out of their pockets, and koalas with their thick fur and round eyes and chic leathery noses, but a not insignificant number of the creatures living on that isolated continent are out to bite, suck, sting, or gnaw the life out of you.

My own move to Australia was rather sudden. Until Tess offered me a job, I'd never once considered moving out of the state, much less the country, much less to the other side of the world, the southern half of the planet where the seasons are reversed and they celebrate Christmas in ninety-five-degree heat and don't celebrate Thanksgiving or the Fourth of July at all, obviously.

It's an easy place for Americans to feel at home since Australians speak the same language, although in a much lovelier tone, adding cute and sometimes inscrutable slang, starting with their own nickname — Aussie. It's filled with tropical birds and surrounded by turquoise water, deadly hot in some areas and seductively sultry in others.

Part of me was uncomfortable about my sudden decision to uproot myself. It's much easier to fly under the radar in your own country. Customs are familiar, and you know the rules of the game. In America, I could more easily lose myself among three-hundred-twenty-five million people. Among Australia's just under twenty-five million, speaking in the distinctive accent of an outsider, I had the potential to be a lot more noticeable.

And there was that passport thing.

I have two of them, and I'd never used either one. I came by the second one somewhat by accident. I'd always felt secure, knowing I had a way to easily adjust my identity, but now I'd be putting a stake in the ground. For my move to

Australia, I chose the one with my real name — Laura Alexandra Mallory. It was the name I'd used at CoastalCreative, the name Tess knew me by. It was the only choice, really, but the other one nagged at me, making me wonder at what point I might be required to shift my identity. The number of people curious about my life was increasing, and part of what pushed me over the edge to Australia was the need to keep an eye on Tess. If her excessive interest in the circumstances of Steve Montgomery's death continued, my involvement might be exposed.

The criminals who populated Sydney in the early days settled in an area known as The Rocks. Now, The Rocks area is all cute shops and upscale restaurants. A tourist mecca with class, but back then, it was crawling with lawbreakers. I might have fit in better two hundred years ago.

Because of their relative freedom, convicted women and men began appropriating land. Europeans moving into the territory of indigenous people pretty much always took that approach. They built houses, planted gardens, and fenced their yards. They started their own businesses, opened shops and pubs, and raised families. Some of them took in lodgers – the next wave of convicts. Some even had the nerve to make servants out of newly arrived convicts.

Leaving the United States seemed like a good idea, the more I considered it. Regular change is important. And the idea of seeing another country, living outside the U.S., especially in the current environment in which a madman was occupying the White House and directing the national conversation, was very appealing.

Not that I was running away. And not that Australia is safe from madmen with access to nuclear weapons. But this madman, bent on pissing off every democratically elected leader on the planet while cozying up with other madmen, well the farther I could get from him, the more I would retain my equilibrium, and possibly my sanity.

Here was a man treating women like his personal possessions, drooling over their bodies, turning his back on female world leaders, and parading up and down the halls of the White House telling women how to dress. He was giving every cretin in the country the idea that women should shut up and take their place as appendages to the male gender after all. Fifty years of progress, wiped out with a single flourish of the magic pen he used to scribble his name all over oppressive directives.

It was a good thing I was gone. Given how he was offering un-evolved men permission and latitude to turn back the clock, I might end up killing two of every ten males I ran into. Really, wanting to kill a very particular man, but the chances of that opportunity falling into my lap was one in three-hundred-twenty-five million.

Tess had been vague about my job description, vague about my salary, and vague about where the company offices were located, so I couldn't do any work ahead of time to set about finding an apartment. The first week would be spent in a hotel. A nice hotel with a view of Sydney Harbor and the sparkling white Opera House. I love hotel living, especially five-star hotel living, so I couldn't complain. Still, the lack of specific details made me wonder what I'd signed up for.

# 2

Traveling for eight months by sea to reach Australia on a ship eating nothing but cured mutton and porridge, sleeping on narrow bunks or pallets, covered by scratchy blankets, using a bucket for a toilet, the smell of shit and vomit, wind and waves battering you this way and that, with the resulting rebellion in your stomach, is beyond my ability to fully imagine.

To a twenty-first century woman like me, the fifteen hours sitting in a sardine seat in the coach section of an airplane was horrific enough. I'd chosen a window seat for easier sleeping and the chance to catch my first glimpse of Australia from the air. The downside of a window seat is the need to climb over the laps of others every time you have to pee. And it literally is their laps. If the plane hits an air pocket while you're gripping the backs of the seats in the row ahead, squeezing your way past knees that are pressed against those same seat backs, you'll be tossed into an unwelcoming lap.

The bathrooms offer the same claustrophobic atmosphere. You can hardly turn around, and the tiny faucet and petite sink are almost useless. Eight to ten hours into the flight, the bathrooms were even less pleasant.

I could count on two hands the number of times I'd been on an airplane. The squashing in of human bodies, the narrow aisles, the closet-bathrooms were vague memories that didn't seem onerous on a two- or three-hour flight. But for fifteen hours? Delusional visions of pressing down on the handles of those supposedly securely locked side doors became an overwhelming obsession as I waited in line for the bathroom. Your education tells you what will happen if a door is opened at forty thousand feet. But some animalistic fragment deep inside longs to know the reality, if only to breathe in the rush of fresh air, if only to fling your arms out to the sides, to move your legs and feel the blood return to your toes. And those doors don't appear all that secure from the impulse of a deranged person who's lost blood flow to her brain from sitting with her legs immobilized. Hopefully, there's more to those locks than meets the eye.

I watched movies. I tried to sleep. I ate tiny squares of lasagna and rectangles of egg mixed with sausage bits pressed into something that resembled a piece of styrofoam. I nibbled on a hard roll and chomped through bags of peanuts and pretzels. I refused to drink a martini out of a small plastic cup. Instead, I stuck with quite a few miniature bottles of vodka and a steady flow of tonic water.

Mostly, I imagined what life was like in first class with luxurious chairs that didn't force you to sleep sitting up, space for your elbows, and real glasses. Maybe. In this post 9-11 world, maybe even first-class fliers drink out of rough-edged plastic and strain to saw flexible knives through a piece of beef.

When I landed, my feet were numb. It was an hour and twenty minutes before I made my way through baggage claim, immigration check, and customs.

Tess stood at the foot of the ramp that led from customs into the food and shopping area of the terminal. Her face was tan. Her hair was several inches longer and she no longer had thick bangs obscuring her forehead. They were brushed to the left, falling over one eyebrow and the side of her cheek. She wore a black t-shirt and Capri-length jeans and silver-edged flip-flops. The forecast for the day was seventy-five, partly cloudy, with a chance of thunderstorms later. I couldn't wait.

She smiled and gave me a light and very brief hug. I didn't recall her ever hugging me before and it seemed rather out of place now. Something about the whole set-up for my new life was tinged with friendship, and there were certainly those elements between us, but I was here for a job and she was my boss. The hug had come instinctively to her, and I think she realized in that same moment that she was my boss, and despite being glad to see me, glad to see anyone familiar, she immediately regretted it.

She moved away, fumbled with her arms slightly, and then gripped the handle of my largest suitcase, tugging it to her side. "Welcome to Australia."

"Thanks."

We started walking, me with my duffel and purse over one arm, pulling the slightly smaller suitcase with my other hand.

Outside, the air was warm and soft. There was no obvious dampness from the humidity like some people complain about. Instead, it just felt pleasant, like walking around in your own skin. The sky was streaked with soft white clouds.

"Have you heard any more about Steve?" she said. "Did they confirm he died from an OD?"

"Is that how we're going to kick things off? I thought this was all about starting over?"

She stopped near the back of a white sedan, popped

open the trunk, and hoisted my suitcase inside. I added the other luggage and she slammed the trunk closed.

"I'm concerned." She went to the right side of the car.

I started to follow her, then paused for a minute, adjusting to the idea of getting into the passenger seat on the left side of the car.

I hoped by the time we settled and belted ourselves, and she backed out, she would return to welcoming me to Australia or start talking about my new job, or suggest neighborhoods where I might look for an apartment. Anything but Steve.

"I don't want to see him labeled an addict," she said. "It's not the truth."

"People will remember him as he was."

"They'll also remember the way he died. It's not right."

"Why do you care? You're seven thousand miles away. And he's dead."

She pulled onto the expressway and I grabbed the dashboard, disoriented by traffic flying toward us on the wrong side of the road. I felt that every car navigating curves was coming straight for us.

"It's not right. That's all."

"You can't do much about it."

"I can make sure they know he would never use heroin, not willingly. Either someone was trying to rob him and forced him to use it so they could disable him, or some other scenario unfolded that wasn't on the up and up."

"The up and up?" I laughed

"It's not funny."

"I honestly thought this move was all about a fresh start. You wanted him out of your life, you didn't even want to work with him anymore. So why are you so fixated on how he died?"

"I'm not fixated."

I didn't respond. She also remained silent as she navigated traffic in the harbor area of Sydney. As we pulled into the valet parking drive at the Four Seasons, I finally spoke. "Should we get a drink and you can give me all the details on what I'm doing here?"

"A drink sounds like a good idea. But first, you can give me all the details about Steve's death."

I closed my eyes. Clearly she was still the boss, despite the hug.

# 3

Alexandra had more chutzpah than any woman Tess had ever known.

Of course, that was why she was drawn to Alex — her strength, the take-no-shit attitude, the harsh, brutal honesty that sometimes felt like a serrated knife slashed across your throat. Although it was irritating to have her concern over Steve's death characterized as a fixation, she didn't regret for a minute asking Alex to join in the new venture. Alex would be perfect for the job Tess had defined for her. Absolutely perfect. Almost as if Tess had imagined the ideal person and Alex had been created in response.

They settled in at the hotel bar and Alex ordered her predictable vodka martini. Most people would choose a mimosa or Bloody Mary at nine-thirty in the morning, but alcohol was alcohol. There was no sense in pretending to drink something more related to breakfast. Tess ordered a glass of white wine.

"You have to understand where I'm coming from with Steve."

Alex was silent.

"He didn't have a partner or even anyone he was seeing casually. And I believe both his parents are dead…"

"You don't know that."

"I would have known if he was seeing anyone. Besides you, if that's what was going on."

Alex moved the olives around her glass rhythmically. She

hadn't taken a sip, even when they toasted their new lives in Australia.

"Someone has to make sure his reputation is kept intact," Tess said.

"In a few months, people will forget how he died."

"When someone dies, those who are left are responsible."

"They're dead. I really don't think they care."

"It's about human dignity." Tess took a sip of wine. She didn't want to argue about it. If Steve didn't die of an overdose, and she was absolutely sure he had not, then it wasn't right for people to believe he had. The reasons why that was important were obvious and shouldn't have to be explained. "So I haven't received a response from HR at CC. I just want you to tell me everything you heard. Did you go to his memorial?"

Alex shook her head. She picked up the glass and took a sip, sighing with pleasure as the liquid flowed into her mouth.

"You should have."

"Why?"

"For respect."

"I give respect to people who earn it. To people who respect me."

Tess leaned forward. She couldn't see Alex's expression and didn't understand why she wouldn't turn to face her.

"So, the details."

"I told you everything I knew when we video chatted."

"I want to hear it again."

"His housekeeper found him dead. Naked. He'd been dead about seven or eight hours. There was heroin on the dresser. They did an autopsy. They found heroin in his blood. No other drugs. No heart attack or aneurism or stroke. End of story."

"What else?"

"There's nothing else."

"There must be," Tess said.

"Maybe you felt more for him than you've led me to believe." A tiny smile fluttered at the edges of Alex's mouth.

Tess adjusted her position on the stool. She stroked the stem of her glass. "I didn't. I'm trying to find out what happened."

"I know you want some dramatic, interesting story. You don't want to think he was stupid, or that he invited the wrong hooker into his condo. But that's all there is. It's not what you expect from someone who was such a success in business, so you want more. But there isn't any more."

"There has to be more. I want to understand how this happened."

"He snorted heroin. He took too much. He stopped breathing. He died."

"But why?" Tess felt as if her blood vessels were calcifying with the frustration of trying to understand something inexplicable. Steve was a lot of things, but he was not a junkie. And he wasn't stupid. He would not try a drug like heroin, even to experiment. "Someone or some situation forced him to take it."

"No one said anything about force. There weren't any needle marks. He snorted it."

"There are ways to coerce people."

"Steve? I don't think so. When was he ever coerced into anything, even buying a cup of coffee?"

Tess laughed. That was true, but still... "Did they find any evidence of someone else being there? Forcing him?"

"He wasn't forced, Tess. You can't force someone to inhale powder."

"Did they find fingerprints? A hooker who…I don't know, maybe a date rape drug in his drink and then… Someone who wanted to burglarize his condo, but he died, so they left?"

"Even if that happened, you can't force someone to snort. They have to exert themselves. And nothing was stolen."

She felt defeated. There was no explanation and it made no sense. The police should be looking into it. They shouldn't just write it off.

"He was not a junkie."

"No one said he was."

"But it's what everyone will think."

"Why can't you let it go?"

"Is that what you would want if something like that happened to you? Your colleagues and friends just blow it off and say, *well I guess we didn't know her*? Would you want the end of your life to be a lie?"

"I honestly don't think I'll care. If I'm dead."

"*When* you're dead. Not if."

Alex shrugged. She ate two of her olives and took a sip of her drink. Still not looking at Tess, she pushed her glass a few inches across the bar.

"Are we going to talk about the future or the past?"

"The future. But if HR doesn't respond to my email today, I'm calling."

"Good idea. Then you can hear the details from someone else. So, when do I start? I need a few days to look for an apartment. Does the company have a name yet, or are we going with what they put on the application for my work Visa?"

"No name. We'll brainstorm that, soon."

Alex smiled for the first time since they'd taken their seats at the bar. "And looking for an apartment? Where will the offices be located? I don't want a long commute."

"Sean wants our environment, our vibe, to be in the mood and tradition of Silicon Valley."

"Okay. What does that have to do with finding an apartment?"

Tess picked up her glass and swallowed the rest of her wine. She signaled the bartender and ordered another. "It's a little different from the norm, but kind of exciting."

Alex sipped her drink. It was only half empty. She must be feeling the jet lag.

"Should we order an early lunch?" Tess said.

"An appetizer. I don't want to eat too much or I'll fall asleep," Alex said.

Tess pulled the bar menu out of the rack and scanned the offerings. "Maybe two? Calamari and deep-fried olives?"

"Ooh. There's such a thing as deep-fried olives?"

Tess smiled. She signaled the bartender and placed the order. "I know how you can be, so please listen and give this a chance. I think it's a really good idea, and it'll be something that gives us a competitive edge."

"That's quite a warning."

Tess laughed. "It's not a warning."

"It sounded like one to me. And besides, how can I *be*?"

"Instant reaction. Stubborn."

"So what's the big secret?"

Tess picked up her wine and took a sip. The cold, sharp

taste made her heart flutter. She was pretty sure Alex wouldn't be excited about the situation. She might even feel she'd been dragged halfway around the planet without being given the full story.

# 4

The calamari and fried olives were served on square plates, arranged with the precision and soul-soothing artistry of a Zen garden. Tess hated to pick up a single calamari ring, destroying the balance.

Alex immediately plucked an olive off the plate and popped it in her mouth. Her expression said it was steaming hot, but she didn't back away from her decision. She chewed and let her eyes fill with tears. She caught the bartender's attention and ordered another martini and a glass of water. Then she ate another fried olive.

Tess nudged the plates closer to Alex. "Part of why Silicon Valley thrives is the hothouse atmosphere. The VCs are right there in Palo Alto, everyone eats at the same restaurants — seeing and being seen, stimulating speculation and gossip. Companies with open office arrangements focus on high-quality team building activities. They take pride in their Lego play areas, giant Tinker Toys, pool, air hockey...all kinds of playful outlets to keep the brain active. Good work and world-class execution comes from creative play. The brain *needs* to play. I think CC lost that."

"And your long vacation made you realize this?"

"Yes. I really do believe what I told you — that time away, goofing off, makes you more creative. Running a business, marketing and selling a product are creative activities."

Alex ate another olive.

"Sean's been trying to think of how we might mirror

some of those features. He was talking about the folklore of start-ups that were born in garages…"

"Those stories are from decades ago. That doesn't happen any more."

"The guys that founded Facebook all lived together at the beginning. That's not so long ago. Work and life and play all become a single stream, nurturing each other."

Alex took several sips of her second drink.

"I guess you see where I'm going with this, so I'll cut to the chase. You don't need to rent an apartment. We'll all be sharing a house. Sean, Gavin, me, and you."

"What?"

"Work, play, and live in the same place. Creativity will be nurtured if we spend a lot of time together."

"Why do you need an overdose of creativity? Isn't the app already complete?"

"Like I said, in some ways, the idea and the product are the easy parts. Getting the world excited about what we have to offer is another ball game. It requires enormous creative energy."

"And that means living in the same house? It sounds like a sweat shop."

Tess laughed. "Far from it. Wait until you see it."

"Who cleans? Who does the cooking?"

"There's a housekeeper."

"A housekeeper is nice." Alex ate two more fried olives.

"Aren't you going to have any calamari?" Tess said.

"These olives are fantastic."

"The calamari is good too."

"I'm fine with olives."

Tess ate a piece of calamari.

"I don't know if I like the idea of living with my employer. It really does seem like a sweatshop."

"Don't be dramatic. It's not. There will be plenty of time off. The hours won't be much different from CC, maybe some evenings and weekends, but the energy of starting something new makes that all worthwhile."

"And you didn't say who does the cooking."

"I suppose we'll share it."

"Grocery shopping?"

"How can you turn something exciting, an incubator for our new venture, into a list of household chores?"

"It's the chores that cause conflict. Haven't you ever had roommates?"

"I guess it's been a while."

"It's very fresh in my memory," Alex said.

"It will all work out."

"Things like that don't tend to work out unless you set the rules up front."

"We can talk about that."

Alex ate the final olive. "You aren't an olive fan?"

"You ate them too fast for me to get a chance. But it's fine. That flight is hell, you deserve to unwind a bit."

"I'm feeling a little sleepy," Alex said.

"We should get up and move around. You don't want to go to sleep until early evening. Or it will take days to get past the jet lag."

Alex nodded her head slowly.

"Getting drinks wasn't the best idea. I should have thought of that." Tess stabbed a tiny fork in two calamari rings and ate them.

Alex sucked up the rest of the olives in her martini and

pushed the half full glass to the opposite edge of the bar. "Are you going to show me this house?"

"Absolutely. Should we head out?"

Alex slid off the stool. "I'll run to the restroom first. Maybe we can stop for a cappuccino or something to keep me awake."

Tess pulled out her credit card. "I'll meet you in the lobby."

Alex walked quickly and confidently, without any wobbling to suggest she'd consumed her martinis too fast or that she was falling asleep on her feet. Tess handed her credit card to the bartender, an aloof guy who hadn't said more words than absolutely necessary to take their order information. He didn't smile. He returned her card, also without a smile. She signed the receipt and picked up her purse. She went to the lobby. She stood near a table that held several arrangements of lilies and orchids that rose at least a foot past her head, but still dwarfed by the vast lobby space that was open to the third level.

Living in Sean's house was unnerving for her as well, but she couldn't reveal that to Alex. She was the boss, after all. She needed to rally her team of one into an enthusiastic attitude toward Sean's plan. At first, she'd wanted to argue with him, express all the same concerns Alex had regarding privacy and feeling like work would be expected by silent, relentless pressure seven days a week and most evenings.

She did see the upside. Ideas for marketing plans or ad copy didn't always spring up between eight and seven on weekdays. Exciting, stimulating conversations over meals, even going running or playing volleyball in the pool would bring out unexpected ideas. It truly was an excellent plan.

Everything in life had an upside. There were certainly negatives to commuting to the office, having to eat all your meals out when you worked late. This was a more holistic approach to life. And she was excited to try it, thrilled and lured by the idea of something she'd never experienced before. Secretly, hardly able to admit it to herself, she was comforted by the thought of the constant companionship.

# 5

It was my house.

That's how I felt as Tess pulled up to the curb in a suburb a few blocks from Sydney Harbor. The neighborhood was populated with large homes, a blend of ultra modern featuring lots of angles and glass beside stately brick near-mansions. The yards were lush with grass and palm trees and birds of paradise. Thick vines covered fences and garden walls. The eucalyptus trees were filled with birds making deep, wild cries that sounded like something I'd expect to hear in a South American rain forest.

The house she'd parked in front of was one of the modern ones.

It was the house I'd dreamed of for years. The property was surrounded by a wrought iron fence. Flowering vines climbed over one section. Along the fence were Queen palm trees, fronds swaying in the breeze. The yard was a carpet of softly brilliant grass and artfully placed flowering shrubs. Leafy banana trees and huge Bird of Paradise plants hugged the front of the house. The walkway was about fifteen feet wide, formed of textured gray stone. The front door was glass framed in dark wood, and the windows surrounding it reached to the second story. As we headed up the walkway, a curving staircase was visible inside.

The desire and sense of familiarity in my bones ached to tell Tess she could get in her car and drive away because I wanted this place all to myself. I knew nothing about

Australian real estate, but I had to guess the price tag was in the vicinity of five or six million dollars.

The sleek appearance, the privacy, the creamy stucco, the large windows, the deep-throated, human-like calls of the birds, the trees and plants, worked together to create a serene atmosphere. Everything felt as if it had grown inside of my imagination for years and now emerged on the other side of the world, a country that I'd given barely a passing thought to for all those years.

"This is Sean's home, obviously," Tess said. "Because we're part of his company, he sees us as part of his family."

"The idea that a family automatically functions well together is over-sold," I said.

"Don't be a cynic."

"I'm not being anything. It's a fact. Probably a third of the human race would agree with me."

Tess inserted her key in the front door. "I asked him to make sure he and Gavin weren't around, so I could show it to you undisturbed."

"Very thoughtful," I said.

She pushed open the door and we stepped inside.

On the right side of the foyer, the staircase rose to an open landing. In the curve of the staircase was a cut out square in the tile floor, filled with rocks and tropical plants. To the left was a half wing with a billiards room, a workout room, and in front of that, two offices facing the street.

On the right side of the foyer was a glassed in area that formed part of the living room. Inside was a pond surrounded by reeds, papyrus growing in the water. Turtles glided through the still water, disappearing under lily pads and re-emerging moments later.

"There are five bedrooms, not counting those two offices you see here, which I suppose could be used as bedrooms." She walked past the staircase and stopped near the glass wall. There are seven bathrooms, four of those are en-suites."

"Nice."

"Nice? It's stunning." She walked straight ahead to the family room that formed a great room with the kitchen. "Wait until you see this."

I followed, feeling as if I should hold my breath to keep the house from bursting like a bubble, evaporating into a film of soap. My heart was beating faster and my mind had flattened into a sheet of ice across which my thoughts cut like the steel blades of ice skates, carving their way into the surface, straining toward the impossible idea of how I might make this house my own.

She led me through the kitchen and formal dining room which was lined with windows looking out onto a backyard that featured more grass, more palm trees, a badminton court, of all things, and a swimming pool with a hot tub and a waterfall.

The most brilliant part of the whole house was the family room. It was large with a sectional that comfortably sat eight, facing a low gas burning fireplace cut into the wall, a flat screen TV mounted above it. Two sides of the room were wood-framed folding glass doors. They could be turned and slid along the tracks until they were flat against the supporting walls, disappearing from view as the room became one with a covered patio. The patio area was furnished with wood chairs and lounges featuring navy blue cushions, a table and chairs for eight, and an outdoor kitchen complete with gas barbecue, and pizza oven.

Upstairs, she showed me the two unoccupied bedrooms. The unclaimed en-suite was mine. We stepped into the empty room. There was a balcony that looked down onto the black bottom swimming pool. It was not my ideal view.

Having somewhat faced down my aversion to water didn't mean I relished the idea of sleeping right above it. And it wasn't as if addressing my dislike of water had miraculously endowed me with the ability to swim. I hoped I wouldn't be tormented by wild thoughts of the structure collapsing and my chair plunging into water that was made dark by the black plaster.

"You can order whatever furniture you need. If you want to see it in a showroom, I can take you, or you can just shop online."

"It's very nice. Really, very, very nice."

"I thought you'd like it."

She smiled as if the house belonged to her and she was gifting it to me.

"The only thing is, I can't drive here, and we're blocks from the train," I said. "It feels a little confining."

"They have Uber."

"I know."

"You saw the workout room, but I suppose we could join a gym. Although I think Sean really prefers we get the complete experience, by working out here. Play and work."

"I hadn't forgotten," I said.

"We'll have our privacy. Discretionary time."

"Will we?"

"It will be an experience. Don't you agree?"

"It will definitely be an experience."

I couldn't reconcile my love for the house with my

thoughts of the constant presence of my boss and the unknown factor of two men I knew nothing about except what had been filtered through Tess's perception.

# 6

For almost half an hour, we stood in the empty bedroom while Tess talked about furniture. It was the most insignificant issue facing us in this gorgeous home, fraught with the potential for disappointment or disaster, but she was very excited about it. Finally she ran out of things to say about interior design tastes and trends in Australia and led me down the hallway to show me her room.

It was indeed filled with lovely furniture — a king bed with a black lacquered headboard and footboard and a white coverlet. Like the other bedrooms, her room didn't have a dresser. All of her clothes were stored in the well-designed walk-in closet featuring drawers, cabinets, shelves, and full-length and half-sized hanging spaces. She had a desk and a softly upholstered armchair with a pink floral pattern. Her balcony lacked the threat of a swimming pool lurking beneath. It was large enough for two lounge chairs and a small table. It faced the front of the house and was sheltered by palm trees.

Her entire room was significantly larger than mine. The desk had its own alcove which prevented the sage green desk chair from intruding into the room. She also had a love seat and coffee table which held a thick, clear glass vase filled with pink roses.

We went downstairs and she opened a drawer to get out beans for the espresso machine.

I looked out toward the back right corner of the yard

where the badminton net was set up. "Who plays badminton?" I said.

"That was my idea. I loved it in college."

"In the 1940s?"

She laughed.

"So how did Sean get the cash to pay for a house like this? And why does he want a bunch of strangers living with him?"

"He started another company before this one. It was acquired...and, you know how that goes."

I nodded.

She ground the beans and packed them into the portafilter basket, put it into the machine, and started it brewing.

"But why does he want his employees living here?"

"I'm not technically an employee." She studied my face. "It's a great opportunity. Don't get caught up with titles."

"What are the titles?"

"Yours is director of social media." She bit her bottom lip. "Anyway, I explained the hot house concept."

The machine finished and she poured espresso into two small white cups. She carried the cups to the patio table, placed them side by side at one end, and we sat down. Tess blew on the surface of her drink while I simply waited for mine to cool. A difference in our approach to life, I thought. She wanted to make things happen, even if her efforts were futile. Most of the time, I was willing to wait for the right timing, allowing the forces of nature to take their course.

"It's an amazing house, isn't it?" She picked up her cup and held it to her lips, blowing again before she took a tiny sip, then putting her index finger to her mouth as if to heal the enflamed skin.

"Yes."

"You need to approach it with a positive attitude. The idea of living together…"

"With people I've never met."

"They're easy to get to know. Especially Sean. Gavin is quiet, so it will take longer, but he's very easy going." She took another sip of too-hot espresso. "Within a few hours of meeting him, I felt like I'd known Sean for years."

"Clearly, since you changed your country of residence and quit your job based on a few laughs on a boat."

"You'll see."

I doubted that I would, but her growing irritation with my attitude was evident. I needed to back off, make her happy, focus on a bit of bonding. "Are you going to teach me to play badminton?"

"There's not much to teach. You hit the plastic bird over the net with a racket. You keep score."

"What about strategy? Even volleyball has strategy."

"To be honest, I loved just hitting the shuttlecock back and forth with my friends, no score keeping. We had some great times, talking for hours. It puts you into a zone, doing something that only takes a bit of mental effort while you have a long conversation in parallel."

I picked up my cup and took a sip. It had cooled to the perfect temperature. The caffeine rushed into my mouth and found its way quickly to my bloodstream. Already I was more alert, my eyelids lighter than they'd been when we were sitting in the bar.

A man's voice called from the foyer. "Safe to come in? Acclimation process complete?"

Tess laughed.

I forced myself not to roll my eyes. So, the infamous Sean was about to make himself known. Stupidly rich boy who wanted to take control of the lives of the people who worked for him. A master controlling his puppets, using luscious surroundings to numb their desire for independence.

He appeared in the family room area and walked toward the patio.

He was very good looking. Extremely good looking — about six feet tall, lean with broad shoulders and long legs. He was tan. His golden-brown hair was wavy and reached to the top of his shoulders. He wore a dark green t-shirt, cargo shorts, and flip-flops. There was a tattoo of a shark on his foot.

"G'day, Alexandra." He held out his hand.

I shook it without standing.

Before I opened my mouth, he continued. "Welcome to Australia. And to the app that will change the face of human decision making."

I laughed.

He took a step away. His eyes did a quick flick across my face, down my body, pausing at my hips before moving quickly along my legs. "I'm very passionate about this," he said.

"So I've heard."

"And I hope you'll feel that passion. We'll get nowhere without it."

"I'm sure I will." I doubted that very much, in fact I knew I would never be passionate about any app. But I was passionate about his house. I wanted his house the way I want a man's body, a good steak, a nice martini.

He pulled out the chair across from me, putting Tess, seated at the end of the table, between the two of us.

"You have an awesome house," I said.

"Glad you like it. I hope you'll make yourself at home. It truly is your home, I expect everyone to feel that way about it."

His expression was open, his eyes friendly and warm. He had no idea that I absolutely viewed it as my home. Of course there was no simple and obvious way to make the house mine, but it had stirred up all my thoughts around the slower-than-I-wanted progress I'd made toward enlarging my bank account, toward becoming comfortably rich and independent from bosses and the requirement of showing up at an office during certain hours of the day. Of course, I didn't have to show up at an office now. Instead, the office surrounded me. It would hear me breathing in my room, it would watch me while I slept.

Apparently Tess couldn't see it, but we wouldn't so much as take a shower or walk out the front door without knowing who was in charge of our lives. For a woman who valued her privacy and independence, Tess was awfully excited about our chummy living arrangement. She seemed completely oblivious to the controlling aspect, determined to recreate a Silicon Valley of the last century in the Southern Hemisphere.

I finished my espresso in a single swallow. "So it's just us four? Two boys, two girls?"

"Yes. Intimate is best."

"Don't you need a CFO or a finance manager or..."

"That function is outsourced."

"So we're like the Bobbsey twins?"

"What are Bobbsey twins?"

"They were characters in a children's book series written in the early 1900s. The books lived on all the way into the 80s. Two sets of male-female twins."

"I don't see that we're like that. But I don't know anything about them." He folded his arms casually across his ribs and leaned back. "Boys and girls are how the dice landed, it doesn't mean anything." He smiled, not at all bothered by the comparison of his leadership and the company dynamic to characters in a dated children's book.

My body responded to his easy pose, the flex of his biceps, the way his crossed arms emphasized the wide, powerful appearance of his shoulders. Every inch of my skin was sticking its antenna in the air, noticing his eyes, his thick hair. I wondered if he felt the same. The cool exterior of him didn't give off any indication of his thoughts.

Still, he might be my ticket to an even better room than Tess's. Although I'd have to share. The idea required more thought.

# 7

Tess had set her alarm for three-fifteen. She woke feeling refreshed and surprisingly alert. She'd expected to be wakeful during the night, rehearsing her phone call in that drifting way her mind took when she was lying in bed, trying to find sleep, her mind oscillating between crisp thoughts about her to-do list and senseless images and strange meandering trips through the surreal world of her subconscious.

Normally she'd be craving espresso, but her heartbeat and breathing acted as if she'd already had two cups.

She took a quick shower and toweled her hair to soak up most of the water. She ran a thin line of gel onto her index finger, rubbed her fingers together, and stroked it through her bangs to keep them off to the side. She closed the balcony door. It had been cracked open all night. She wasn't sure exactly why, but she didn't want to be overheard by Alex on one of her pre-dawn runs.

Since the day Alex moved into Sean's house, the atmosphere had shifted. The house crackled with energy, as if Alex brought a host of other people with her and they were all pressed for space, jockeying for position. For several days, all of Tess's attention had been sucked into the logistics of Alex settling into her space, trips downtown to buy towels and sheets, a few vases and lamps and prints for the walls, alongside longer expeditions to Domayne, selecting a bed, desk, and armchair. There still hadn't been any discussion over the details of Alex's role, she'd become completely absorbed by her concerns over decorating and the ground rules for living together. Beneath the buzz of activity and concern with rules, Alex didn't seem all that happy to be in Australia.

It wasn't what Tess had expected.

Yes, Alex could be high strung, but she was usually fairly adaptable. She'd seemed excited, anxious even, to make the move to Australia, to change jobs. When they'd spoken on the phone, she hadn't seemed to even care what the job entailed. During their final video chat, Alex had given the impression she couldn't wait to leave the U.S. Tess had the feeling Alex was pleased that this move had come along at the right time, as if she'd been ready for a big change, but wasn't sure which direction to jump. In person, she was ambivalent, at best.

Maybe Alex had realized how close she'd come to the fire with whatever went on between her and Steve. Maybe, in some strange, Alex-way, she was upset about Steve's death. It could be she was running away from the emotions, escaping grief, if you could call it that when it was a colleague. But somehow that word seemed to fit more a family member, a person you'd loved.

With this, what did you call it? Forget Alex, her own feelings weren't what she would consider grief. She wasn't bereft, she didn't feel the vast emptiness that she'd felt when her father died. Grief was intimate and personal, possibly as personal as making love. It was an experience shared by the entire human race, and many parts of the animal kingdom, but each instance was so private no one else could truly understand another's experience.

Was *anyone* grieving for Steve? His parents gone, no

partner, no children. Did he have close friends? Like her, most of his life was spent working — into the office early, catching up on Saturdays, dinners with customers, many Sundays spent on airplanes and checking into hotels. Traveling for business had so many tedious components. It became your entire life, and there was so much to keep you busy when you weren't working. Locating preferred places to eat in new cities, navigating unknown streets, exchanging currency and waiting for elevators from hotel rooms on the sixteenth floor — the floor she always tried to book, no matter what city, what country, what hotel. Lots of relationships with acquaintances and colleagues and business partners, some bordering on friendship, possibly.

Her mind roved as if on the verge of sleep, except she was sitting at her desk, supposedly wide awake. The initial surge of energy was dissipating and she felt her body calling out for caffeine. It would have to wait. Grinding beans risked waking the others, despite the long hallways and well-constructed, sound-deadening walls and the noise reducing floor plan.

She wasn't just calling the HR department, she was calling Cynthia Latimer.

Cynthia was the HR rep who had been assigned to Tess at CC, the one who handled salary and personal issues for the marketing organization. The one who listened to all of Tess's thoughts about job candidates. She helped Tess follow company and state and federal guidelines when she had to discipline an employee, or terminate someone. At the same time, she helped Tess sort out her priorities for herself and for her organization.

There was only one time Cynthia had called it wrong in

the hiring arena. Except for that one instance, Cynthia had always gravitated toward Tess's top one or two candidates before Tess even made her own inclinations known.

But Cynthia hadn't liked Alex. She felt Alex was arrogant. When Tess argued that she liked to hire people with a lot of self-confidence, Cynthia said this was not self-confidence. Tess disagreed. They'd argued for twenty minutes, talking in circles, Cynthia finally saying there was something else, but she couldn't put it into words.

"She wants something, maybe that's the way to put it."

"Everyone wants something," Tess said.

"Not like her. She looks like she could eat you alive. It feels like she *would* eat you alive, if she were given the chance."

Tess laughed. "You make her sound like a mythological creature. She's just a very confident, mildly aggressive woman. I like her."

"You don't hire on *like*. You know that. You remind me all the time."

"I just used that word because it was simplest. It's an instinctive sense that she'll be an asset to me and my team. She'll breathe some new life into my organization. And I feel like I can trust her. I don't know why, but I do."

"All very poor reasons for a hiring decision," Cynthia said. "I *don't* trust her…at all."

Tess became convinced that not only was Alex the woman she wanted to hire, she came to understand that Cynthia was opposed because she was jealous. At well past forty, Cynthia was threatened by Alex's not-too-subtle sexuality. It wasn't flamboyant or offensive. It wasn't that she dressed provocatively, at least not at work. But it was there, like a pan barely simmering on the stove, little movement on the surface of the liquid, but you felt it cooking anyway, despite the almost non-existent physical signs.

# 8

Tess put in her earbuds and plugged them into the phone. She picked up a glass of water off the shelf above her desk. The water had been sitting overnight, but she needed something to help her feel more alert and she didn't want to spend time going downstairs. Even a trip to the tap in her bathroom seemed like a distraction. She took a few sips.

Cynthia was in the office by eight every day of the week. Tess had waited until eight-thirty California time, giving Cynthia a chance to get her coffee, chat with her colleagues, settle down, and skim through email.

At three-twenty-nine, she tapped Cynthia's phone number. Cynthia answered after two rings.

"Hi Cyn. I'm sure it's a shock to hear my voice — it's Tess."

"Tess! Are you still liking Australia?"

"Love it."

"That's great. You're so lucky. I hope I can make a trip there some day. It's on the bucket list."

Tess ran her finger across the keys on her laptop. She tried not to laugh at the bucket list. It was such a trite expression. It turned amazing experiences and destinations into something silly, almost childish. Why did everyone have to use that ridiculous term after that semi-sappy movie came out? The whole concept was about finally living when you were facing death. That was not how she wanted to approach life.

"What can you tell me about your new company?" Cynthia said with a slight cooing tone to her voice. "I'm dying to hear."

"Nothing yet. Actually, I called for a reason."

Cynthia was silent for half a moment. "Yes?"

"I wanted to ask about the investigation into Steve Montgomery's death. I want to talk about CC's role."

"Investigation?"

"Well there was an autopsy, wasn't there?"

"Yes."

"And the police were called to his condo."

"Yes."

"So what is the status?"

"I'm not too involved in the details. But I don't think there is a status. They said it was an accidental overdose."

"Not possible."

"I don't know anything about drugs," Cynthia said.

"Neither do I, but I definitely do know Steve wasn't into that."

"It surprised me, too," Cynthia said.

"Did you say anything?"

"Who would I say anything to?"

Tess swallowed to push back the enormous sigh that rose up, filling her lungs. "The police. Did you tell them he would never…"

"Oh, I didn't talk to the police."

"Who did?"

"I guess Ted. But I didn't hear that directly."

"So no one at CC was interviewed?"

"About what?"

"Am I the only person who thinks something is off when

a man who experimented with drugs maybe once or twice in his entire life, and then swore off weed, suddenly turns up dead from heroin? It's insane. It makes no sense."

"Calm down."

"I'm calm." She took a long, slow breath. "But I'm frustrated he seems to have been memorialized already…or whatever. And there's no discussion."

"About what?"

"That this wasn't accidental."

"You think someone killed him? How would you even do that? Force it up his nose?" Cynthia laughed. "Sorry. That's inappropriate, it just struck me funny."

"I don't know how. All I know is that Steve did *not* do drugs. And Ted knows that. Why are they accepting a lazy, incompetent assumption from the police that he OD'd? I don't believe that and no one who worked with him should believe it."

"I told you it surprised me," Cynthia said.

"Being surprised, and taking action are two very different things."

"What do you expect me to do?"

"At least talk to Ted. Ask him what was said. Ask why there isn't an investigation. Ask every question that's already bothering you, if you stop to think about it."

"Steve was kind of a jerk."

Tess was silent.

"Sorry. I don't know why I said that. But he was, and it was right there, so…"

"That doesn't mean he snorted heroin. And I hope it doesn't mean you think it's no loss that he's gone. It's a huge loss to the company."

"And to you?"

"We worked together a lot, yes."

Cynthia made a sound that Tess couldn't decipher. She decided to let it go. Finding out what had happened was more important than taking offense at an offhanded dig.

"You'll talk to Ted? Find out what the police said?"

"Oh sure, Tess. I can do that. A mid-level HR rep calls the CEO and chats with him any time she feels like it."

"You've communicated directly with him lots of times. If you're bothered, don't call him, send an email and ask for a quick phone call."

"I'll try."

"Thank you."

Cynthia changed the subject to offer a run down on how Tess's former organization was adapting to her absence and the new leadership. From HR's perspective, all was going well. No resignations, no rebellion showing itself in the form of people requesting out of cycle raises.

Tess closed her eyes. It all seemed so long ago. Only two months, and she felt as if her career —the rise to Senior VP at a global software company was nothing but a bullet point buried in a résumé. The faces of her colleagues and the people who reported to her were blurred. A few names sounded foreign when Cynthia spoke them. How long until she could no longer match a name with a job title? These were people she'd relied on every day, people who felt like an integral part of her life, almost like family. But she wasn't grieving.

# 9

*Portland, Oregon*

From as far back as I can remember, it was made clear that all the Mallory children would go to college. The expectation was the same for girls and boys. And all of us would attend Mount Zion Bible college, only two hours from Portland. We would live in the dorms where we would experience supervised independence. We would emerge after four years with the ability to earn a living, and the added glow of contributing to the human race — ideally in a way that brought them to their knees in repentance.

Of course, it was unlikely a girl would need to earn a living. For a girl, the four years were a controlled hunting ground for finding a husband. The boys too, but more critical for a girl. That was made clear.

I did not want to go to a Bible college. I'd had enough of the self-righteous and cliquish kids in the youth group at Pure Truth Tabernacle. Teenagers at our church could be vicious to kids they deemed ungodly. I didn't really care how they labeled me, but the girl who got pregnant when she was sixteen sure cared. That girl might as well have had the scarlet letter tattooed right on her forehead — *F for fornicator*. Or maybe *S for slut*, since no one knew who the guy was and it all came down on her.

It wasn't just the supreme sins of sex and drinking and drugs that resulted in near shunning.

There were so many minor infractions that got you labeled ungodly. The failure to bring a Bible to youth group said you didn't care as much for god's word as you did for your social life. There were sins of gossiping, unless it was deserved because of the gossip victim's sins, as well as bragging, not submitting to the youth leader's authority, and skipping youth group for a school function were a few.

By the end of my freshman year in high school, I knew I wasn't spending four additional years in that environment, looking for a mate. I kept my intentions about Bible college to myself and waited. I was hoping, and I thought the odds were slightly in my favor, that they would rather have my soul rot at a secular college than see it rot out in the wide wicked world, which was my destination if they tried to force me to Bible college.

My father printed off the application for Mt. Zion. He placed it on the kitchen table and handed me a pen. "I'll help you work through this, in case you have questions."

I smiled. "The thing is, I'm going to UCLA."

He laughed.

"I'm serious."

"What on earth for?"

"To explore my options."

"The option is Mt. Zion."

"It's not what I want."

"We're paying for your college education. You, of all people, need to be in a controlled environment until you gain some maturity."

I pushed the papers toward him and placed the pen on top. "I'm not going there. I'll just move out on my own then. I don't have to go to college."

"Yes you do."

"I'm not going there." I smiled and patted his arm.

He yanked his arm away from the table. "This is for your own good."

"What do you think is going to happen at Mt. Zion? I'm going to fall on my knees and see the light?"

He held my gaze. His pupils seemed to jitter slightly and for half a moment, I felt like a veil was pulled back and I could see into the workings of his mind. That was exactly what he thought. He believed he'd failed to raise me to be the woman the Bible told him I should be. Outsiders, more sophisticated preachers and teachers with more highly developed brainwashing skills would have at me now. They would succeed where he had failed.

He probably thought my hunt for a godly boy would succeed as well, and my hormones would transform me into a woman fit for this mythical boy. My father would believe he'd accomplished his goal and been redeemed from wherever he'd gone wrong in trying to mold me.

It weighed on him, I could see that. Not a weight that made him sad or guilty or disappointed, but a weight that he had a job to do and he hadn't done it. There was a constant low-level burning rage inside of him that I'd prevented that. Raising a girl should not have been so much work.

"College is important," he said.

"That's what everyone says."

"Eighteen is too young to be out in the world on your own. Especially…"

"What? For a girl?"

"Well, yes. Maybe you should be talking to your mother about this." He picked up the pen and clicked the cartridge so

*43*

the tip showed. He clicked it back into place. Clicked again. Click. Click. Click. Click. Click. "I'm trying to do what's best for you. There are a lot of very ungodly men in this world. You have no idea. A fair amount of outright evildoers — possessed by Satan. You want to meet a man who will cherish you, and take care of you."

Wrong thing to say, if this was his sales pitch. "I don't need taking care of."

He didn't argue. His thumb twitched. I could see he wanted to ease his tension by clicking the pen, but he thought he could hide the anxiety from me by remaining still, not giving in to his compulsion. He placed the pen on the table and folded his hands. "It's a good school. Eric loved it there. Tom and Jake think it's terrific. Won't it be great to be close to them again? Instead of just during the summer?"

"You're not going to convince me. I want to go to UCLA. I won't fit in at Mt. Zion."

This conversation continued until my mother went to bed, it lasted through a pot of coffee my father made for himself. It didn't wind down until twelve-thirty in the morning. It involved graphic threats of men who cheated on their wives, men who fathered multiple children then walked out, and men who made their wives do despicable things in bed. It involved drugs and forced prostitution. This bit surprised me — that he had the nerve to say it to me. He didn't look me in the eye with those jittering pupils when he mentioned this. He went on to talk about men who beat their wives with fists and belts. All of these men might be lurking in the halls of UCLA. They were definitely living in apartments and working at any job I managed to get without a college degree.

It ended with him telling me to sleep on it. I think he was hoping for nightmares.

# 10

*Sydney*

I'd been living in the palatial yet inexplicably confining house for two days and I still hadn't met Gavin. He spent a lot of time in his bedroom. When I stepped into the backyard to enjoy the tropical evening air, I saw his balcony, devoid of furniture. His shutters were closed tight, not even a slight angle to let in fresh air, or a bit of filtered light. He was a software coding geek, so I understood the need to eliminate screen glare, but as far as I'd seen, the shutters never moved a fraction of an inch. It was a little disturbing.

Sean and Tess acted as if it was perfectly normal that this guy was a recluse in our house of work-play-create togetherness. What was the point if twenty-five-percent of the team wasn't there?

It was just past four o'clock on Thursday. Tess and I were finally going to have a formal meeting to go over my job description. She'd made it clear, almost giddily so, that nothing was set in stone. She'd sketched out rough ideas, but I was welcome to provide input. Lots of input. She was counting on my strong opinions. She craved my suggestions. She wanted to brainstorm about how we would function as a two-person marketing department. I hoped she realized she would have to actually work. No more delegating and spending her days reporting on what other people were doing.

I took a bottle of Pinot Grigio out of the fridge and unscrewed the cap. Most Australian wines came with a metallic, grooved cap that snapped as the seal broke. It was horribly unsexy, but Australian winemakers prided themselves on its superior efficiency. Corks can cause oxidation. They can cause the wine to become tainted. Australia's loss from wine going off was a fraction of what was lost from corked California wines, according to Sean.

Tess wouldn't consider a martini meeting a good idea, but I was sure she'd be happy with a glass of wine. Our meeting would be wrapped up before we'd finished two glasses. And I was showing my team spirit — simultaneous work and play.

I filled each glass about a third of the way, screwed on the cap, and put the bottle back inside the antiseptically clean sub-zero refrigerator. I picked up the glasses and turned.

A guy stood four feet away from me.

"Oh. Hi." I gave him a tiny frown to reprimand him for startling me, and raised one of the glasses slightly.

He didn't say anything.

"Are you by any chance Gavin? Or should I call the police to report an intruder?"

"Gavin." He didn't smile.

"I'm Alexandra. I'd shake your hand, but you can see…" I raised both glasses.

He said nothing. I could not see this guy being a *let's-all-play-badminton* or *lounge-around-the-pool-table-until-two-in-the-morning* kind of guy, but maybe you had to get to know him.

"Well, I'm off to my meeting," I said.

He gave a single nod of his head but didn't move out of my way.

"Did you want a glass? The bottle's in the fridge."

He moved slightly, but not enough to allow me to easily pass by.

"Excuse me. Off to meet with Tess."

"You're not a developer."

He'd finally spoken enough words for me to hear his lovely accent, but the rigid set of his jaw fought against the charm and easy grace of his voice. He had light brown hair, including a small goatee without the accompanying mustache. He was slim and muscular, obvious even with his baggy t-shirt and slightly loose jeans riding low on his hips. He was barefoot. He was kind of hot in a cold, cruel way. It was the kind of personality that made you want to turn a man into an obsessed, attentive lover.

"Very astute observation," I said.

"Seems a bit out of whack. Two marketing people and only two developers. One and a half. But what do I know. Sean knows what's best."

"Let's hope so." I smiled.

He stepped around me. I started toward the family room.

"So what, specifically, is your role?" he said.

I turned. Again, I lifted the glasses. "I'm off to meet with Tess, talk later."

"Tess is talking to Sean."

I took a sip of wine from the glass in my right hand.

"Can't wait to get started?" He smirked.

"With the wine or my meeting?"

He opened the fridge and pulled out a mango smoothie. He broke the seal with a quick flick of his wrist and drank some. "We haven't met. Tess can wait a few minutes."

I smiled. "I don't like to keep someone waiting when we've scheduled an appointment."

"Not ever?"

"Not if I can help it."

He swallowed more mango smoothie, leaving some smeared above his upper lip. He licked it off with slow, careful sweeps of his tongue. "I don't know anything about you."

"Ditto." I took another sip of wine.

"Gavin Dirkson. Born in Werribee, Victoria. Graduated University. MIT — Melbourne Institute of Tech. I write code."

"Alexandra Mallory. Born in Portland, Oregon. Studied at UCLA, didn't graduate…" The next bit of my bio that rose up in my mind was that I kill misogynistic men, if they're extreme cases. It was the desire to shock, to end the conversation dramatically, and to shatter that hard mask across his face.

"You didn't finish University, and you hesitated. Looks like a lie is coming my way."

"Not at all. I was a project manager in my last few jobs, but…"

"I don't think we need a project manager for only three people and one project."

"Four people. I won't be doing that anymore."

"Then what will you be doing?"

I took a sip of wine. My glass would be empty by the time I was sitting across from Tess. "That's why I'm meeting with Tess."

"So we're paying you for no definitive reason? For no apparent job skills, at least nothing relevant to our product?"

I smiled. "I'm late for my meeting."

I turned and walked through the family room and foyer

toward the offices at the front of the house.

Tess was not talking to Sean. She was seated at a small round table in the corner of the office, typing furiously on her laptop. She didn't stop until the wine glasses were in the center of the table and I was settled in the chair facing her.

Her fingers stopped moving, but remained on the keyboard, stroking the keys as if words were still running through her head, itching to come out so badly they made the muscles and tendons in her fingers tremble from the pressure.

"I met Gavin." I picked up my glass and took a sip. In a few minutes, I'd have to return to the kitchen for a refill.

"Oh, good."

"He's different."

"Is he?"

"Kind of socially awkward, or something."

"I haven't noticed that."

"He doesn't seem thrilled to have me in the company."

"I'm sure that's not the case. Don't jump to conclusions based on a five-minute conversation."

I raised my glass toward her and smiled.

She returned my smile, seeming to take it as agreement.

I always jump to conclusions, sometimes based on a one-minute conversation, sometimes based on a smile or a handshake or a look in the eyes the moment contact is made. All of us do — human animals, wary and alert to threats.

# 11

The subject of Gavin faded. Tess sipped her wine and set the glass to the side. She moved a sheet of paper across the table, angling it to face me. "This is the role I envision for you. We're kind of jumping ahead...I need to demo the app for you, but we can go into depth later. You get the basic concept."

"Reading the user's gut instincts." I smiled, thinking of her chastising me for jumping to conclusions. I was very in touch with my gut. You might say my life was driven by my gut. I didn't need an app. But I could definitely see that millions of people did need that very thing. Maybe if they all jumped to conclusions a bit more frequently...

"I don't think traditional marketing, like we did at CC, is what we're after. First of all, because it's consumer instead of B2B."

Her tone was condescending. The earnest, welcoming shape of her lips and her ever so slightly enlarged pupils didn't compensate for that. I already knew this wouldn't be the same as marketing from one business to another. Why was she acting like she knew nothing about my background, as if she had to teach me Marketing 101? I took another sip of wine, keeping it very small so I didn't have to immediately jump up and go back to the kitchen, running the gauntlet of Gavin, if he was still there.

"Social media will be a significant piece of what we do to generate buzz, and that's where I think you'll be fantastic. But

I'll stop talking…read the description." She settled back in her chair and drank some wine, turning to look out the window.

I scanned the introductory paragraph and the list of bullet points. Half my mind was circling around her belief that I would be fantastic at social media. She knew nothing about how I behaved on social media. The first point being that I avoid Facebook like the proverbial plague. I do like Twitter and I've used it on and off, but lately it seemed like the conversational aspect had withered and it was all links to long articles and overpopulated by bots shouting at each other. It defeated the point of having a tool for global *conversation*. But maybe I followed the wrong people — people who wanted to convert others to their political views, or sell something.

Which of course, was exactly what I would be doing.

The challenge was enticing. There's shoving products in people's faces, which the clueless consider sales. And there's the alluring dance of generating desire. That, I would excel at.

"What do you think?" She was still looking out the window.

"It could be interesting."

"That's all you have to say? I thought you'd be excited. Social media is a challenge. And it's something most companies struggle with, so this is a chance to figure out how to do it right. Depending on how long you want to be involved here, it will be a ticket to lots of future opportunities."

"Maybe." Marketing in any form was not my long-term plan, so opportunities weren't that interesting. Still, there was no long-term plan, just the end results, and this would do for now. Who knew where it might lead.

"Do you think it's enough to challenge you?"

Not many work assignments are enough to challenge me, but this could be entertaining. "I think so. The idea of getting anyone to pay attention to you on social media is a challenge." Surely Tess and Sean would have opinions about what I was allowed to do in order to get that attention. But maybe not…

"It's much more creative than the things you did at CC. And I thought you were looking to get out of the analytical, project management side of things. You seemed bored the last few months I was there. To be honest, I thought you'd be more excited about this."

I looked around the room. There was a small desk under the window. There was a boxy coffee and sand colored sofa with a very narrow low table in front of it. The round table where we sat was surrounded by three black chairs. Those chairs were an interesting message to a company of four people.

In Gavin's view, I was the one the newbie company could do without. But perhaps the CEO never sat in meetings and it was only for the other three. Sean's conferences would be held in the swimming pool or around the pizza oven, emphasizing his vision for the path to success. Or maybe the missing chair was because Gavin preferred whatever entertainment he had in his bedroom to other human beings. Or maybe it was just an artistic statement — the unbalanced, yet connected nature of three that offers such a pleasing aesthetic.

"To be successful, we need open communication," Tess said. "You can't sit there with that distant, conniving look on your face and not speak up."

"When have I ever not spoken up?"

"I have no way of knowing."

"I think the job you described sounds interesting, and challenging." I nudged the paper toward the center of the table. "Social media is a wasteland, but people still crave the connection. They crave having the hottest info."

Tess smiled.

"It seems like I have three bosses, though. I'm definitely at the bottom of the heap."

"We're a team."

"Do we all have the same salary?"

"No."

"And since there are no plans to go public, I'll never hit a jackpot. So the salary is everything."

"Yes, although we're working on developing a bonus structure."

"But you and Sean and Gavin share in the profit."

"Not Gavin."

"Really? Why not?"

"He's only interested in creating cool stuff, as he puts it. He didn't want to be a principal."

This didn't fit with his aggressive attitude toward me, challenging whether I had anything worthwhile to contribute. Was he rich on his own and didn't need any more? Then why would he consent to live in a house with strangers? If he could do as he pleased and didn't need the job and Sean's approval? It certainly wasn't loneliness, since he was working overtime to make sure his contact with others was minimal. The rest of us had shared two meals, Sean barbecuing and Tess and I running to the deli for sides. Gavin hadn't shown up and no one commented on his absence. Now, I wished I'd asked, to see how Sean justified it. "Seems hard to believe, but okay." I finished the rest of my wine and scooted my chair away from the table. It moved easily on the sand-colored tile floor.

"I thought we'd start with Instagram, Twitter, and Facebook, obviously," Tess said. "And I want you to feel free to modify the description of your role as we make our way forward. Nothing's set in stone."

It seemed she was taking my silence as agreement. The job would give me something intriguing to focus on, and it wasn't as if I had a job in the U.S., or any cause to turn around and fly back home.

My lot was with her for now. Keeping a watch on her effort to repair Steve's reputation, and figuring out how to get the screaming, deluged world to pay attention to a little app from Australia would keep me entertained. "First, we need a name," I said.

She finished her wine and without talking further, we stood and went to the kitchen. We took the bottle out of the fridge and went to the patio, settling into lounge chairs and waiting, presumably, for the creative juices to stir inside our heads.

# 12

There's an old saying — *A man chases a woman until she catches him.*

It strikes me as very sexist. It implies women are manipulative. Although I'm certainly that, not all women are. I also don't like it because it implies men have deluded themselves into thinking they're in charge. It implies women are running the show, but men don't realize that, which is not the case at all. It suggests that women and men can't have balanced relationships, and the woman needs a man more than he needs her, and the only way to get what she needs is to trick him. It doesn't really say that, but the trickery is between the lines — a woman plotting while the man thinks he's pursuing her, a woman unable to express what she wants and so she relies on tricks.

How curious that women are assumed to use tricks to catch a man and the customers of prostitutes are called tricks. Is there any history to that, or just a coincidence? I really don't know, but it's suspicious.

There is definitely some chasing going on. And I think if half the male population wasn't busy believing women are some sort of secondary, slightly sub-par human beings, designed only for the purpose of pleasing the male, it would be agreed the chasing is equally balanced between women and men.

Deep beneath the layers of consciousness is the need to hunt. The *imperative* to hunt. When the drive to hunt wanes, people lose their edge. They grow bored and lethargic and flaccid.

I love the thrill of the hunt. I don't like to manipulate a man into paying attention to me — because I really don't feel the need to catch one and pin him down. Rather than trick and contrive, I like to entice. Seduce. It's so much more fun.

In my new home, there were two men and two women. Not the Bobbsey Twins at all, but four adults with a rich vein of hormones flowing through our luxuriously seductive home. Something was bound to happen, eventually. Although I couldn't see Tess having sex with either of them even if the hunting desire rose up inside of her. She wouldn't want to compromise her role. After making that mistake with Steve, it was unlikely she'd let her natural desires win out over her career again. On the other hand, with her longer hair, lighter make-up, and usual attire of jeans with bare feet, who knew where her head was at.

It's fun to put on dramatic make-up and blow dry your hair until it's so silky you want to lap it up like a kitten lapping cream from a bowl. I like painting my toenails and fingernails in a color that says I'm ready to have fun — usually red, but purple or blue, or anything tropical. I like shopping for clothes. I like changing clothes. I like figuring out what outfit will make me stand out in a crowd, but in a way that men like, not to impress or intimidate other women. Although that seems to happen occasionally as a by-product.

At some point in my life, I'll no longer be the kind of woman that men and other women look at twice, or three times. I'll no longer be a target in anyone's hunt. Will it be like the flip of a switch? One day I'll feel eyes on me, the next, I'll fade into the scenery, no more noticeable than a parked car you've passed a hundred times.

Looking at the two fine lines extending from Tess's left eye in the pale, light-filled room had made me think of these things. Tess might know the answer to when it ended. Did you see it coming? Did you only notice long after you'd passed that point? I wondered whether I should ask her if she thought of these things.

The hunt starts when you first make eye contact. In that instant, you know whether there's an attraction. You don't have to make a decision. There's no need for a gut-checking app on your phone, no need to think it through. Either the spark is there or it's not. Sometimes, you see it in the other's eyes. Often, you only know it's inside of you and the desire to find out if it's inside the other drives you forward.

When the spark is there, words are spoken with a slightly altered tone. Your body changes — one part thrumming and aware of the proximity of the other person, and the second part softening, almost as if it's drawing the other to you. I suppose for men it would be a hardening, pulling the other to him. I like setting my eye on a man and seeing whether I can get him to respond, watching to see how long it takes.

With these two guys, I was torn. I would end up with one of them, unless Tess and I started leaving the house and I had the chance to meet other people. But as long as we were hostages to playing with our co-workers, the chances for that might be rare. Setting my sights on Gavin offered a much bigger challenge. Just getting him to stop putting off a vibe of wanting me out of the house entirely would be fun. But going after Sean might get me into a palatial bedroom. I still hadn't decided whether sharing would be worth the presumably larger room. I'd need to see how magnificent the master suite was before I decided.

The other problem was that sex with Sean would be more difficult to hide from Tess. And if she found out, she would be pissed. She'd get all maternal, telling me how I *am*, telling me to listen to her, giving advice. Hearing these thoughts inside my own head, I sounded rather childish, but my inner brat and her inner mother seemed to be drawn to each other.

Sean was cool and placid and didn't seem particularly drawn to me. But this knowledge sent adrenaline rushing through my nervous system, thinking through how I might behave differently to entice one or the other, the thrill of not knowing what might happen.

Hunting is in our blood. We're built to be always moving forward, perpetually hungry — hunting for a social structure, better living conditions, a greater sense of security, and most of all, a mate. I didn't want a mate in the traditional sense of someone with whom I shared my entire life. But I did need a man. It had been too long.

# 13

Tess woke to the echoing, haunting cry of two kookaburras. They were drawn to the eucalyptus trees dotting Sean's property and the surrounding homes. They began calling, raucous laughter breaking out frequently, as soon as the sky was light. Magpies joined in, and occasionally the cockatoos and lorikeets, until the yard was swollen with their vocalized passion.

She checked text messages, voicemail, and email. There was nothing from Cynthia. Realistically, it would take Cynthia a few days to connect with Ted, but Tess had half expected an update on the progress — something about sending him email and waiting to hear back, or mentioning that a call was already scheduled, or that he'd asked her to pop by the following day. Anything.

She refused to consider the possibility that Cynthia might push the request out of her head. When Tess messaged her in a few days, Cynthia might announce she'd done nothing. Maybe it was worth checking the status now. She tapped out a message and sent it.

After a quick shower, she put on her one-piece swimsuit and grabbed a large pink and yellow striped towel. She glanced at her phone — no new messages. She crept down the curving staircase to the foyer. The house was silent. There was no odor of coffee or sounds of breakfast cooking.

She dropped her towel on a chair near the deep end and dove into the pool without sticking in her toes to test the temperature. It was always warm enough, bordering on too warm. Sean kept the temperature steady and the black bottom helped it retain heat.

Water flowed over her skin as her body glided almost to the center of the pool, propelled by the angle of her dive. She began swimming the crawl, remembering how they used to call it the Australian crawl. She laughed and choked on a mouthful of water. She stopped and turned onto her back for a moment, staring up at the sky. It was filled with soft white clouds, the space around them a pale gray. As she watched, the growing light transformed the color to a faint, barely perceptible blue.

She turned over and began swimming again, keeping her eyes on the bottom of the pool. The pool was familiar enough now that she knew by instinct when she was close to the end and needed to prepare for a turn.

How had she forgotten the pleasure of swimming? She'd loved it in high school and college, and then let it slip out of her life during graduate school. She could probably count on one hand the number of times she'd been in a swimming pool during the past ten years. Swimming relaxed your mind completely, your thoughts moved at a slower pace, and the exertion was just enough to drain out excess adrenaline without leaving you exhausted. After a swim, she was invigorated. It was partially the effect of the water, but also the movement that didn't require heart-pounding effort.

As she made her turn at the shallow end, a flash of dark blue stabbed at the corner of her vision. She turned her head slightly. Someone else was in the pool. By the time she stopped, she was far enough along that her feet could no longer reach the bottom. She cycled her legs and swept her arms through the water, keeping herself afloat.

Sean stood on the bottom step leading from one corner into the shallow water. "I thought I was an early riser, until you came along."

"Years of habit." She'd woken before dawn because she wanted the pool to herself. Having him here was tipping her morning toward a bad start. She needed time alone to think, to review her day, to simply wake up.

"Mind if I join you?"

She laughed. "It's your pool."

"That's not how I want you to look at things. I've said that heaps of times."

"You have."

"So do you mind if I join you?"

It was a controlling question. Manipulative. She hated being asked that. The requester always knew what he or she was doing, knowing full well they were intruding, thinking their presence was cherished and welcomed and desired. They were so certain, they phrased their pseudo request in the positive. She'd never been asked — *Do you prefer to be alone?* It was so simple to respond to that question with a *yes* It was the rare individual who would say *yes* to minding, in almost any activity. Minding came across as fussy and antisocial. The only time she freely and easily said *no* to that question was when she was sitting in a bar and a man who gave off a disturbing vibe approached. Otherwise...

"Not at all," she said. It really didn't matter. He'd already broken the mood.

He stepped onto the bottom of the pool and launched himself into a rather stiff-limbed breast stroke, straining to keep his neck and head above the surface. The ends of his hair dragged through the water. He tucked his hair behind his ears and almost sank in the process. He swam toward her.

She turned onto her back, floating with her head raised slightly, which forced her hips and legs to angle downward. He clearly wasn't planning on joining her to swim laps. So he wasn't *joining* at all. He was disrupting. If they were going to talk, she preferred to get out of the pool, or at least have an inflated mat so she didn't have to work so hard simply to maintain the ability to breathe.

He stopped a few feet away from her. "How are things going?"

"Fine. I'm getting a sense of what needs to be done, and what our first steps should be."

"Good. Good. No issues?"

"No."

"And your team member?"

"She's excited about the role I outlined for her."

"Good. Good."

Tess sighed. Clearly he wanted something. Why didn't he get to the point before her ears filled with water and his voice became a clogged, echoing sound that she couldn't quite pick up on?

"I'm not sure about her," he said.

"Not sure about what?"

"She's…it seems as though she's after something."

"Everyone's after something."

"I get the sense she has an agenda."

"For what?" She made a sculling motion with her hands near her hips, trying to lift her lower body closer to the surface. "Why don't we get out. It's hard to carry on a conversation like this."

"I didn't want to interrupt your swimming."

She turned over slowly and swam in a modified breaststroke toward the steps. He didn't seem aware of the contradiction in what he wanted and what he'd done. She reached the steps and straightened. She stepped up out of the pool and walked around toward the chair holding her towel.

Sean hadn't moved. He floated on his back, eyes closed.

Tess glanced up at the balcony outside of Alex's room. It wasn't a good idea to talk in the pool anyway. The water created a megaphone effect. Even without the water, if Alex's doors were open, there was a chance she'd overhear. Not that Tess planned to say anything she wouldn't say to Alex's face. But it was still upsetting and insulting when you became aware of people talking about you.

She toweled herself dry, bending forward and flipping her hair over her head to pat and rub the soaked strands. She wrapped the towel around her waist and returned to the shallow side of the pool.

"Did you want to talk?" She glanced again, unwillingly, at Alex's balcony. It was impossible to tell from this angle if Alex was outside, standing back from the railing. If she was, Tess imagined her looking down, a tiny smile on her lips, her eyes wide and staring. She did always seem to have an agenda, but that wasn't a flaw. Perhaps her wants were more pronounced, but everyone went into every situation with some sort of wanting inside of them — wanting information, wanting answers, wanting attention, wanting money, wanting sex, wanting admiration…

"It's not important." He didn't open his eyes.

"You said…"

He waved his hand at her, then immediately lowered it to

the water to paddle himself into a more comfortable position.

She folded her arms across her ribs.

He'd interrupted her lovely swim, he'd complained about Alex, and now he wasn't going to tell her what the problem was. Maybe he couldn't articulate his thoughts, but still, it was something for him to bring it up, and now she was uncomfortable that he didn't trust her judgement.

There was a thing now, hanging in the air. It cast a sickly glow over the environment — the pool, the house, their shared meals and games.

# 14

Splashing water woke me. I slipped out of bed and walked to the doors. I tilted the shutters. The shallow end of the pool was visible, but not the deep water that was closer to the edge of my balcony. I couldn't see anyone. I stood there for a minute or two, listening to periodic splashes, the slap against the tile trim, followed by silence. And then another splash, a slap.

I moved away, adjusted the shutters until they were parallel with the floor, letting in more of the quickly spreading light. I dressed in running shorts and a sports bra. I put a tank top over it to keep the chill off at the start. It was already late May — the middle of autumn across the Southern Hemisphere. But without the polar air that sweeps over the Northern Hemisphere, and with the Southern Ocean mitigating cold air from Antarctica, Australia's weather is mild in the winter. Most days so far, once the sun came up, were almost summery.

Carrying my running shoes in my left hand, I walked slowly down the curving staircase. The kitchen was thankfully empty. I drank some water and put the glass in the dishwasher. Sean was very tidy. He hadn't demanded tidiness, but with the total absence of clutter, it was difficult to leave even a knife lying on the counter, marring a perfect surface. I didn't mind, I like tidiness.

I went out to the front patio, put on my shoes, and stretched. I opened the running app that would track my route in case I lost my way. This was only the second time I'd been out of the house alone, and the strangeness of that experience truly did make me feel like I was some sort of willing prisoner. It was a completely oxymoronic sentiment, but I couldn't shake the sensation.

Within half a mile, I had my tank top off, the bottom edge tucked into the back of my shorts. I wished I'd sucked it up and tolerated the initial chill. Running with a shirt flapping at the backs of your thighs dampens the freedom that comes with running.

After another half mile, I stopped. I took off the shirt and tucked it under a pink flowering shrub near the sidewalk. The house was brick, three stories, with large curtained windows. The lawn was perfectly mown and there wasn't a stray palm frond or dried leaf anywhere. It looked slightly uninhabited with all the curtains closed, so I figured my t-shirt was safe. If someone stole a mildly sweaty tank top, they needed it more than I did. To be sure I didn't forget, I took my phone out of its holder and snapped a picture of the shrub, the stately house in the background.

I started running fast, but found myself slowing against my will, caught up in admiring the huge homes fanned out around me. The older ones were mostly brick, a few with wood siding that gave them a look like plantation houses in the Southeastern U.S. The style of the newer homes resembled Sean's. They were all sharp lines, rectangular entries, lots of glass and tile with flat roofs.

Everything looked so clean. This was partially caused by the lush plants, but it seemed as if the soft quality of the air contributed to it as well. It might also have been the lack of cars parked along the street and in driveways, as well as the obvious touches of professional gardeners, and the rich flow of money that means a house never suffers from fading paint or tired shingles, chipped tiles or dirty windows.

The running wasn't squashing my thoughts as much as I'd hoped. I paused and pulled up a Chopin playlist, increased the volume, and started again. So far, I'd passed two other runners, both male, and a couple pushing an elaborate baby stroller that looked like something equipped for a moon landing.

I ran for three and a half miles more, my mind finally easing into a blank slate, nothing pressing on the flesh of my brain except the ping and crash of piano keys.

I stopped and looked at my digital map, studying the path I'd taken, and figured out my way back. I pushed myself to a full sprint for a quarter mile, then resumed my normal pace. When I passed the brick house where I'd left my shirt, the drapes were still closed and my shirt was folded in a trim little rectangle as I'd left it.

At the end of Sean's street, I slowed to a walk. No one was outside, but after seeing Sean's elaborate backyard paradise, I understood why. According to Tess, living space that flows unbroken into an outdoor patio which is furnished like an interior room is a common architectural design in Australia. There was no reason to hang out anywhere else.

As if to prove me wrong, three girls rounded the corner on bicycles, flying past me, helmet-less, hair streaming behind them.

The house immediately before Sean's was also a modern design. It looked like it had been built more recently than Sean's — everything sparkling new. The landscaping appeared recent, not quite filled out the way it was at the other nearby

homes. The structure was stucco, painted the palest green.
Two parallel rows of palm trees led up to the entryway. The
front patio was flush with the lawn. It ran the entire length of
the house, furnished with an entire suite of furniture.

As I stood gawking, and there was no other word for it,
the front door opened and a man stepped onto the tiled
patio. He was older — fifty, or so — but in good shape. As if
shape is something that applies to a human being. It seems
more like the description of a blanket or a house or some
other inanimate object that you wish to preserve, or re-sell.
Good shape. She's in good shape — for her age. He's in very
good shape for an old guy. As if human beings that stay in
good shape are also adequate for resale.

This guy wore jeans, flip-flops, and a white collared shirt
that hung outside of his jeans.

He hurried down the walkway and stopped. "Are you
looking for someone?"

His eyes were blue. An almost turquoise blue, startling in
their brightness, forcing you to look directly into them instead
of letting your glance graze across the rest of his face.

"I was admiring your house."

"You're American," he said.

"So are you," I said.

He smiled without showing his teeth.

"I'm staying next door. Sean Farmer's," I said.

"Yup."

"I just moved in a few days ago."

"Why are you staying there? Holiday?"

"An extended visit."

"How extended?"

I smiled. "Not sure yet."

"He seems to have several house guests."

"There are three of us."

He nodded. His eyelids closed slightly, showing only a gash of that bright blue. "You're a runner?"

I nodded.

"So am I."

"It's a nice place to run. Wide sidewalks. Quiet. No traffic."

"Indeed," he said.

"Well, I should get back. I'm hungry. Need some water."

"What's going on over there?"

"What do you mean?"

"Two good looking gals, two healthy males."

He smiled, his implication clear. I wasn't sure if I should mention our startup company. Did Australia have zoning laws that prevented such things? "Don't read into it," I said.

"I'm John North, by the way. Maybe I'll see you. Running."

Not if I could help it. I returned his moderate, lips-sealed smile. I'd have to start setting an alarm, make sure I got started with my run before the sun came up.

Before I turned toward Sean's house, John winked.

# 15

I stepped into Sean's foyer. The house was as silent as when I'd left. I slipped off my shoes and went into the kitchen. There wasn't a plate or coffee cup in sight. The family room and patio were deserted. I walked into the billiards room and looked out at the pool. The water was still. No towels suggested someone had just finished swimming. The pavement was nearly dry.

I took off my socks to climb the polished wood stairs. At the landing, I looked down both sections of the L-shaped hallway. All the doors were closed.

Then, the door opening with a flourish, Tess stepped out of her room. She wore a red sheath dress and red sandals.

"Are you going somewhere?" I said.

"No. I felt like getting dressed up."

"I think it's supposed to rain."

"As I said, not going anywhere, so this is fine."

Her hair was damp and uncombed.

"I was going to make breakfast," she said. "Are you hungry?"

"Where's our house master and the independently wealthy recluse?"

"Don't."

I grinned. "What are you making? I just need to jump in the shower."

"English muffins and bacon."

For half a second, I was excited about biting into crisp,

thick bacon. Then I remembered. Australian bacon was essentially Canadian bacon, more like a slice of ham. It was tasty, but I love my American bacon. I missed it before I'd even taken a bite.

"And a smoothie sounds good," Tess said. "For the healthy part."

"So just us?"

"Yes. Sean and Gavin left about twenty minutes ago."

I went into my room and closed the door. I folded back the shutters and looked out on the swimming pool. I really did not like that thing smack in the center of my view. Never wanting to admit my aversion or that I'd be helpless in a pool of water, left me with no options for fixing the situation.

Downstairs, Tess had the bacon sitting in the warming drawer beneath the oven. Four English muffin halves stood in the toaster, ready to descend. She was dropping strawberries into the blender, which was partially filled with yogurt, orange juice, and banana chunks. "Can you make coffee?" She put the lid on and flipped the switch. The blender roared, preventing me from asking whether she wanted straight espresso or a latte.

When the blender stopped, Tess said, "I'll have a double espresso."

We sat in the dining room, Tess at the head of the table and me at her left. The English muffins, buttered and spread with raspberry jam were divine. Neither one of us spoke as we chewed our way through the comforting food, with a sweet, creamy chaser of fruit and yogurt.

"I'm still a little disoriented," I said.

"You should be over jet lag by now."

"It's not that. The layout of the house is difficult to get

used to."

"Why?"

I laughed. "It's a little strange that I haven't seen all the bedrooms."

"They're private."

"I know. I don't want to go inside, but just a peek, to get a sense of how the whole thing fits together."

"There's absolutely no reason why you need to see their rooms in order to find your way around the house." She slurped her espresso quite loudly, as if to emphasize her point.

"Have you seen them?"

"No. And I can make my way around perfectly well."

"Doesn't it feel strange when you're outside, looking up at the second floor, and you can't quite get your bearings?"

"That never happens to me."

"You never look up?"

"Why would I?"

"I'm always curious about my surroundings."

She scowled.

Suddenly, I realized why we'd been snappish with each other. We were together twenty-four-seven. It was easily forgotten that she was my boss — between living in her condo, seeing her ex naked, sleeping down the hall from her now. Our lives had grown together like two plants that started out spaced quite nicely, but no one anticipated where the branches might extend, or in what direction the roots might travel, and now, we were tangled up as if we were a single entity. When I paused to think about it, we didn't know each other all that well. She was a friend and a stranger at the same time. "I don't want to snoop in their rooms. But since they're out…I just wanted to see the size and shape, so that I don't feel out of whack when I see the house."

"You're weird."

"I don't think I am. I think it's weird to live in a house where you haven't seen parts of it. And I think it's weird to see the outer shape of the place and not be able to piece it together inside. It makes everything seem disconnected, like there are gaps in the building."

"That's your imagination."

"No, it's not."

"I'm not showing you their rooms."

"It's not as if I need a guide."

"I think Gavin keeps his door locked."

I laughed. "Now how would you know that?"

She took another sip of espresso. "I saw him lock it."

"I'm not sure why I even asked. It's not like I need your permission."

"You're not going snooping in Sean's room."

I pushed out my chair and stood. I walked through the family room, into the entryway. I climbed the stairs two at a time. Tess was calling after me, but she'd been holding her cup when I stood, so I imagine it took her a moment to settle it on the saucer, push away from the table, and hurry up the stairs after me. I was halfway down the hallway before she caught up with me. She took my wrist in her hand, loosely, but not loose enough for me to break free easily.

"Don't do this. It's not right."

"Assigning me a room and then not even allowing me to see the house isn't right. I thought we were supposed to treat it as our home? I thought we were all a team? Playing together, sharing our lives?"

"We don't know each other well enough yet. Give it some time. You don't need to see his room right this minute."

The thing was, I did. And the more she threw out reasons why I shouldn't, telling me my confused, gap-riddled sense of the house was in my imagination, the more I wanted to see the other rooms. It's an unsettling feeling to live in a place that's half closed off. I suppose half-closed is an exaggeration, but it was a good portion of the second floor. It truly did give the house an unbalanced atmosphere. And it reeked of classism, or something. Entitlement, maybe. It was his house and I was invited to live there rent-free, and grocery-free. But at the same time, it sent a message that I wasn't an equal.

What the hell did they have in those rooms that was so damn private? Posters of nude women? Devil worship icons? Evidence of an interest in S&M? All crazy thoughts, but if not something like that, then why the crazy behavior?

I wanted to see those bedrooms but I regretted mentioning it to Tess. Of course I could peek all on my own. Maybe I'd thought she had already seen them and was holding out. Or that she hadn't and was equally curious so she'd be up for a little bit of girl-bonding or something silly like that.

I would absolutely find a way to see those rooms.

# 16

Tess tracked my movements for the rest of the day, making it impossible to sneak off for a look at Sean's bedroom. Based on what I estimated from the size of his balcony, his suite was massive. Part of the sleek design of the modern homes in the area, including Sean's, was the balconies were more like open rooms. There wasn't a deck jutting out, but rather openings adjacent to the rooms, a continuation of the interior space, which made them mostly dry and usable during a warm rainstorm.

Sean and Gavin returned home together. It turned out they'd been playing basketball. It was surprising they didn't have one of those portable hoops in the side yard, there was more than enough room. Going off on a boy-bonding trip seemed counter to Sean's desire for the hothouse environment of *work-play-eat-talk-blow-your-mind-create*, but I kept my opinion to myself.

I was sitting on the patio, the doors open to the house. The weather was warm. There were thick gray clouds overhead, shoved up against each other without a speck of blue peeking through. The forecast predicted an eighty percent chance of rain, but so far, nothing. I scrolled through Twitter, letting my mind drift over the question of how this newbie company could find a footing there. I looked at ways to promote products that were fun and enticing. Tess kept mentioning that I hadn't experienced what the app had to offer, telling me I needed to try it out, but she kept not doing it, bringing it up during meals, then seeming to forget all about it. It almost seemed as if she was avoiding it.

The two men emerged together through the billiards room door, raced to the edge of the pool, and threw themselves into the water — Gavin dove, Sean jumped. My first thought was that I now had a perfect opportunity to check out Sean's room, both rooms, actually. I couldn't believe Gavin locked it every single time he left, even for a quick swim or a cup of espresso.

I scooted forward on the lounge chair and put my feet on the tile floor. I glanced at the kitchen, hoping to see Tess moving around, getting snacks or doing something that suggested she was coming outside, leaving me a clear path to the second floor. The room was dark, all I saw was my own reflection on the glass.

I settled back and picked up my tablet.

"Come on in." Sean's voice was too loud, commanding. There was a tinge of annoyance in his tone.

"No thank you."

"We can play volleyball."

I decided to cut to the chase. Being coy would open the door for a repeat of this scenario on a regular basis. "I'm not a swimmer."

He moved to the edge of the pool. He crossed his arms and rested them on the edge. "What does that mean? Not being a swimmer? Do you mean you don't know how to swim?"

"That's right."

"I'll teach you."

"No thanks."

Gavin climbed out of the pool and grabbed a towel. He

went to one of the chairs near the waterfall and settled down, as if he was ready to watch a show play out between Sean and me.

Wet and wearing nothing but board shorts, he looked thinner than he had fully clothed. The curve of his body in the chair formed a concave arc from his shoulders to his waist, shoulders thrust forward. He picked up dark glasses off the table beside his chair and shoved them onto his face with force that would have given him a painful jab in the eye if he'd miscalculated the angle.

I returned my attention to Twitter. It was early evening in America and since my older accounts all followed Americans, my feed was a steady stream of political complaints — people screaming that the other side was ignorant, others screaming back about who was really ignorant. I wondered how many were real people and how many were robotic trolls. They say fifteen percent of the people on Twitter are bots.

"Alexandra!"

I looked toward the pool.

"I'm a really good teacher," Sean said. "I'm happy to teach you. No one should live in Australia and not be adept in the water."

"Why is that? From what I've been told, your water is filled with creatures that want to kill me."

"Not true. Not true at all. Let me teach you."

"I'm not interested."

He heaved himself up onto the edge of the pool, swung his legs out of the water, and stood. He walked toward me, water streaming from his hair and dripping off his fingers. He wore a speedo style swimsuit. Lots of European and Australian men do, but to my American eyes, it was intriguing and seemed a little show-offy. The outline of everything inside the thin strip of fabric was quite distinct. When he stood by the lounge chair, his balls were in my face. I didn't turn away.

After watching me stare at his crotch for several seconds, he stepped back and turned slightly. "Why don't you like to swim?"

"Not everyone does."

"Really?"

"Yes."

"Are you afraid of drowning?"

"No."

"It's better to learn. Knowing how gets rid of the fear. It's ignorance and lack of ability that makes water seem scary."

"I'm not afraid."

"Perhaps you should be."

"Thanks for your concern. My life is fine without water sports, and I can't imagine why I would ever be around enough water to be in danger."

He pulled a chair closer to mine, the heavy wood legs scraping at the tile, causing gooseflesh to erupt along my legs and arms. He sat down. "Did Tess explain my vision?"

"For what? Teaching swimming lessons?"

He smiled. "My vision for our team developing creative synergy, making this app, and the demand for it, world-class by sharing our lives. Playing together, not hiding out in our separate rooms."

"You might mention that to Gavin."

He looked blank, as if he truly didn't understand what I was talking about. "How can that happen if we're splashing about in the pool and you're sitting over here?"

"We can play badminton. Or basketball."

He leaned forward and stabbed his elbows against his knees, propping his chin in his left palm. "Tess is quite smitten with you."

I smiled.

"You know that?"

"Yes." I wouldn't have used that word, but I knew she was drawn to me. She depended on me, almost as if I filled some missing part of her.

"She said you were a team player."

I couldn't imagine Tess saying that. I wondered if she really had. When it's beneficial, I can be a team player, but I didn't think Tess viewed me that way at all. I thought she viewed me as stubborn and uncooperative, and those were the things she valued about me, in the right context. Otherwise, it annoyed her.

He straightened. "I'm not going to pressure you to swim. But if you're truly that afraid, I've found it's better to face up to your fears."

"I'm not afraid." I removed my sunglasses and smiled. I widened my eyes at him, holding onto his gaze until his eyelids began to flutter with a desire to escape.

# 17

We ate tuna salad sandwiches for lunch, sitting around on the patio, everyone tapping their phones between bites. Gavin seemed to be playing a game, judging by the rapid stabs at his screen and the set of his shoulders, tense and ready for action. His sandwich sat half eaten on his plate. Several flies had begun circling. One landed and was marching boldly across the bread. Gavin ignored them, the game more urgent than any concern about fly shit going into his body when he finally broke from his trance and finished the sandwich.

Sean talked about the company name. Mostly he talked about how he was counting on Tess's years of marketing experience, her inherent genius, and her astute insight that would allow her to come up with the perfect name. A name that would be descriptive of what the product did for you, but also enticing and pithy and easy to remember.

He had a lot of ideas for someone who wasn't required to actually come up with this all-around brilliant description and embodiment of the app's function.

He went on to explain what he meant by the name capturing the functionality. "The name has to express the customer benefit. The *why do I want this*. The *why do I NEED this*."

"I get it," Tess said.

"I suppose in corporate marketing, it wasn't as challenging. Business buyers don't care much about the kind of feeling a product name elicits."

"You'd be surprised," she said. She stood and picked up her plate, she gathered Sean's and mine and stacked them. She was still wearing the red sheath, but her feet were bare, her toenails painted an identical red.

"I think we need the name this week," he said. "Not having it is holding us up."

"I know. But we don't want to rush," she said.

"Of course not."

"It's important to get it right," she said.

"How about *Self Knowledge*," Gavin said.

He didn't look up from his game. It hadn't been clear he was listening to the discussion. Maybe the guy wasn't a sullen recluse, maybe he was quite sharp. I suppose he had to be if he could write software code, coming up with something useful and functioning that a regular person could use and interact with.

"That's not a name," Sean said.

"Yes, it is."

"It's not what we're going for."

Gavin didn't respond. His thumbs tapped across the screen of his phone and he seemed to slip out of the space, disappearing into another world, not caring that his idea was rejected.

It was a ridiculous name.

Sean stood. "Well, I have confidence, Tess. But Friday. I think next Friday should be the deadline."

"No problem." She walked through the family room area to the kitchen and opened the dishwasher. She slid the plates into the rack and closed the door. She ran water onto a sponge and wiped the counters, the faucet, and the inside of the sink. She wrung it out and ran it lightly over the handles of the dishwasher and refrigerator. She rinsed and wrung it again and left it in the receptacle on the lip of the sink.

While I became engrossed in reading an article about female billionaires, Sean and Gavin went into the house. I didn't even notice they were gone until I finished the article and closed the cover on my tablet. I wanted a cigarette. I scooted out of the chair, but before I could stand up, Tess reappeared holding two badminton rackets.

"Let's play a bit," she said.

"I was…"

"We need a name. It's a good way to get your brain into a rhythm, stir up our creativity."

"Don't we need a white board? Or at least a piece of paper?"

"We'll know it when it hits us."

"How will we remember the ideas? Besides, sometimes seeing the words on a board helps you put different concepts together."

"This is better." She stepped around me and went to the grassy area where the net was set up. She pulled a shuttlecock out of the pocket of her dress.

"You're going to play in that?"

"It's not a strenuous game. And we're not playing a competition, just batting it back and forth. You'll see, it's quite Zen-like."

I put my tablet on the lounge chair and walked to the lawn. I kicked off my flip-flops and pushed my hair back, lifting my face to the sky. The clouds were still full and gray, like sodden sponges ready to start dripping water at any minute. "It's supposed to rain."

"If it does, we'll stop. It's always supposed to rain here. You'll learn."

I took one of the rackets and went to the opposite side of the net. She swatted the bird over the net and I whacked it back. It felt light and easy and I was surprised by how far it flew. And I hardly had to move at all. "You seem very East Coast, being into this game. The upper crust."

She laughed. "It's fun. I don't understand why it's not more popular."

The bird flew toward me and I hit it again. It was so much easier than tennis — there was more time to register where the object was headed. Each contact with the racket was a soft tap, and I didn't need a carefully prescribed and practiced form with proper hand positions and moves that involved all kinds of jumping, running, and pivoting.

We continued hitting the bird, not talking for several minutes. We rarely missed since neither one was trying to trip up the other or outsmart with a strategy to win. It was more of a team effort to see how long we could keep the thing moving. Or flying, rather.

I whacked the bird. "It's hard to see Sean being so excited about this game that he's willing to devote a section of his yard to it."

She tapped the bird back at me. "It's not his. I bought the net and equipment and told him I was putting it up."

I smacked the bird at her. She reached up with liquid grace and tapped it back over the net again. "I thought it would be something for you and I, to give us a chance to unwind."

"That's what martinis are for."

"Not all day long."

"True."

Again we swatted the shuttlecock back and forth in silence. She was right, my mind was settling into a peaceful state, caring about nothing but the flight of the bird, the contact of it against the center of my racket. The white plastic piece sailed back and forth, truly resembling a bird when it was high in the air, swooping down toward our rackets like a small white dove. The yard was quiet except for the soft chirping of a few real birds. The large, more vocal birds appeared to be napping. All around us, the yards were silent — no voices, just the gentle splash of the waterfall. The heavy cloud cover increased the feeling of quiet, the whole neighborhood waiting for the rain, or waiting for something.

"So, names," Tess said.

"I hardly know what this thing does, so it's not possible to think of a name that conveys how it improves user's lives."

"I decided it's better that you know less. You'll see the big picture more clearly. The problem with Gavin's suggestion was that it tried too hard to explain."

"Okay."

"Any ideas?"

"True You," I said.

"That's actually pretty good. Let's say we have to throw out a name each time we hit the shuttlecock."

"I'm not sure I can think of new ideas that fast."

"That's the challenge and fun of it. You can't censor yourself."

"You go first."

"Gut Check," she said.

"Mind Check."

"Mind Your Gut."

"Natural Instinct," I said.

"Instinct. Period."

I hit the bird.

"What's your name suggestion?" She batted it back over the net.

"My mind is blank." I returned the shuttlecock.

She hit it again.

"What's your suggestion?" I said.

She laughed. "This isn't working as well as I'd thought."

"No."

We started laughing. Soon, we were laughing so hard, our arms grew weak and we couldn't manage to hit the shuttlecock. It fell to the ground. Tess picked it up and we went to the patio, setting our rackets and the bird on the table.

"Want a martini?" I said.

"Sure. I'll go get a pen and a pad of paper."

I went into the glistening kitchen and took two martini glasses out of the cabinet. I had a feeling that Sean was going to overrule any name we came up with, so I wasn't enthusiastic about working overtime to think of something clever. He probably already had a name and was waiting for someone else to say it, or to dismiss every idea and roll out his brilliant suggestion.

# 18

*Los Angeles*

**D**uring the drive from Portland to LA, with an overnight stop in Santa Rosa, California, my mother was silent. Even during our rapidly consumed roadside meals, she didn't speak. She cut her food with precision. She placed each bite in her mouth, using the tender roof and insides of her cheeks and her tongue to determine the shape of the food, exploring as if she were blind and lacking taste buds, so that her mouth had to work out whether it was egg or toast, pickle or onion slice or beef patty.

When her eyes met mine, they were glassy and almost frozen. Nothing escaped from behind the dark blue iris. The blues shimmered like shards of glass, giving the impression of a kaleidoscope, but she wasn't about to let any of its inner workings show in even the tiniest lift of her brow, or a tear falling out of her eye.

I couldn't make out whether she was grieving because I was going away, scared of the threats lurking in the dorms and classrooms and fraternity houses of UCLA, or if she wasn't sure who she was with her children leaving the house, one by one.

My father was a different matter. He had a lot to say, although none of it came from his own mind. His running commentary consisted of words from the Bible, filtered through his editorial system, some embellished, some quoted out of context. I was reminded that all the earth, even the students of UCLA, should fear god. He went on about the pleasures of the flesh and the harm that came from indulging them, and he talked about how life was hollow if it wasn't built around following god's directives. The attributes of a godly woman were repeated every few hours — silent and eschewing the wearing of fine jewelry, or styling her hair like a temptress — whatever that meant.

Despite the firm, authoritative, *don't-argue-with-god* tone of voice, his hands shook when he pulled cash out of his wallet and placed it on top of the restaurant bills. The closer we got to LA, the more noticeable the tremor, as if his body was fighting to prevent the release of his grip on me. His fingertips were white, the blood retracting into his body. I imagined they were icy and hard to the touch.

I spent most of the drive looking out the window, first at forests crowding close to the highway. After we crossed into California, the landscape was more open, farms and miles of grazing cattle. Each house — some weather-beaten shacks, some large ranch-style homes with a few nearby trees and nothing for miles — made me wonder about the people who lived there.

What was it like to be so far from the rest of society? How did families cope when they had no one else to talk to for days at a time? Or maybe it wasn't like that at all. Maybe they got in their cars every morning, just like the people of Portland. Unlike people in cities or suburbs who traveled only a few miles, they drove thirty or forty or fifty miles to find a small town, simply to escape the claustrophobic presence of their blood relatives.

I tried not to let my father's words grate on me. I tried to numb my eardrums so that his voice became a faint droning while my mind wandered off to imagine life in college.

Some girls who were escaping from the restrictive world I'd grown up in might look forward to drinking and sex. Those things were definitely on my mind, but I had no intention of getting involved in drunken orgies and puking my guts out. I was actually interested in classes. The array of things I could learn about was mind-boggling. The online course catalog went on forever.

The school encouraged you to declare a major, but I didn't like the idea of making that commitment. I was barely eighteen years old. I wanted to try everything.

At home, most of my literature came from the Bible or church-approved writers. The movies I watched were family entertainment. Art pretty much meant sewing and needlework or religious paintings — not messy things like pottery and sculpture. I wanted to get my hands dirty, I wanted to take yoga and fencing and horseback-riding. I wanted to read novels I'd never heard of and study the history of film and history that went beyond that of North America and Europe.

My parents didn't know about my desire to sample the entire world, at least as much of it as was on display at UCLA. They thought I should pick a solid major like business or marketing or better yet, pursue a teaching degree. To keep them happy, I'd written down marketing as my declared major. My father hovered over me, practically covering my hand so he could move the pen for me, but they wouldn't have that kind of scrutiny over my actual classes after the first quarter was over.

Again, to prevent any sudden roadblocks in my goal of

escaping Bible college, I registered for English composition, a math class that I've long forgotten, Introduction to Psychology, a drawing class, and tennis. The only one that sparked a raised eyebrow and a slight cough was the drawing class. It sounded frivolous, they said in a single voice. I don't think it crossed my father's mind there might be nude models. I smiled to myself, glad that I'd deferred yoga for now. That would be viewed as a practice that dabbled in Eastern religions and would have been very upsetting.

My dorm was a six-story building that looked pretty much like a parking garage. I was on the fifth floor — girls only on my floor, but the building was mixed gender.

The first order of business for my father was to pull aside the Resident Advisor and tell her in a firm, resonant voice that he wanted to be assured that she looked out for the safety, both physical and spiritual, of the girls on her floor. The RA looked confused about the spiritual part, but nodded along with him. Her eyes were wide, staring into his, making me think of the hundreds of times over the years that I'd heard the story of Mary sitting at the feet of Jesus, drinking in his words.

There was no chance this RA, twenty years old, would be able to look after me or guarantee my safety, but she sure managed to assure my father of her vigilance.

We carried boxes and dragged suitcases up to my new room — bare except for basic furniture, waiting to launch me into my real life.

# 19

*Sydney*

**D**arkness was approaching by the time Tess and I finished our second martinis. It never had rained, but the sky remained swollen with the promise of a deluge. Soon. Just like we would have a company name. Soon. Currently we had three pages in a legal-sized yellow pad filled with words, none of which seemed quite right. They were pretentious, vague, too long, too convoluted, too cryptic.

The second martinis probably hadn't helped, because a lot of the words were ridiculous — The Gut Game — but we'd laughed quite a lot.

I ate the last olive out of my glass. "I'm hungry."

"Me too." She stood, picked up the pad, and took it back to the office. She returned and swallowed the rest of her drink, probably warm and quite salty from the olives.

I'd rather not finish the drink at all when I let a martini sit too long and it gets that taste that makes you think of seawater, or tears — warm and gamey.

"Should we order pizza?" I said.

"How about meat pies?"

"Like Sweeney Todd?"

She gave me a grim smile. "Did you have to mention that? I was craving one and now…"

"So meat in a pie? Instead of peaches or pumpkin?"

"Yes. They're delicious."

"I guess like a chicken pot pie."

"Exactly, but so much better."

"What about the others?"

"I'll text Sean." She picked up her phone.

"Really? We live in the same house but we have to text each other? We dare not knock on his bedroom door?"

"This is easier."

"I'll run up there."

"No."

"We're supposed to be a chummy little family. Why are you acting like half the house is off limits?"

"I'm not." She tapped a message on her phone. "And it's not *half* the house."

I stood and headed toward the family room.

"Don't bother him...them," she said.

I turned back. "This doesn't seem bizarre to you? Who's in charge here? Are we a team or are we some kind of marketing indentured servants?"

"Don't dramatize. Here...a message from Sean. He said go ahead without him. He's not hungry."

"And Gavin?"

"Nothing," she said.

"Then let's go. I need to get out of here anyway."

We met in the foyer a few minutes later.

While Tess drove to the pie shop, I looked down at my phone, scrolling through headlines. It was better than looking out through the windshield, watching the distorted view of cars making left turns, hugging the curb, and right turns that swung out around oncoming traffic.

We ordered small pies with homemade crusts that appeared flakey and moist at the same time. Two of the pies were filled with mushrooms and beef with gravy. The third was stuffed with chili. We planned to share the chili pie. It was a lot of food, but Tess said the chili was the best and I couldn't remain in Australia for another day without trying it.

The first floor of the house was bursting with light when we returned, suggesting Sean or Gavin had been downstairs to stock up on snacks and alcohol, or just to take a peek at our scribbled notes for naming the company. Upstairs, there wasn't a single light turned on.

We took our pies to the dining room. While I put out placemats, plates, and utensils, Tess opened a bottle of Zinfandel and filled two glasses.

She was right — the pies were fantastic and I almost wished I'd eaten two. But I probably would have regretted it. While we ate, we talked about Australia. She filled my ears with details about the Sydney aquarium, the Great Barrier Reef, and the bits of history she'd read while she lounged around her hotel room trying to decide where her life was headed.

We were finished eating, the plates wiped clean except for a thin smear of gravy, when Sean appeared in the entrance to the dining room. Gavin hovered behind him.

"How about billiards?" Sean said.

We refilled our wine glasses. Gavin got out two beers for him and Sean. We walked single file to the pool room, following Sean like he was some sort of pied piper. He racked the balls, we chose our cues, and the game began.

They were all very good pool players. I held my own, but it took all my concentration. Midway through I exchanged my glass of wine for water.

After five games, Sean called off the competition. It was

convenient for him — he'd won two, Tess, Gavin, and I had won a game each. It was getting close to ten and I figured everyone would head off to the privacy of their rooms, but now Sean proposed a movie. The evening was taking on the atmosphere of a pre-teen slumber party — all activities planned according to a precise timetable, moving smoothly from one event to the next, no time for goofing off, also known as causing trouble.

The three of them sat on the couch and I picked a chair to the side, hopeful that a loud, action-filled movie might give me a chance to pretend exhaustion so I could slip away to check out their rooms. I hoped the two martinis and wine and the chips and dip, and more wine being consumed right then, had dulled Tess enough that my desire to see the rest of the house had sunk to the back of her mind. Besides, she was slightly tense from our lack of progress on finding a solid name for the company. Nothing could move forward until we figured it out. My curiosity no longer concerned her.

The movie he chose was Guardians of the Galaxy. Tess seemed excited about it and I couldn't get a sense of whether she really liked that kind of entertainment, or if she was kissing up to her boss. I'd already seen it. Once was more than enough. It was okay. Just okay. I know I part company with most of my generation in saying that, but it's true.

First, I stood for half a second and moved the chair back a foot or so, which put me out of the range of their peripheral vision. I waited fifteen or twenty minutes, then stood and moved toward the kitchen. No one turned. No one asked if I wanted the movie paused.

I slid my feet out of my flip-flops and walked quickly toward the foyer. At the entrance, I paused and looked across the room. They were motionless, facing the screen, occasionally sipping their drinks.

I ran lightly up the stairs, my toes gripping the wood. On the landing, the carpet was warm and comforting on my bare feet as I hurried down the hall. I tried Gavin's door. It was locked, as I'd expected, but it hadn't stopped me from hoping. The guy was paranoid about his privacy if he believed he couldn't even go downstairs for a game of pool and a movie without locking his door. I pressed the handle again, in the absurd hope that it was stuck, or I hadn't used enough force. I stepped back and listened for anyone following me up the stairs. Of course, if they were also barefoot, I'd never hear them until they were speaking in my ear, demanding to know why I was so nosey and disrespectful.

I walked toward Sean's door. I pressed the handle and the door swung open.

His room was nothing like I'd imagined. I'd expected several computers, maybe, one with an enormous screen. I thought there would be a TV and a mess of discarded clothes and a pile of diving gear.

Instead, it was minimalist. Extreme minimalist. But it was even larger than I'd imagined.

There was a bed with a simple dark oak frame, a white comforter and black throw pillows. A white ceiling fan turned slowly. Across from the foot of the bed was a narrow table like you'd see in an entryway, also oak, beautifully polished with elegant curves in the top and legs. There was a smallish chocolate brown leather chair in the corner near the doors to the balcony and in the opposite corner a life-sized polished oak statue of a naked woman. Dark veins ran through the wood, a few of them curving around polished knots. It was so smooth and inviting, it gave the appearance of human skin.

She stood flat on her feet, her arms up, elbows bent, her hands clasped near the base of her skull. Her back was arched, her face raised to the ceiling.

I shivered. There was something unsettling about the chair facing the statue, suggesting that Sean spent his time alone in the room doing nothing but staring at this naked, lifeless woman. There were no tables beside the bed, no books, no tablet, nothing. Even the table across from the foot of his bed was empty. It seemed pointless to even have it there.

All that unused space was calming and unnerving at the same time. I was no longer sure I wanted to find a way to move myself into this room.

The closet was as sparsely filled as the room— a few pairs of slacks, jeans, and a handful of button-down shirts, a leather jacket and two sport coats. The palatial bathroom had a shower large enough for five or six people, flush to the tile floor with a grate for drainage along the opening, and a free-standing tub, gleaming white.

I returned to the bedroom and approached the statue. I touched the space between her eyebrows and drew my finger slowly down the slope of her nose. I'd expected the surface to be cool to the touch, but it was warm.

# 20

Rain finally let loose about two a.m. It pounded the house until daylight. It was drizzling when I woke on Sunday morning. I'd slept late, since *Guardians of the Galaxy* had been followed by over an hour watching Australian stand-up comedy, quite a lot of which I didn't get. Sean and Gavin snorted occasionally while Tess tried for some half-hearted giggles. I wasn't sure if it took a lot to make the two guys laugh or if the show wasn't all that funny. Comedy can be that way, more often than not, which is sad. Good comedy that makes you laugh until your belly clenches into a knot and your chest aches is like an out of body experience. It's an orgasm for your brain. But it's also difficult to achieve, to hit those perfect notes, to tell a story that leads an audience to an outbreak of hysteria when they were laughing all along, thinking the setup jokes were the good ones.

The others had also slept late.

They'd left the folding glass doors open to the patio and the great room area smelled fresh and damp, but it was also cold. I ran upstairs for a long-sleeved shirt.

Back in the kitchen, I poured a glass of water and went into the workout room. I hadn't used it yet and I hadn't noticed anyone else using it either. The equipment was nice — a universal machine that enabled lat pull-downs, leg presses and extensions, and a few other exercises. There was a rack of dumbbells in one-pound increments starting at six and going up to forty pounds, a bench with a barbell and a stack of lead plates, and a stationary bicycle.

An anonymous gym would have been preferable, but why spend money on that when I had all this rather nice equipment sitting right here? I just had to get into a routine and start using it. So far, the start-up incubator wannabe, was mostly about playing and nothing about a regular routine or work.

Despite his Friday deadline for a name, Sean seemed in no real hurry to get the product to market. Even Tess wasn't her usual driven self. It was as if the house, with all its lovely amenities, had cast a pall over us, dragging our minds down into the tropical moisture of bodily needs — nothing but eating, drinking, sleeping, and playing. The only thing missing was sex.

Since I was wearing leggings, it seemed like a good time to try out some of the weights. I couldn't use the dumbbells with my bare feet, but the bench press would be fine. I found a pair of gloves on a table near the floor-to-ceiling window that looked out onto the side yard — a jungle of plants that blocked the fence, as well as most of the sunlight, which would be a nice feature in hot weather.

I strapped on the gloves, slid the iron plates onto each end of the bar, replaced the clips, and laid on my back, my knees bent and my feet flat. I lifted the barbell off the rack and raised it until my arms were straight, careful to keep my elbows from locking. I lowered it slowly and raised it again.

Blood surged through me, warming my body as I raised and lowered the bar for eight reps. On the last lift, my muscles burned and my feet clenched involuntarily. I lowered it slowly and took my hands off the bar. I rested them on my belly and closed my eyes.

"Impressive."

I sat up too fast, barely avoiding whacking my head on the barbell. For half a second, I was light-headed and my vision blurred, then I saw clearly. Sean stood in the doorway, arms folded over his middle, one ankle crossed over the other. He was barefoot and wore shorts and no shirt. Clearly he didn't find the rainy morning chilly at all.

"You're strong," he said.

"Yes."

"That's unusual, for a girl."

"Is it?"

"I'm glad you're using the equipment."

"It looks brand new."

"It is. Tess used it once."

"And you and Gavin?"

"Gavin's not into it."

I let the unanswered portion of the question lie there, wondering if he'd bought the equipment only for Tess and me. Once again I was overcome with the sense that he didn't really want us leaving the house. Everything we could want was at our fingertips. The fridge and the cabinets and wine fridge and liquor cabinet were always fully stocked.

"Sausages and eggs for brekky?" he said.

"Sounds good."

He uncrossed his arms and turned. "I'll get it started. Finish your workout." He stepped back and the door closed behind him. I did two more sets of bench presses and then stood and did some stretching.

Sean cooked and served us breakfast at the bar. "I want to have a team meeting this morning," he said.

"It's Sunday," Gavin said.

"I know what day it is." Sean smiled with a slightly condescending shape to his mouth. "This will only take ten minutes at most. Let's go into the dining room."

Like obedient students, each of us followed him into the room, pulled out a chair, and sat down.

"Tess has come up with a name for our fledgling." Sean grinned, directing his gaze to each one of us, lingering for a moment before moving to the next. "And she's way ahead of the deadline."

Tess slowly, and rather dramatically opened a leather folder sitting on the table. She removed a thick, glossy sheet of paper. The sage green words in a font that filled most of the paper read: *TruthTeller*. "My thinking," she said, "well, our thinking…Alex helped me quite a lot with the brainstorming process, but we couldn't quite get to the right feel. Then, it came to me just as I woke up this morning. A kookaburra was making a lot of noise, chattering and laughing. The idea came up out of nowhere, as good ideas often seem to. I think it embodies the customer benefit of the app — knowing the truth. We all crave people who will tell us the truth. And our own truth is deep inside, in many cases, still waiting to be recognized. It also suggests something larger — that society overall is in desperate need of truth, both on a personal and a political level. Without truth, you can't have real relationships, and we can't progress as a human race."

"I agree completely," Sean said.

"It doesn't have the same sound as most app names, but I think that's a good thing," Tess said.

"Sets us apart," Sean said.

They grinned at each other. Neither seemed to notice, or care much, that Gavin and I hadn't erupted with enthusiasm.

"So. We're ready to hit the ground running." Sean pushed his chair back. "And thanks for the brainstorming, Alex. Good job."

The condescension turned my stomach. Praise wasn't necessary, and praise that isn't deserved is like something slimy and smelling awful, like something dead. It makes you feel you need a shower and an internal cleansing to burn away the rot inside of you.

Gavin pushed out his chair, stood, nodded at Tess, and walked out of the room.

# 21

Tess looked at her phone for the third time since waking up. There was no word from Cynthia. Phone, text, email, and Cynthia had avoided all three. How hard was it to text a status update? It wasn't as if it was Cynthia's personal phone, charging her an international data fee. She knew Tess was waiting. It was so fucking rude to leave her hanging like this. If Cynthia hadn't connected with Ted yet, she could let Tess know that. If he was traveling, or...whatever. But the echoing silence was passive aggressive. There was no way Cynthia had forgotten.

She put on workout clothes. She brushed her hair into a ponytail and checked her phone. Nothing.

The more time passed without someone objecting to the easy dismissal of Steve's death, the more likely it was that nothing would be done, ever. She tapped out a message to Cynthia: *Any update?*

Nothing came back. She went downstairs and got a glass of water. She went into the workout room. Maybe yoga would be better than lifting weights, it would center her thoughts and provide equilibrium. There were several yoga mats stored in the spacious closet that also contained weight-lifting gloves, tennis rackets and balls, two basketballs, and a rugby ball.

Doing something physical would get her mind off Cynthia. She checked her phone again. It would have chimed if there was a message, but she couldn't resist the desire to make absolutely sure. Sometimes she didn't hear the ping, sometimes it came in while the phone was still active and it didn't ping at all.

She got out a turquoise yoga mat. She unrolled it and closed the door. Feeling watched was the perfect way to destroy a yoga routine. She wished she could lock the door. Maybe she should bring the mat up to her room. She stretched her arms overhead. Something caught the corner of her eye. She picked up the phone and pressed the home button. No message. It must have been the light catching the screen, or a brief flutter inside her eyeball.

Lying on her stomach, she straightened her legs behind her, pointed her toes, and pushed her torso up into the cobra position. She held it for what felt like two minutes, but when she released the pose and looked at her phone, only a minute had passed, maybe a bit more. She sat and pulled her legs into the lotus position. She picked up her phone and checked the news. Obviously yoga wasn't helping to center her mind.

Now she was not only annoyed at Cynthia's failure to communicate, she was angry that she'd allowed her own restlessness to sabotage a strenuous workout, and that she was on her way to failing at an easy few minutes of yoga.

Forcing herself to concentrate was the only solution. Action. Sitting here waiting accomplished nothing. She could either call or do some yoga and then decide what to do. She turned her phone face down and shoved it across the carpeted floor. It slid close to the closet door and stopped. She got on her hands and knees and raised herself into downward facing dog. She held it until her arms ached. She worked through ten more poses, including the warrior pose which was her favorite. She smiled at herself every time she performed it, because in some mysterious way, the stance truly did make her feel powerful and in control. The perfect way to end the sequence, and the perfect attitude for dealing with Cynthia.

It wasn't as if she mourned Steve. But it was so wrong to have the facts of your life slip out of your control after death, the wrong impression left, and not be able to correct the lies. It wasn't fair and she felt that someone had to fight for him. She wished it didn't have to be her, but no one else, so far, seemed inclined to take up the fight.

She rolled up the mat and drank the rest of her water before picking up her phone. She pressed the home button and was greeted by a photograph of the sunset a few weeks earlier. No banners indicating new messages.

After making a cup of espresso and carrying it up to her room, she sat at the desk and opened her laptop. She took a sip of espresso and checked her phone. No messages. She unlocked the screen. There were no new emails.

She left the phone on the desk and picked up the small white cup. She carried it to the balcony and sat down, looking out at an endless sea of greenery. A cockatoo soared over a palm tree and landed on the branch of a eucalyptus tree a few feet away. It was so regal. The white so absolutely pure and the pale-yellow crown feathers giving the impression the species had sunny personalities and carefree lives.

Watching the bird made her think of Damien. She'd spent a considerable amount of time talking to him, dissecting her relationship with Steve while Damien pecked at his bowl of seeds or nibbled on fruit, walked around the room, and hopped on and off his perch. Occasionally, he'd comment on the weather or his desire for mangos, but mostly he was quiet. He would tip his head to the side, lowering his crown feathers into a welcoming, fearless position, and gaze at her with his dark, calm eyes. She missed him.

She took a sip of espresso and rested the cup on the palm of her left hand, letting the warmth spread through her skin.

Either Cynthia didn't give a shit about Steve's reputation, or doing Tess a personal favor for that matter, or she was too hesitant about bothering the CEO with concerns over a man who was no longer an employee.

It was such a simple task. Even if Cynthia didn't care about the unbelievable circumstances of his death, all she had to do was write a short email to Ted. Two lines, maybe three. It was possible she'd written the email or made the call and Ted was blowing her off. Although that wasn't Tess's experience of him. His time was in high demand, every minute accounted for, like all CEOs, but he cared about the human beings who were employed by his company. He was one of the reasons she'd enjoyed working there. He didn't just spout caring comments scripted by HR, he genuinely wanted his employees to be happy, to know they were valued.

The thought made her throat seize up for a moment. She hadn't valued Ted and the opportunities she'd had a CoastalCreative as much as he'd valued her. She'd thought only of her own career, her own timeline, her own desires. Still, she didn't owe him or the company. And maybe a new marketing director was a good thing, bringing fresh life to the company. Maybe she'd done something valuable for Ted by leaving. He didn't need an executive staff that had lost their enthusiasm.

Her drink was cooling fast. She took several sips and tried

to remember how she'd felt the first time she met Steve. Looking back now, it seemed like a manufactured thrill. Good sex, around which she'd imagined something more for a short time, but hadn't ever truly felt. Maybe their whole relationship had been like that.

So why was she so concerned with his reputation? She hadn't even liked him. Her life returned to normal the minute she broke up with him. He was controlling and condescending. He was good in bed, but that didn't cause her to have meaningful feelings for him. They had some good times, he could be funny and charming. But that was it. The thing she had with him was wanting and satisfaction, not anything that came from her heart. Why did she care that he not be labeled a drug addict? Besides, had anyone actually said that? Had those words been used? She doubted it. But it was the aura of suspicion, the suggestion of something wrong in his life. It was an accusation he couldn't defend. More than anything, it was the lack of control over how he was remembered, down to the smallest detail.

Maybe, she didn't care at all about Steve's reputation or legacy or whatever you wanted to call it. Maybe this was all about imagining her own death, and the feeling that she had no control over what happened — to her money, to her accomplishments, after she was gone. Fighting for him gave her hope that karma would provide her with the same dedication to a truthful portrayal of her life from someone who had known her.

She finished the espresso and went inside, closing the glass door. She sat at the desk, clicked on her email, and typed in — TedHutchins @CoastalCreative.com

She lifted her hands off the keyboard and stared at the

image above her desk — a sixteen-by-twenty framed photograph of a blue whale off the western coast of Australia. Steve, Ted, and CoastalCreative felt very far away.

She lowered her hands to her lap and gazed at the whale for several minutes.

# 22

On Monday morning, I snuck out of the house just before six-thirty. And it absolutely *was* sneaking. After Sean's unexpected appearance in the workout room, after being blind-sided by a Sunday team meeting and Tess's heroic results that completely cut me out of the picture, and too much eating and drinking and hanging around the swimming pool, I needed space. Lots of space.

How could a gorgeous home with such exquisite decorating — not to mention a nice bedroom, delicious meals, and all the martinis I wanted, everything without charge — give the impression it wanted to swallow me whole? This living arrangement was supposed to be fun. Instead, it was tense and contrived. I couldn't stop thinking that Tess and Sean had some sort of plan going behind the scenes that I was not privy to. I wondered whether Gavin knew anything more. Or if I was imagining things. My confinement was turning my thoughts on themselves, eating themselves like that snake devouring its own tail.

The air outside was muggy and damp, but the pavement was dry. Birds called and chirped and cooed and chattered. The distinctive staccato laugh of the kookaburra was the loudest. It sounded like a chorus of conversation discussing the imminent arrival of the sun, the likelihood of thunderstorms — none forecast — and the sudden appearance of a woman from America on the front patio wearing navy blue spandex shorts, a matching cropped running top, and a white hoodie. Even the navy blue stripes on her shoes were part of the outfit. Was that what caused the kookaburra to laugh its crazy head off? That, or I was the crazy one.

I stretched my calves and quads and hamstrings and started off in the same direction I had the previous time. Trying a new route was appealing, but that desire was overruled by the knowledge that a familiar route meant I could run for several miles without consulting the map quite as frequently, checking the pulsing blue dot in order to navigate my way back to the house.

The beauty of running is not thinking. Checking street names and using conscious brain cells to remember landmarks drained some of the pleasure. It's the silencing of the mental chatter, feeling nothing but heartbeat and lungs and the movement of my legs and arms that I love. It's addictive, really. A healthy addiction. When I don't run for several days at a time, my whole body cries out for it. The sensation isn't much different than when my body cries out for the touch of a man. And it was also doing that, but running was easily accessible, a man was not. Well, two men were accessible physically, but socially, mentally, not quite yet.

I ran faster to push the thoughts out of my head. Although I wanted the challenge of seeing which man I could lure into my bed, or rather lure into inviting me to his bed, the risk to our hothouse environment might be too great. Keeping my income was a higher priority.

After a mile and a half, my brain was pleasantly relaxed. The birds had quieted now that the sun was higher in the sky. I assumed they were busy eating or perhaps cleaning their feathers after a hearty breakfast. Now that I no longer had their background noise, I stopped for a moment and stuffed my earbuds into my ears. I selected a Queen playlist. It wasn't the most ideal for running, but I like the mind-tripping quality of some of their songs, so it seemed like the best choice given the mind-tripping quality of my current situation.

I ran faster, building up to a sprint. The pavement pounded through my bones, vibrating my whole body. The muscles in my legs burned and I was breathing hard. Sweat eased across my back, making its way to the indentations along my spine where it settled, cooling my skin slightly when the air brushed across the moisture.

As I rounded the corner past a park that was the marking point for turning back toward the house, I sensed someone behind me. I'd slowed to a steady jog now and wondered if the other runner would pass me. The music blocked out most of the sound and the pavement was too solid to give off any awareness of other feet pounding, it was more of that instinctive spider sense that tells you you're not alone. It's the same as that creepy, almost supernatural feeling you have when you know another driver is going to come into your lane without warning.

Suddenly, he was beside me. He grabbed the cord from my earbuds and yanked the white orb out of my left ear. The bud tapped against my arm as I ran. I veered to the right and onto the edge of a lawn.

"Hey, slow down," he said.

Now he was beside me. I didn't turn, but I saw enough from my peripheral vision to know it was the neighbor, John. I picked up my pace.

"You can't hear anything with those things in your ears."

His voice was steady, unaffected by the effort of keeping up with me.

I didn't turn or respond.

"I'm talking to you."

I continued running, slightly faster.

"I called to you when you first went out. I thought you needed some company." He moved slightly ahead of me and turned to look at me.

I continued with my head facing forward.

"Don't be pissed off. I'm just being friendly. Those things pop right out, I didn't hurt your ear."

I said nothing.

He laughed, an edgy sound in his voice that was even creepier than his words or his behavior.

"So how about some company?" he said.

"I'd rather not." I pushed harder but I had a good mile or more before I would be back at the house, and I couldn't keep up a sprint for that distance. Hopefully he'd wear out or give up before I reached my end point.

"Well I'm already here. And we're both headed in the same direction."

"I prefer to run alone."

"Are you sure that's safe?"

"Yes."

"You're a very good looking woman."

I stuffed the dangling earbud back into place. Why do men say that as if they're giving you new information? Do they really think women aren't aware of how they look? Do men like him think women need their opinions, as if their stamp of approval is required to let you know you're someone worth paying attention to? It wasn't a compliment, telling me I looked nice at a particular point in time, from a person with whom I had a relationship. It was a grade, a categorizing me into a slot on his list of females.

"Brrr." He laughed. "I can feel the chill from here."

"Then move away."

He laughed, then gasped slightly for air. "Don't run so fast."

I maintained my pace.

"Did you hear me? You're very good looking."

"I heard you."

"Most women would say thank you."

"For what?"

He sighed. "You're also a bit difficult. Like most attractive women."

"Thanks for the info," I said. "Now please take a different route so I can finish my run in peace."

"I'm going the same way."

I needed to stop speaking. It was the best way to shut him down, but then, I couldn't help myself. "Does your wife know you follow female runners?"

"My wife is in the states."

I said nothing.

"Kids. She visits the kids for the summer."

He remained beside me, but at least he was breathing with more effort, no longer able to keep up the flow of words. He wore a white t-shirt and red gym shorts. His shoes looked just worn enough to prove that he went running, or did something athletic, on a regular basis.

I wanted to tell him to fuck off, but it might not be a good idea to have a man living next door with a wounded ego. From what he'd said earlier, I didn't think he knew Sean at all, but I couldn't be sure.

Another reason this whole situation was too claustrophobic.

I thought CoastalCreative owned too much of me when they'd provided an apartment in San Francisco. I wasn't sure I would have accepted Tess's offer if I'd known the situation in Australia would be even more controlled. But I was here now and it was good for my financial future. Besides, I certainly wasn't leaving before seeing a kangaroo.

# 23

The aroma of coffee filled my nostrils and washed over me as I stepped inside the front door. It closed behind me and I felt my muscles unclench, pleased to be rid of John running a few inches closer to my side than he should have, close enough that I'd felt the heat of his skin and smelled his sweat. Getting away from him was easy, I'd simply kept running. He'd called after me, assuring me it would be safer to run with a partner if I insisted on going out before it was fully light. Apparently, he'd been watching me from the moment I'd left the house.

My impression of Australia so far was a lower threat of violent crime compared with the U.S., and I seriously doubted there were a lot of rapists and muggers in the neighborhood where I was living. In those kinds of communities, where the cars cost as much as some people's homes, the rapists aren't lurking in the shadows of buildings ready to attack. The rapist is sipping a cocktail at a party, popping a piece of sushi in his mouth, and eyeing your drink while fingering a roofie in his pocket. Or simply topping off your glass every time you take a sip of champagne until you forget how much you've had.

Maybe John was speaking out of his American sensibility, assuming a level of violence that he'd been aware of throughout his life before landing in the Southern Hemisphere.

At any rate, I clearly needed to start running well before

dawn, in full darkness, which was less threatening than being watched by him.

I removed my shoes and peeled off my socks, stuffing them inside my shoes. I left them near the foot of the staircase and went into the kitchen. Steam was coming from the espresso machine. Gavin stood with his lower back pressed against the center island, his legs extended, ankles crossed. He was looking right at me as I walked into the room.

"Smells good," I said.

He smiled, barely.

The machine continued performing its magic of transforming ground up beans and cold water into hot, delicious, eye-opening coffee. "Is there enough for me to have a cup?"

"Certainly."

I went to the cabinet and took out a cup. I put it beside the one already sitting on the counter. "Are you making breakfast?"

"This isn't a B&B," he said.

"I didn't mean it's your job, I was just asking."

"Why don't you make it?"

"Certainly." I smiled. "What would you like?"

He didn't answer.

The espresso machine finished. He pulled out the carafe and filled both cups. He replaced the carafe and gestured at my cup. He picked up his own and walked toward the family room couch.

I took a sip of espresso. "Do you want me to make enough for you or not?"

"I'll have whatever you're having."

"I don't know what I'm having."

He shrugged. He settled on the couch and put his cup on the table. He immediately stood up again, walked to the doors, slid open one panel and turned it ninety degrees, ready to push back along the track to the wall if the weather grew warmer.

I opened the fridge. All I wanted was a cup of yogurt, maybe a bit of granola, but now that I'd offered, it seemed like I should put out more effort. "Sausages and scrambled eggs?"

"Sounds lovely," he said.

I pulled out pans for the sausages and eggs and a bowl for scrambling. I got the sausages cooking and returned to the fridge to look for something to dress up the eggs. There was one large tomato and half an onion. I chopped both. I cracked and beat four eggs, adding a splash of milk, while a pat of butter slowly melted in the pan. I sautéed the onion first, then poured in the eggs. I stirred for a minute or two and dropped in the tomato.

When the eggs were finished, I split the egg and sausages onto two plates and set them on the bar. I found a bottle of hot sauce and put it near my plate. "Food's ready."

He walked over and pulled out a chair. He settled on the edge, leaning slightly over the counter, and began eating. I sat beside him, close enough that my skin was instantly aware of his presence. His forearm was inches from mine, the soft, pale brown hair making it look vulnerable despite the movement of well-defined muscles. He was wearing jeans and a t-shirt and his feet were bare.

"Good eggs," he said.

I looked at my plate and smiled, unsure whether he was

suggesting I was a so-called good egg. I laughed softly.

"What's so funny?"

"Glad you like the eggs."

That forearm with its luscious soft hair and those muscles that moved and tightened each time he cut off a piece of sausage was consuming all my attention. I could feel him there, I could feel the warmth of him and the casual presence of him, and the silence of him.

"You don't talk much," I said.

"Neither do you."

I saw how my silence is interpreted as coldness more often than not. I don't intend to be cold. I just don't see the point in talking when I don't want to, just because it's expected, or because someone else is nervous and wants to fill the air with words in order to prove that they exist. And I certainly don't talk when someone I don't want to be around is talking at me. John came to mind.

Gavin's arm was still inches from mine. Had it moved closer? Maybe he was also considering the structure of the household with its obviously balanced genders. I couldn't be the only one who was feeling the lack of sex, but I was still on the fence about whether I was more drawn to Sean or Gavin, and which one would be more satisfying over time. And although I hadn't necessarily been treated like a valued member of the new little company, I still didn't want to piss away the only job prospect I had right now.

I let my arm relax slightly on the edge of the counter. His was definitely closer than it had been, finding a new position each time he laid down his fork to pick up his cup.

I finished my eggs and speared the last bite of sausage. I popped it into my mouth and slid of the chair while I continued chewing.

He stood and set my plate on top of his, stacked the utensils on the plates, and carried them to the other counter. He put everything in its place inside the dishwasher and closed the door.

"Very good. Thanks," he said.

I smiled.

"Now what should we do?" He looked slightly lost, as if he genuinely needed the answer to that question.

I walked around the island and stood in front of him, my bare toes close to his. I looked up at him. He stared into my eyes, still with that suggestion of cruelty, but it was very appealing, exciting, almost. I moved my mouth into a barely perceptible smile, waiting for him to kiss me.

# 24

Tess had been staring at the blank window of the email to Ted for over ten minutes. She should have a little bit of sympathy for Cynthia now that she'd seen how long it was taking to put her own thoughts in the right order. She wasn't even sure what she was asking. Every time she typed out a phrase, it came across like a veiled accusation of murder. Or negligence. It was possible Ted would read it as an indictment of him. But she no longer worked there, what did it matter how he felt? Still, never burn bridges and all that.

She wished she had another cup of espresso, but that was just further procrastination. She put her fingers on the keys and started typing again. Spit it out, adjust for tone after she got the words down, that was the key.

*Ted — I understand Steve's death has been categorized as a drug overdose. In all the years I worked with him, I never knew him as a drug user and he never did anything to make me think he had issues even remotely related to addiction. I think the police have brushed it off too easily. Is anyone putting pressure on them to dig deeper? Regards, TT.*

She lifted her hands off the keys. That was actually perfect. She hit send and closed the laptop.

There was a knock on her door. She pushed the laptop toward the center of the desk. There was another knock, slightly louder and several raps longer.

When she opened the door, Sean stood there, his hand raised for a third knock.

"What's up?" she said.

"Can I come in for a minute?"

She glanced at the rumpled sheets on the bed, the comforter hanging off one side covering part of the floor. "I suppose."

She led the way to the balcony and they sat at the table.

"How are things coming along?" he said.

"Great, now that we have a name. I'm putting together a launch plan. It should be ready tomorrow."

"And what's Alex up to?"

"She's reading some books on effective social media marketing."

"I've never seen her reading a book."

She laughed. "What does that mean? You're doubting what I said?"

"Not you…"

"She's reading ebooks…on her phone, if you're doubting my word. She'll be great at this. I promise."

"I'm concerned that she's…What did you say she did for you at CoastalCreative?"

"She was a project manager."

"And that's the best candidate you could come up with for social media? It sounds completely unrelated. The way you described it, a lot of our success hinges on effective social media engagement."

"I promise, she's a natural."

"She doesn't seem all that sociable to me." He leaned back and stretched out his legs.

"You'll see I'm right."

"Maybe."

"So you are doubting me. You don't trust my judgement after all?"

"I do."

"Good. What else did you want?"

"The atmosphere in the house has changed since she arrived."

"How so?"

"It's tense. I don't think she's a team player."

"That term is over-used, it doesn't mean anything."

"I think it means a lot."

"She has strong opinions. She has a strong personality. I suppose people either like her a lot, or don't like her, with equal passion."

"There's something about her energy or her vibe or whatever you want to call it. She seems like she's hungry."

Tess laughed. "Hungry?"

"A little predatory."

"Oh come on, Sean. Are you serious?"

He sat up straighter. "I feel like I need to keep my eye on her."

"I really have no idea what you're talking about. You need to give her a chance. She's very smart, and she knows how to sell. With class. It's a natural thing with her, and I think she'll be able to sell in the way it needs to be done on social media."

"There are a lot of people in the world who know how to sell with class."

"I'm in charge of marketing and I hired her because I think she'll be very good at the job. It's my call and I don't like you questioning my decision because you have some ridiculous idea of her being predatory. I don't even know what that means in this context."

He stood and went to the railing. He leaned over and looked across the front yard. He stood there for several minutes, not speaking. He turned to face her, his expression expectant. He crossed his arms.

She refused to say another word. He needed to apologize. None of them knew each other very well yet. Four strangers trying to start a company without understanding the strengths and weaknesses of the others. He'd asked her to join based on one conversation on a boat in the middle of the ocean. But they were in it now, and he had no right to put barriers around her. She knew how to market a product and she knew how to surround herself with the right people, with good people. He'd only allowed her one employee for now. Her choice was Alex.

Magpies chattered in the yard. She pictured them hopping around the lawn, digging insects out of the earth.

Sean uncrossed his arms. He put his hand to his mouth and coughed, then shoved both hands in his pockets. "I think you know what predatory means. In any context."

"Well she's here to stay."

"Then keep your eye on her. I'll be doing the same." He walked back into her bedroom. As he crossed to the other door, he looked rather predatory himself, bare feet treading on her carpet. He glanced at her unmade bed, secure in the knowledge that this house belonged to him and they were all beneficiaries of his generosity.

He'd seemed so easy-going when they met, when they explored the Reef together, ate several delicious dinners, and had lengthy follow-up meetings. Had she mis-read him that fully?

She stood and went inside. She yanked the comforter

over the rumpled sheets. As she straightened her back and looked at the photograph of the whale, she remembered Alex's desire to see the other bedrooms. Had she gone into Sean's room and he'd caught her? Or seen her leaving his room and Alex didn't realize it? Sometimes dealing with Alex was like dealing with a rebellious teenager, not that she had any first-hand, or even second-hand knowledge of that. The woman did have a mind of her own. But that's why Tess respected her.

   She opened her laptop. There was one new email message — from Ted Hutchins.

# 25

*Los Angeles*

My first college roommate didn't show up at our dorm before my parents had to leave to start the drive back up north. My father was very agitated about the fact he hadn't met her. God only knew what kind of person she would be, what terrible influence she'd have on his innocent daughter.

All those years he'd known me, battled nearly to the death with me, told my mother to figure out how to reign in my tongue and ensure that I understood what god required of the female half of the human race, and yet in his imagination I remained a fragile and delicate gossamer-winged angel.

His lips contorted into an expression I'd never seen on his face. The flare of his nostrils above those deformed lips made me think he was ready to be sick to his stomach. He put his hand on my shoulder, then removed it as if he'd been given an electric shock. He shoved his hands in his pockets and looked at the toes of his shoes. He rocked back on his heels slightly. "Remind me — how did you choose this girl that's sharing your room?"

"Roommates are assigned."

"But I remember you filling out a form."

"Just my habits and things I like to do. I didn't get to pick her. They match you."

"I hope you wrote down that you're a woman of God."

I didn't laugh, but it was difficult.

"Did you?"

I held his gaze, keeping mine steady, my expression unsmiling.

"Surely they asked you to indicate your religion. You should not be unequally yoked. Common faith is critical for a wholesome living situation."

I considered these last moments under his rule. With him providing tuition and room and board, I would continue under his rule for years, but it was a remote kingdom I'd inhabit. If I lied, he'd be happy, but I'd view myself as a coward. If I told the truth...well, I had no idea how he would respond.

Lying is such a fraught subject. Everyone hates liars, yet everyone lies. Who hasn't given a false answer when asked if a new haircut looks good? People lie about whether they're sick — not at all or worse than it really is. They lie about their taste in food, their feelings about their relatives, their income, the performance of their investments, and their past.

Some wouldn't label all of these minor adjustments to the truth as lies. *White* lies. They want to put a good spin on something, or they want to elicit sympathy or envy or admiration or affection. They want to be liked and so they create stories that are close to the truth, but not the truth.

The population goes ballistic when government officials hide what's true, make up what's "true", re-position what's "true". All of us want these people, entrusted with our votes, to tell the fucking truth about what's happening in our city, our state, our country. The world. It's considered a breach of public trust. Congressmen and women who lie are loathed when caught. But then, the lies are forgotten or overlooked or explained away and they receive our votes once again —

*The lesser of two evils.*

Truth-telling has become so problematic that there are gradations of truth accepted when a politician's statements are dissected — *mostly true, mostly false, partially true, partially false, pants-on-fire liar.* It's accepted that they all lie, all the time.

When a manager asks if a project is done, the employee says *almost.* That alone could be a lie. It's certainly open to enough interpretation that the manager assumes it will be ready in an hour and the employee knows it will be ready in a day. The manager views the answer as a lie, the employee feels virtuous in her honesty.

People lie to traffic cops and they lie to friends.

It's a lie to tell a dinner host you're full and then proceed to eat two servings of chocolate cake. It's a lie to say you're perfectly fine to drive after three martinis. A traffic cop will disagree, the person you hit with your car will be furious with your lie, and maybe crippled or dead because of your lie.

A lie can grow, starting with a half truth and entrenching the speaker further every time she opens her mouth. First, a tiny lie about not being able to work late because you're visiting your mother in the hospital. It gets a little larger when you're seen at a bar after work. It grows again when it's clear you're on your second drink. It explodes in your face when your mother posts a picture of her vacation in Hawaii on your Facebook page.

It's hard to lie in the twenty-first century. Social media trips you up. Technology with its vigilant tracking reveals your location. Time stamps on emails reveal you were away from work for hours, not the thirty minutes you implied.

And yet, people seem to lie more. Politicians certainly do. They don't seem to care that you know they're liars. Lies can be proven with taped interviews and tweets. It's almost a badge of honor — getting away with telling bald-faced lies that can be proven wrong with a quick tap of computer keys, and yet, winning support over and over again.

Most of all, people lie to the ones they sleep with. *Yes, I had a glorious orgasm. That was the best ever. You're an amazing lover, I couldn't ask for better.*

I told plenty of lies in my childhood and teenage years. All kids do. Most were for self-protection, and I suppose most lies in general are for self-protection, making sure you don't lose your position in a job or the world or in another person's mind.

If I lied, my father would leave my room without too much additional drama. My mother would sleep better at night. I looked at her hopeful eyes, studying me, her lips half-smiling in anticipation of me finally admitting I cared about the god they'd shoved down my throat for eighteen years. She looked ready to be vindicated, knowing that I truly believed after all, knowing that I'd simply been contrary because I was stubborn and independent and argumentative.

I lie easily, without even thinking about it, when it's necessary to achieve what I want. I'll lie about the smallest details and the most monumental events. I've lied to men I had sex with and I've lied to cover up the people I've killed. I've lied in bars to get free drinks and I've lied at work. I lied repeatedly to Steve and I've told a few to Tess.

In the last years of high school, I'd learned how effective lying is in keeping your life moving smoothly in the direction you desire. But this seemed different. It wasn't really about saving my ass from my father's anger, risking a change of mind that would cause him to drag me back outside and lock me in the backseat of his car for a two-day drive back to Portland.

He needed to know, once and for all, who I was.

# 26

*Sydney*

I stood in the kitchen, my bare toes inches from Gavin's, waiting for him to kiss me. For several seconds we remained in that position, neither of us moving. I wasn't sure what he was waiting for. His eyes didn't give away any thoughts. It wasn't that he hesitated or seemed disinterested. He was just...there. Like most of my experiences of him had been so far. He was there, not reacting to the world, just holding his place in it.

The seconds stretched to a minute.

I reached up and placed my hand on the back of his neck. Gently, I pulled his head toward mine. I put my lips on his, not hard — a gentle pressure, testing the temperature of his skin, the moisture around his mouth.

When I slid my tongue between his lips he reacted. I can't say how, exactly. He didn't grab me or start kissing harder or gasp or change his position at all. But there was a sudden shift of intensity, maybe just awareness that he was finally doing more than simply holding a place. He actually had something to say, with the touch of his mouth rather than the sound of his voice.

We didn't kiss for long. When we drew away from each other, the intensity was still there.

"Okay," he said. He went to the fridge and took out a smoothie. He raised the bottle in my direction and walked around the center island and out of the room.

Okay, yourself.

It was the strangest lead-up to a kiss and the strangest aftermath I'd ever experienced. But the kiss did the job. I was enticed. I had to get inside his head. I had to figure out this guy who didn't want the money or the importance that came with being a principal of the company for which he was one of two creators. He locked everyone out of his room, he kissed like a god, and he hardly spoke. I had to know more.

I pulled the basket out of the espresso machine and rinsed it. I put in more coffee and filled the milk pitcher. I started the espresso brewing and put the steam wand into the milk. More caffeine was not what I needed, but the milk would hopefully smooth the coffee's entrance into my stomach and keep me from getting too amped up.

When the latte was ready, I took it out to the patio.

Kissing is such a weird thing. Strangely human, for the most part. Animals lick one another, even the non-domesticated, so maybe it's not human, we're just more discrete with our tongues.

Still, it's a difficult thing to navigate. When you're fucking, you can talk. Not that talking is desirable, but you can make gentle suggestions, or express your satisfaction with words. Kissing shuts you up, seals off your lips, binds your tongue, and all you can do to communicate pleasure is moan, and if you get too carried away with that, it's weird. You certainly can't make suggestions. They have to be physical — a shift of your jaw, a slight pulling back.

It's not that I spend my time telling lovers, and friends with benefits, and whomever, how to do things in bed. I'm not talking the entire time. It's just an observation that you're silenced when you kiss.

Putting your mouth on another's is intimate in a different way. Maybe it's because the connection is between your heads — the core of you swimming around inside that bone enclosure. You open your mouth and join your flesh and your brain and all your thoughts are right there, inches away. Kissing is usually the starting gun. You test the waters, a light kiss to see if there's a response. You find out if your bodies work well together without giving direction and having any associated conversation.

I love kissing. I've loved it since my very first, and I lucked out because that guy was a good kisser. I'm not really sure what makes a good kisser. There are the basics such as not allowing your mouth to generate buckets of saliva. And there's finding the right touch, firm but not hard enough to grind teeth into the insides of lips. And not putting your mouth over the entire mouth of the other, swallowing their lips so they feel they have a leech on their face.

After that, it's personal taste. Compatibility, I suppose. When someone is labeled a good kisser, are they inherently good or are they right for that individual?

Gavin's kissing was nice. I would categorize it as good. Excellent. I was a little surprised that he hadn't started things when he so clearly wanted to, but then, it's back to that placeholder nature he has.

Starting things myself was kind of fun. It's a good change of pace from time to time, and I think he was surprised. Or maybe not. Maybe that's why the pause — he was waiting for me and I hadn't realized it. I could have gone on longer. I didn't care if anyone saw us. Possibly, he did care.

Sitting on the lounge chair, taking tiny sips from my latte,

I still felt the warmth of him through the center of my body. I wanted to do something, to shake off the desire that was creeping out farther, ready to take me over. Weightlifting would be good, yet here I was, drinking a latte and lying on my back.

I sat up. I put the cup on the tile and stretched my arms over my head. I tipped my head side to side, stretching the tendons. I picked up the cup and drank the rest of it rather quickly. I went into the house, put the cup in the dishwasher, and went upstairs to change into workout clothes.

Lifting at my maximum capacity would hopefully drain out the urge I had to knock on Gavin's bedroom door.

# 27

Tess was a little surprised Ted had responded so quickly. It was ironic that Cynthia was still ignoring her while the CEO managed to find time to tap out a few words. She supposed that's why he had the position he did. No matter how a CEO might go off the rails after too many years in power, sinking into ever-worsening decisions as those around him failed to tell the truth about what was going on in their organizations — everything from shielding employees who were risks for revealing proprietary information, to product development problems that would leave the CEO having to scramble with press to paint a positive picture explaining the delay — they didn't get there by being lazy. And they didn't get there by failing to respond to honest inquiries, or failing to stay on top of their email in general.

Most of them, that is. In her first job after grad school, Tess worked for a man who couldn't seem to manage any aspect of his life. Even his super-efficient administrative assistant was unable to make much impact. The guy needed a text message to tell him to read the six emails you'd sent trying to get his attention. And not just one text message. It wasn't unheard of that you had to leave a voicemail, or four, to get him to read the text messages telling him to read his email. And when finally confronted in a conference room before a meeting, he was startled that he hadn't seen any of your communications, his eyes widening in disbelief. He stared in a very unnerving way, saying without the slightest movement of his lips into a chagrined smile — *I wonder why I didn't see that sooner?*

Tess had wanted to scream — *Because you're incompetent. If you can't manage your in-box, how can you manage a company of twelve hundred people?*

She clicked on Ted's email.

*Tess — Good to hear from you. I hope life is treating you well. I spoke with the detective investigating Steve's death. He said they're satisfied with the cause of death, and the autopsy confirmed it. The quantity of heroin in his system was enormous. Thanks for your concern. Enjoy your visit down under! If there's anything I can do for you in the future, please do let me know. —TH*

She tapped the mail tool closed and picked up her cell phone. His response was unacceptable. Of course Steve died from heroin, of course the toxicology report confirmed it! The point wasn't the agent of his death, it was the source of the heroin. It was the person who persuaded him to get naked, the person who convinced him that multiple snorts of something that was a known killer was a good idea.

It was nine-fifteen — two-fifteen on Sunday in the U.S. She had his cell number. She'd used it frequently over the years, mostly right before a big product launch when they were in contact on an hourly basis as the event drew close.

Getting an answer on the weekend was easier. He might assume she was calling in response to his offer to do *anything*. He might also remember her tenacity and know she was calling to object to his refusal to prod the detective into more action.

Still, he would answer. She was sure of it. He wasn't one to dodge confrontation, and if he thought she had an impassioned demand, he wouldn't try to run away from it.

She tapped his name and waited for the call to connect.

He answered before it rang on her side. "Tess, good to hear from you. What's up?"

"Sorry to bother you on a Sunday…"

"I have a moment. What is it?"

"I'm calling about Steve."

"What about him?"

"You and I both know he wasn't a drug user," she said.

"Correct."

"Then how could he…"

"An experiment, I imagine."

"You really believe he would do that?"

"It doesn't matter what I believe, he did it."

"What if someone, I don't know, injected it or…"

"There were no needle marks. The detective said it was snorted."

"No needle marks proves he wasn't into it."

"He obviously was."

"Someone might have forced him."

"I don't think that's possible, to force someone to snort powder up his nose."

"I just know how he was, he would never…"

"Tess. Surely you know by this point in your life that none of us ever really knows what anyone will do. It's not possible to say *never*. We only know what others choose to show us."

"Aren't you the philosopher."

"It's the truth."

"I don't believe he would have snorted heroin without some kind of pressure or influence."

"The police made their final call and I'm comfortable

with it. If there's nothing else I can do for you today, I'll say good-bye now." He paused for a few seconds, and then ended the call.

Tess threw the phone onto her bed. It buzzed. She picked it up and saw a message from Cynthia.

*Ted said some questions are never answered. Steve OD'd and we'll never know why. Sorry.*

She tossed the phone back into the center of the comforter where it sank like a kitten burrowing into a fluffy pillow for an afternoon nap.

She went out to the balcony. The air smelled of damp eucalyptus. A few of the slender leaves had floated onto the front lawn. A magpie swooped down and began strutting around the yard as if surveying it for future development.

It amazed her how Ted had managed to be patronizing and factual in the same conversation. She couldn't understand why everyone simply accepted the results. Were they cowed by the authority of a police detective? She couldn't imagine that. The people at CC weren't meek or deferential in any way. Of course it was true that no one knew others as well as they thought, that you never knew everything about a person. But you had some insight, some experience of a person — you knew their tastes, their typical behaviors, opinions, hot buttons, and daily routines. You knew their beliefs and their personalities and their dreams.

She needed to bounce this off Alex. She needed someone to agree that something wasn't right about his death. Alex had been dismissive before, but she'd been jet-lagged. Alex kept complaining she wanted to get out of the house for a few hours, that she felt trapped.

Tess went into the bathroom and turned on the shower.

A lunch out was called for. And no matter what Alex said, she would provide some insight. All that was needed was a pair of ears to absorb her thoughts. It didn't matter whether Alex disagreed. She was not letting this go.

# 28

Alex's response to her lunch invitation was immediate, coming before Tess had finished speaking. Alex didn't ask where they were eating. Instead, she ran up the stairs calling back that she'd be showered and dressed in less than ten minutes.

In the curve of the staircase was a small bench. Tess sat down. Looking at the staircase from that angle, the structure was almost a piece of art in itself. That's what she loved about the entire house. The artwork was dramatic. Every room had abstract paintings in bold colors, bronze figures — an ibis, a dolphin, a collection of sea turtles among leaves of kelp — and large glass vases placed in corners and on tables. The art enhanced the fact that every tile and line of grout was also an artistic expression. Even the placement of windows and bifold glass doors and the garden areas functioned like works of art. She loved it, and she'd loved Sean's idea that they live and work together so their collective energy around TruthTeller was made stronger.

She rolled the name around in her head. It had the same acronym as her initials — Tess Turner. Was that why her subconscious came up with the name? It was a little embarrassing. She hoped no one else noticed. She wasn't sure why she hadn't realized it earlier.

Friday she would present the marketing plan to the group. It would be the first substantial meeting they'd had. Sean seemed to be drifting, unsure what he was supposed to be doing to lead their small team. Gavin was busy working out final bugs in the app. Often at night, the two of them met alone, Gavin updating Sean on the minutia of each tweak he'd made that day. Tess was glad they hadn't invited her to those meetings.

But maybe that wasn't a good thing. The four of them hadn't formed a solid connection, they hadn't formed a connection at all. Sean was outspoken in his distrust of Alex. Gavin closed himself off in his room, and even when he was with the rest of the group, he was aloof.

The experience so far was the polar opposite of what he'd proposed — shared energy kept at a high level through laughing together and talking about life, letting all of those meaningful conversations feed into their work. They were supposed to be collaborating informally, building enthusiasm. Except for Gavin, lethargy pervaded the atmosphere. She'd spent several hours a day working on the marketing plan, but it was nothing compared to the number of hours she used to put into a crucial product plan at CoastalCreative. Did that mean she wasn't passionate about this after all? She had been when she made the decision, what changed?

Sean was right — Alex.

She closed her eyes. Alex needed to mold her attitude into one that supported this venture. She needed more drive and less stubbornness. Maybe this lunch would be good for more than verbalizing her frustrations about Steve's death, getting her views clear in her own mind. It could turn into a bona fide business lunch.

Alex was headed down the stairs, spreading mocha tinted gloss across her lips as she walked. Her lips looked fuller than normal. Swollen. Maybe it was the humidity.

Tess drove to Sydney Harbor where they found a restaurant along Circular Quay near the Opera House. The area was covered with an enormous overhang, so even if a drizzle materialized, which rain often did out of nowhere in Sydney, they'd be completely dry. A low heat lamp sat beside their table. Right now, the sky was a cloudless sapphire. She smiled. It felt good to be outside, to be away from the house, lovely as it was. She liked watching the crowd — tourists and people pouring out of office buildings for lunch. She felt the energy of the human race, the excitement of lunches and love affairs happening around her. She felt bathed and cleansed by the ever-moving froth of human life.

They both ordered crab and shrimp salads with dressing on the side and Voss sparkling water with lemon.

"Too bad I'm driving. I'd love a glass of white wine," Tess said.

"One glass won't matter."

"Maybe. But what if I want a second?" She shifted in her chair, crossing her legs.

"So what's the business we couldn't discuss at the house?" Alex said.

"That's not why I suggested this."

"You wanted to escape?" Alex said.

Tess laughed. "Maybe, a little. We need to get out more. I like the concept of the incubator, if you want to call it that, but I don't think it's meant to be exclusive."

"We're cheating on the company when we go out and meet other people?"

"Yes and no. Anyway, I'll get to the point." She unwrapped her straw and stuck it in the glass. Suddenly, her mouth craved the comfort of closing tightly around a straw, sucking in the liquid, giving her time to think. But she shouldn't think, she should charge in. "I'll be blunt. You need to be more of a team player."

"I am a team player, when I'm with the right team."

"Well this is the team, it's not going to change." She gave Alex a tight-lipped smile. "So get on the team or we'll need to figure out something else."

"What did I do that's so terrible you want to fire me?"

"I'm not firing you."

The server delivered their salads, a relief because now she could give her attention to the food, a respite from Alex's eyes.

"You seem hostile," Tess said. "It's palpable."

"Not with Gavin."

"Gavin's not important."

"So I don't really need to be a team player, I need to kiss the boss's ass?"

"Don't put words in my mouth."

Alex didn't say anything.

"Can you just be a bit more pleasant?" Tess said. "I know you can be, I'm not sure why you're so…difficult. Australia is a wonderful place and you act like you hate it here."

"What did I do that's difficult?"

"It's the air you give off."

"Well, I'll have to get some different air, then. I wonder where I find that?"

Tess laughed, wishing she hadn't. "I know you can be charming, why can't you charm Sean?"

"He's too superior."

"Superior to what?"

"He thinks he's morally superior. To everyone."

"No he doesn't. Not at all. You're completely misreading him. Anyway, I'm not going to get sidetracked into analyzing his personality. I know you can be charming, be charming."

"Is that a command?"

"Take it however you want." Tess put a piece of crab leg in her mouth. It was so sweet, she was glad she'd drizzled only a little vinaigrette across the entire plate so the taste of the crab came through clean and pure.

"Duly noted."

Tess looked down at her plate. She longed for a glass of wine.

"What else?" Alex squeezed lemon into her water and stirred it with her fork. She licked the fork.

Most people would look tacky doing something like that, but she managed to appear smooth and classy and perfectly well-mannered.

"I wanted to talk about Steve."

Alex smiled. "This isn't about me being charming at all. Or escaping from the house and being outside on a perfect day."

"Yes it is."

"It's about your obsession with Steve. You really should let it go. Why are you thinking about anything related to CC at all?"

"I'm not obsessed."

"He's dead. What's there to talk about?"

"I told you, I don't believe…"

"Don't believe the police?"

"Will you hear me out, please?" She put down her fork. She took a long sip of water, feeling the carbonation dance down her throat, the cool liquid clearing out her thoughts.

Alex stabbed a slice of avocado and put it in her mouth. She stabbed her fork again, this time into half a piece of shrimp. She put that in with the avocado.

"I asked Ted Hutchins to tell the detective that Steve wasn't a drug user. He refused. Even though he, and Cynthia Latimer, both agree with me that Steve would never have done something like that. They were shocked."

"You can't possibly know what someone would never do."

"That's basically what Hutchins said. Yet, he agrees with me! It's so frustrating. How can he agree but refuse to look into the situation? It seems they could care less that Steve's life ends with this black mark on it."

"I don't mean to be cold, but a few years down the road, what will it matter?"

"That is cold."

"But true. You know it's true."

"I can't let it go."

"Because you're obsessed."

"No, I want to do the right thing. And it doesn't need to be labeled. I just wanted your take on whether I should contact the detective. Not your take, exactly, I'm not asking for advice. I'm curious what you think of the idea, though."

"I think it's a waste of time. And you have a product to launch. And you live in Australia. You should put all of that behind you. I have."

"I can't just cut off my whole life. Part of me is still there. I worked at CC for over ten years. And I still have a home there. And Damien."

"I thought you were moving Damien here?"

"I'm not sure I can, as long as we're living in Sean's

house. But I suppose I should ask him."

"How long do you think that's going to last?"

"He hasn't said. But I would expect we'll be there at least until the app gets traction, until we have solid sales."

Alex poked her fork into a piece of crab leg. She admired it, turning her fork at different angles, before putting it gently on her tongue.

Tess smiled. Sharing a meal with Alex was fun. She worshipped her food. When she chewed, her mouth moved in a way that showed the pleasure she experienced from the variety of tastes. Her eyes were soft and glazed as if she and the food were having a sexual experience. She laughed.

Alex lowered her fork. "What?"

"Nothing." She'd been right — it didn't matter that Alex thought there was nothing worth pursuing. She didn't even care that Alex viewed her as obsessed. Talking about it had cleared her head and made her realize there was no reason not to call the detective. The worst he could do was what they'd done so far, what Ted and Cynthia had done — nothing.

"You need a new man in your life," Alex said.

"Probably."

"Then you wouldn't be obsessed with Steve."

"I'm not obsessed with him."

"You absolutely are."

"I'll touch base with the detective. That's all."

"And what will you say? How will you explain your inordinate interest in something that's obvious and has already been resolved?"

"Stop making it more than it is. I have a simple concern. A colleague. Doing the right thing, as I said."

"So you're going ahead with it?"

"Yes."

"Then why did you even ask me?"

"I told you I wasn't asking. I'm thinking out loud."

"If you're so determined, maybe you should let me do it," Alex said.

"Call the detective?"

"Yes. I knew Steve. I could ask the same questions. Or question."

"I don't think that would make any difference."

"You don't want them finding out you had a relationship with him. They might wonder why you care so much."

"What are you talking about?" Tess signaled the server and ordered two glasses of Sauvignon Blanc.

"Perfect," Alex said.

"What?"

"A glass of wine will be nice. Anyway, if I call, I can be more detached."

"I don't care what he thinks of me," Tess said.

"But he might think you're..."

Tess waited for nearly half a minute. "He might think I'm what?"

"I don't know, never mind. You're kind of emotional about it, and the results might be better if someone who's more removed makes the call."

Tess rolled this idea around in her mind. The wine arrived and she took a quick sip. This was why Alex would be good with social media. She was persuasive, even when the reasons for her point of view were flimsy, something you could barely grasp, as if she made it up as she went along. But she might be right. Alex would be more aggressive and she wouldn't give the impression she cared too much, that she was looking at Steve through a filter of sex and grief over a dissolved relationship. They might take her more seriously.

"I'll think about it." But she already knew the answer. And then she thought of the app. Was this a decision she might have posed to the app? It hadn't even crossed her mind. They had a long, uphill battle to make this product appealing to the masses. People were used to making decisions by bouncing them off other human beings, not by plugging data into a smart phone.

# 29

The morning after Gavin and I kissed, I skipped my run. I hadn't woken up while it was dark and there was no point going at six-thirty as the sky was growing light and John was standing by his front window watching for me.

When I finally went downstairs, the first floor was deserted. I made the route through all the rooms twice to confirm it. I went into the garage. Tess's sedan, Gavin's restored British sports car, and Sean's SUV were gone. I couldn't believe my good fortune. They must all be feeling as claustrophobic as I was.

I scurried, literally, back inside the house. I closed the door and darted up the stairs two at a time. I knew better, but tried Gavin's door anyway, pressing on the handle as I passed by. It didn't give an inch. Or a millimeter as the Aussies would say.

I continued on to Sean's bedroom.

This time, I wasn't looking for his secrets, and I wasn't all that disappointed Gavin's were still hidden from me. What I wanted was that statue. Running my finger down her nose wasn't nearly enough. The wood was as smooth as human skin, like satin, but with a solid feel that made it even more desirable. I wanted to touch it, run my hands over it. I wanted to feel every inch of that woman's body.

The door was unlocked and I went inside.

Beautiful artwork is always displayed in hands-off environments. If you walk up to carved marble or wood or bronze in a museum and stroke the arms and legs of a human or animal figure, caress the face, feel the solidness that's like bone and muscle, or touch the textured color of an abstract painting, a security guard will be on you in a minute.

I left his door cracked open so I'd hear the sound of vehicles, the front door, footsteps on the stairs. Surely they didn't go out in the car barefoot, and they weren't the types who lined up shoes inside the front door.

First, I sat in his leather chair. It was very comfortable for a rather small chair. Spending an hour or two in it would be pleasant. I studied the form in the corner and wondered what Sean thought about when he sat in the same chair, gazing at his possession. And she was that — a possession that he didn't want to share in a prominent area of his house. Who has a five-and-a-half-foot statue in his bedroom?

After a few minutes, I stood and walked toward her. I touched my fingertips to her mouth. I ran them around the shape of her lips. I closed my eyes and let my fingers move across her face — the indentations of her nostrils, the surface of her eyeballs, and along her hairline. I traced the outline of her ears and put my hands around her neck as if to strangle her.

I ran both hands over her shoulders, down across her breasts, to her belly and hips.

"What the fuck are you doing?"

My hands fell away from the seductive wood of their own volition.

I turned. Sean was standing in the doorway. I hadn't heard a car or the door or even the intake of breath.

"Admiring your statue."

"It looked as if you wanted to fuck my statue."

I laughed.

"And why are you in my room at all?"

"I was interested."

"Please leave."

I thought of John, the roles reversed. Did Sean view me with the same revulsion I had toward John, entering my space uninvited and refusing to leave? I gave him a friendly smile and walked toward him. He moved out of the doorway so I could pass through.

"You have no right to be here. I don't enter your room without permission."

"How would I know that?"

"Because that's not what people do. We respect each other."

Did he think I wasn't a person. I laughed softly.

"Is this funny to you?"

"I shouldn't have invaded your space, you're right."

He glared at me.

"But it's strange, living in a house where half of it's shut off. It makes me feel disoriented."

"So you entered Gavin's room also?"

"He keeps his door locked."

"This is a complete betrayal of trust. We're a team here."

"I know. And I said, I shouldn't have done it."

"And you won't do it again."

"I hope not."

"What kind of answer is that?"

"The truth."

"Well stay out. This is so very disappointing. It's not the kind of…"

"I know, we're a team."

"Do you always go into people's private space without invitation?"

"Not always. But it happens."

His lips were parted but no breath seemed to come out of them. He moved closer. "I don't like this at all." He spoke in a low voice, on the edge of a whisper. "It's rude, disrespectful, and honestly kind of creepy."

"I said…"

He held up his hand. "I know what you said. If it happens again, there will be consequences."

He was threatening me? I wanted to point that out, but again, the thought of giving up everything in this luscious house along with a very nice income was not something I wanted. Was he threatening to fire me? I couldn't see Tess going along with that, but I could absolutely see Tess's face when he told her I'd been hanging out in his room, running my hands over his statue.

"I don't trust you, Alex."

"Well you didn't trust me before, so nothing has changed."

His eyes widened but he didn't say anything.

I returned to my room, longing for a cigarette. It was early in the day, not the time I usually like to smoke, but the desire was intense. Sean wouldn't like it if I smoked on the property. According to Tess, they sometimes smoked weed, but he wouldn't want me out there smoking regular tobacco. I could feel it in his monk-like bedroom and his long hair and his utopian view of a startup.

# 30

I wasn't going to miss another run, so on Wednesday morning, I was out the front door and running by four-fifty. My hoodie was warm and soft. The air was as quiet as night, and I liked the thick, brooding presence of it. I could feel the same silence inside the unlit houses as I passed. I imagined I heard the birds sleeping on branches around me, beating hearts and rapidly moving nervous systems. Some of them might already be awake, aware of my passing but not threatened enough to raise an alarm that would wake every bird for a quarter of a mile, filling the neighborhood with their laughing, chirping, squawking sound.

The familiar landmarks looked different in the darkness. Some of the houses I'd noted before now looked identical to each other — brick siding all the same, large windows and flat roofs equally similar — and I wasn't sure where I needed to make my first turn. For the start of my route, I wanted to make sure I put as much distance as possible between me and John.

I ran unmolested for over an hour. As I started up the street toward my temporary home, John was visible from the corner. He stood near a decorative lamppost set into the lawn in the space where the front path met the sidewalk. He wore jeans and a black button-down shirt that hung open, revealing a strip of skin. I couldn't see his skin from that distance — still six or seven houses away, but the movement of the sides of the shirt let me know it was there.

Obviously he hadn't planned on joining my run, which made me think he'd seen me leave after all, but hadn't had time to change his clothes and catch up to me.

I started running faster, planning to pass by with a quick nod, up the walkway and into the foyer, closing the door before he could open his mouth.

He shouted at me when I was two houses away. "I don't even know your name."

I didn't shout back.

As I drew close to where he was standing, he moved onto the sidewalk, almost blocking my way, but not quite, just enough to make me feel crowded, forced to adjust my path.

"Can I talk to you for a minute?" he said.

"Some other time. I need a glass of water."

"I can offer you a glass of water. I'll show you around the place. It's only two years old. Tore down the old place and started completely from scratch. There are a lot of nice custom features."

"I'm sure." It was hard to say no. I didn't like him at all, but I loved the exterior of the house. And I'm relentlessly curious about the insides of nice houses. I love contemplating floor plans, looking for flaws so that by the time I build my own house, I'll know in my gut what works best. I love to see what's done right and I like noticing features like the location of a wine cabinet and the design of storage closets. Sean's indoor-outdoor family room that Tess said was popular all over the Sydney area was fantastic.

He buttoned his shirt, starting at the bottom.

My resistance ebbed further.

"You want to see it, I can tell."

"Is that right?"

"There's a craving look in your eyes."

"I don't think you can assume that."

He smiled.

I was also annoyed that he could read me, annoyed at myself for letting my thoughts show on my face.

"I don't bite," he said.

"I have no doubt."

"Then come on in. I didn't mean to get off on the wrong foot with you. I can tell you like your space. I shouldn't have snuck up on you and pulled out your earphones."

"You got that right."

"So all is forgiven?"

He still rubbed me the wrong way, still gave off a slight air of creepiness, but I did want to see the house, and there's no point in creating premature conflict with the people around you. He was an ass, but the men inside my house had tendencies in that direction also. His apology seemed genuine, and buttoning his shirt helped. Maybe grabbing my earbuds had been one of those impulse things that he truly did regret once he saw how controlling and aggressive it was. Or maybe I was making excuses for him. Either way, I wasn't going to turn down a chance to see the house. I might not get another.

"Okay. But I only have a few minutes."

"What's the rush? I never see any of you leaving for work."

"I work from home."

"Everyone does now. I don't see why companies put up with it. The whole setup is a recipe for anarchy."

"That's a little strong."

He turned and started up the walkway. At least he hadn't made a big show of insisting I go first.

The front door swung open and I stepped inside.

Everything was white. The tile floors, the walls, the staircase, and the countertops and appliances in the kitchen. It could have been quite dramatic and very chic, especially with some white furniture, maybe a few startling reds to intensify the drama. Instead, the furniture looked like it could have come from any department store in the U.S. The artwork was too small for such massive amounts of wall space, and the images were pedestrian — paintings of farms and fields of wild flowers, oceans and forests.

I followed him on his grand tour of living room, dining room, and two downstairs bathrooms. Another room contained nothing but bookcases and a chair. The one next to that featured a TV and two reclining lounge chairs. There was a billiards room and another room with a leather chair, two sets of speakers, and an iPod in a dock.

He led me to the great room and then out to the patio. The backyard was filled with blooming shrubs and swaths of flowers in every color of the rainbow. It was laid out exactly like a rainbow, with red hibiscus at the left side of the yard, moving through to lavender agapanthus and shrubs with tiny dark purple flowers along the far right.

"No swimming pool?" I said. "I thought it was practically a requirement for luxury homes."

"My wife, Karen, doesn't like the water. She can't swim. She doesn't even own a bathing suit."

I nodded, feeling a great affinity for her. She didn't have to look out her bedroom window at a dark pool of water nearly seven feet deep. I do like bathing suits, though. I followed him back inside.

On the second floor there was a lounge area that opened

into a deep set balcony. The outdoor space was enclosed by concrete walls that made it look like a shoebox turned on its side. It was very dramatic, but didn't allow for enjoying much sun. I supposed it was designed for sitting outside during thunderstorms.

In the back corner, well away from any place where rain could get at it, was a large white telescope mounted on a tripod. In front of it, pushed up against the wall, was a small table and beside that was a matching wooden chair, neither remarkable, just plain and functional.

I gestured toward the telescope. "That's slick."

"I'm an amateur astronomer."

I nodded.

He began talking about the wonders of looking at the planets and constellations, the seductive beauty of the night sky, the utter silence of space. "Looking at the stars transports you away from the earth. The endless nature of it is even more evident than with the naked eye. The mathematical precision is breathtaking." He paused. "You're welcome to come look at the sky. Any time."

"Maybe I will."

He didn't push it, which was surprising.

There were six bedrooms on the second floor. Like Sean's house, four were en-suites. I wondered if it was an Australian thing or a twenty-first century homebuilding trend in all developed countries.

In the first three rooms, I made comments about the light, the placement of the windows, the spaciousness, the closets. I couldn't say a word about the decorating because it was so incredibly disappointing and I honestly could not come up with anything complimentary. The dull furniture didn't even look particularly comfortable.

The master bedroom contained a double bed and a single dresser. The two remaining bedrooms were empty. When I asked why, he shrugged. We were halfway down the stairs when he said that maybe if the kids came to visit, they would use those rooms.

We returned to the kitchen and he filled two glasses with water. He handed one to me.

"So you have kids in the US?"

"Two." He gulped some of his water.

The empty bedrooms made no sense, if he only had two grown children. Why would they use the unfurnished rooms? The other three were already set up as guest rooms.

He put down his glass and wiped the back of his hand across his mouth. "Two girls. One with a girl of her own."

"That's a lot of girls."

He laughed.

"Then your daughters are adults?" I said.

"Of course. One of them has a kid."

"So they aren't really girls, then?"

He furrowed his brow but didn't say anything.

"And your wife spends the summer there?"

"Not all of it. She goes in May, comes back in late July."

"You can't get away from work to go with her?" I drank half the glass of water in several long gulps, already bored with our conversation, even my side of it.

"I'm retired. From the oil and gas industry."

It seemed odd that he didn't travel with her, but I wasn't interested in finding out why. He was strange, I'd just add it to the list of oddities. I finished the water and put the glass on the counter. "Thanks for this."

"Any time."

"I need to get going."

"To work?"

"Yes, pretty much."

"I still haven't heard your name," he said.

"Alex."

He gave me a thumbs up. He walked with me to the door but let me open it myself. We said good-bye and I walked quickly down his walkway and over to Sean's.

I was sick over that gorgeous house. The structure was spectacular — the garden lush and the patio like it belonged at a resort. The patio furniture was very nice, what you would expect. Maybe he spent all his time out there and didn't care about the rest of the rooms.

Still, it could have been amazing.

What did he do all day? Retired, his wife out of the country. Maybe he spent the time making a pest of himself whenever his neighbors went for a run or walked around the neighborhood.

# 31

I'd been asked by Sean, via an icy text message that contradicted our cozy little work-play community, to meet him in the largest of the offices at two o'clock. It was more of an order than an ask. There were a lot of orders flying around this tiny company. Given all the togetherness, I'd expected it to be more equality-based than the massive organization that was CoastalCreative, but Sean and Tess seemed to have executive privilege down pat.

He wanted to meet so he could demo the app to me.

Finally.

Not the app, *our* app. I was supposed to think of this as a team, so the app belonged to all of us. It was our baby.

Maybe that's part of why I was so on edge. It wasn't just being trapped and it wasn't just needing sex, it was boredom. You can only sit in a lounge chair, and you can only lift weights and run so much. Especially when there are only three people, not counting John next door, to keep you entertained.

I dressed in black skinny jeans, black ballet slipper shoes, and a white button-down shirt with the tails out. I decided the outfit looked a little Katherine Hepburn, so I used a curling iron to put some dramatic waves in my hair.

I waited until two before heading downstairs.

He wasn't in the office. In fact, it didn't look like he'd been there at all, leaving for a moment to get a beverage. The lights were on but the computer screen was dark and the shutters were closed from the night before. Unless he liked to work only with artificial light. I took a deep breath. Charm. I needed to charm. I wasn't sure why I was so antagonistic toward him. There was his superiority. But it was more than that. It was something below conscious thought. Maybe because he seemed very controlling. Or maybe I was intensifying the feeling by focusing on what I didn't like — his attempt to control our free time, and pissed at him for highlighting that I'd contributed nothing tangible when he issued that forced and empty thank you for helping with Tess's naming exercise.

When he walked into the office twenty minutes later, I knew two things.

He was deliberately late to put me in my place.

He was better looking, more alluring, and a greater challenge than Gavin and I wished I'd gone after him.

Too late for both things, for now.

"Sorry to keep you waiting, Alexandra."

Gone was the look of horror in his eyes when he'd found me in his room. Gone was the rather paternalistic attitude toward me, acting as if I not only worked for him, and was beholden to his generosity, but also that I was some sort of junior employee, or even a child who needed to be taught rules of social behavior.

I did not view the house and food and beverages as generous gestures on his part. I viewed them as perks that I was earning, or would be soon. I was earning them already by going along with his fanciful, junior high school fantasy of incubating a start-up in a house.

"Take this." He handed his phone to me and took a seat at the opposite side of the small round table, identical to the one in the other office.

The phone was warm from being in his hip pocket. I let the heat seep into me and waited.

He dug around in his front pocket and pulled out a small disk, the size of a checker but thicker. He placed it on the table. "You need to hold this so it can read your body's reaction."

"I thought this was all about a phone app?"

"It is."

"I don't think people will rush to download it if they have to buy this thing."

"That's your job."

"What?"

"To make them want to."

"Well the buying behavior is different. You aren't going to get the impulse crowd."

"It can still be impulse, for people with more discretionary income. They'll be able to order it off our website and have it overnight in all major metropolitan areas. Or from Amazon."

I picked up the disk and held it in my other hand. It was also warm. It was smooth with rounded edges, making it pleasant to hold, comforting despite the hard plastic shell. They'd done a good job on the design. It was very Apple-like. "Who's working on this product?"

"It's outsourced."

I nodded.

He unlocked his phone and explained how I should enter a question and tap through the questions the app gave me.

The question I posed was: *Should I hook up with Sean?*

I figured, what the hell. If I really wanted the app to run

through its paces, to get a true picture of how well the thing worked, I couldn't give it a softball question about my job or whether to move out of the claustrophobic house. If I was going to sell this thing on social media, I needed to get some sort of enthusiasm about it. I really didn't think I should pursue Sean, but I wanted to and it seemed an excellent test for how well it could read my true instinct.

The questions were intrusive.

"Where does this data get stored?"

"Your responses?"

"Yes."

"In the cloud."

"And people will feel comfortable releasing very intimate pieces of their lives into the cloud?"

"I think most app buyers, technology users in general, aren't paranoid about the security of the cloud any more. As long as they're savvy about protecting their data."

"Really? When the headlines scream about major hacks every other week?"

"People have accepted that's a risk for modern life, but overall, they know that it's poor personal security measures that open the door for those breaches to happen."

"If you say so." I turned my attention back to the app.

There were questions about my sex life, my satisfaction with my financial situation, including detailed requests for how much money I currently had and whether I was pleased or angry or detached when I typed in that figure. It asked about my workout habits, sleep habits, and my diet. There were a few basic questions about my health history, and my age, of course. It asked about family relationships and friends and marital status and whether I was happy with all of that.

Happy is not a word I tend to use, or a concept I think about much.

I'm always enjoying my life. When I'm not, I work fairly quickly to change things.

When I was finished, the app crunched the data and returned a startling result — *No.*

"You look surprised," Sean said.

I shrugged. I would have to take some time to think about why this answer was my deep, instinctive response. I would have to think about how valuable this app was.

Even if it wasn't that useful in many situations, I needed to figure out a way to imagine other people hungry to use it. And it had to be ongoing. Not something they'd perceive as a one-time use, and simply share it with friends rather than encouraging friends to purchase their own device.

"So where does this data go now?"

"I told you…"

"I mean the information I put into your phone."

"Oh, just delete your session."

"It's not drifting toward the clouds?"

He laughed. "No."

I deleted my question. The answers disappeared and the welcome screen returned. I tapped through, checking to make sure there weren't any little breadcrumbs lying around that would allow Sean to follow my train of thought.

I placed the phone and the sensor disk on the table.

"What do you think?"

"It's very intriguing," I said.

"I was hoping for a little more enthusiasm."

"What's wrong with intriguing? Better intriguing than *it's fun*, don't you think? You want people to be seduced."

"Are you seduced? By the app?" he said.

"I'd like to try it again."

"Gavin will have a new rev by early next week."

I smiled.

"So, now that's out of the way…are you feeling like part of the team?"

I shrugged. "Give it time."

"We need to establish trust. It was very disturbing to find you in my room. It showed a total disrespect for my privacy."

He said privacy with a short *i* sound — priv-a-cee. It was so charming. It sounded so formal and so British and so upper class. I was charmed. "That statue is beautiful and I couldn't help myself. Why don't you have it displayed where everyone can enjoy it?"

He was quiet for several seconds.

I wondered if he wasn't going to answer.

He turned and looked at a photograph on the wall adjacent to the windows. It was gorgeous, bursting with blue — an aerial shot off the northeast coast of Australia, the coastline, the ocean, and the Whitsunday Islands. I knew this because I'd spent quite a while studying it while I waited for him. There was a tiny label on the wall beside it, like an art gallery label, stating it was Queensland.

He looked back at me. "If you really want the truth."

"Of course I do."

"It seems inappropriate for a work environment. Especially one where there are women present. It might be offensive."

I laughed.

"Why is that funny?" he said.

"It's art."

"Yes. But it's a nude woman."

"I think we're all adult enough to know art versus something offensive to women."

"I wasn't sure. I know how American women are."

"Do you?"

He looked annoyed, as if I were questioning his opinion even though he believed I should know for myself that American women were a certain way — touchy, lacking humor, easily offended, strident.

"It seems unbalanced. To only have a female nude," he said.

"So you need to buy a male statue?"

He pushed his chair away from the table. "I don't think this is a productive discussion."

"We're talking about art. How is that not productive?"

"Well, it's my statue and I enjoy having it in my room. There's plenty of other very nice artwork in the house."

"There is, I agree."

"Good. So you'll be setting up a Facebook page? Twitter? What about Instagram?"

"I'll start with Facebook. That's where half the planet hangs out."

"You'll show it to me by Friday?"

"I'll have it done before then."

"Friday is fine. Be sure you give it some thought before you start throwing things up there."

"Absolutely."

He held out his hand. "Good meeting. Thank you." He shook my hand with one downward stroke, then walked out of the office. His formal attitude contradicted everything he said he wanted.

# 32

Setting up a Facebook page for TruthTeller would be simple. Figuring out what to do with it would be something else.

People use Facebook to share pictures of their pets and kids and vacations, and to emote. I suppose that's why I don't like it all that much — I'm not an emoter. I like Twitter where people are snappy and sharp and you can interact with strangers, at arm's-length.

Of course Facebook needs to make money to pay for storing all the random thoughts and pithy quotes and cat and dog videos and personality "tests". Hundreds of petabytes of data are filling servers, heating up the planet as we busy ourselves posting images and warnings about the planet growing too hot. Facebook runs advertisements on everyone's page, and you can never escape. Facebook hounds small businesses to run their ads, so someone must be clicking for more information. If you click to get rid of an ad, they demand to know why, and another takes its place. It's a never-ending community of ants pouring out of a hole in the ground. You can step on the first wave, and another will follow, their delicate bodies racing like maniacs, not even noticing that two hundred of their friends are gone.

Every modern business that's trying to operate with one foot in the virtual world and one foot on the rapidly warming earth, has a Facebook page. Even the Sydney Opera House has a Facebook page. It's insane. TruthTeller would be fighting for attention among the forty million others promoting their products and passions.

It was easy to set up my first ever Facebook account which was required before I could create a page for TruthTeller. Instead of Alexandra Mallory, I used the name Alex Teller, grabbing half the TruthTeller name for my own. I didn't want to be easily located on Facebook. I don't like to be easily located anywhere. The next post was a profile picture of the four of us, one where I was on the left side, partially in the shadow of a palm tree. I posted a banner image of a blue whale, which Sean had suggested.

Setting up links to the website Gavin had developed and loading screenshots of the app interface and photographs of the device — all of which could have been done by a ten-year-old — took about half an hour. But the next task was monumental — figuring out how to stand out among those forty million others. I needed to be interesting, informative, and friendly. I needed to figure out how to drive sales in a virtual world where you're immediately tuned out if you put one sliver of a toenail over the invisible line of *too much self promotion*.

I sat at the computer in the front office closest to the side yard. It was drizzling, which made it easier to keep my attention on the large screen in front of me. I entered the location and description information for TruthTeller and the names of the employees. Some people might not want that info made public, but if we were going to interact, we needed to be human beings. Not the little TruthTeller logo, hiding our humanity.

Over the previous few days I'd taken some casual photos of Tess, Sean, and Gavin. For my photo I'd worn dark glasses and a Great Barrier Reef hat I'd swiped out of the downstairs closet where we kept jackets and umbrellas. I put my hair in a ponytail, looped it through the back of the hat, and snapped a few selfies. They might give me grief for an unprofessional photo, but I was the one setting it up so I gave myself creative license. They, meaning Sean, could complain all they wanted. It was doubtful he'd go to the trouble of snapping a picture of me and getting the log-in details for the page.

I'd also taken some discreet photos of the house — nothing recognizable, and nothing showing off its more extravagant features. There might be an angle of interest for the way we were living and working together. I could imagine that concept, and posts about our experiences, getting some traction. We might be able to get people discussing the pros and cons as we posted tips for making it work well, if it ever started working *well*.

When the page was finished, I thought about creating an ad right away to get some people liking the page, but Tess would want that sort of thing carefully scheduled and the expense planned out. She wanted it all spelled out in PowerPoint slides. With spreadsheets. And she was right. To make this work, I needed a detailed strategy for expansion.

Still, I was so excited with the little virtual store I'd created, I wanted to see *likes* piling up, our page a sought-after destination. Posting good stuff was the way to get there, not just promoting the skeleton which was like every other page skeleton.

When I was finished tweaking the details, I ran upstairs, changed into workout clothes, and went down to the weight room. I spent an hour lifting weights. The workout energized me. My body was as solid and hard as the carved wooden woman in Sean's room.

I returned to the front office to see whether we'd magically generated any *likes* from people randomly stumbling across the page. We hadn't.

I skimmed through the first draft of Tess's marketing plan and found some of her research about the psychology of decision making. I posted a quote on the Facebook page: *Decisional balance sheet — complicated name for a pro and con list.* I added an editorial comment — *Truth shouldn't hide behind inflated terminology.*

Figuring out relevant video clips was also on my list, to be included in my plan. According to the helpful tips provided by Facebook, video content received a lot more interaction. But it had better be good video. Not a ten-minute clip of a droning head. When I'm surfing online, my attention span for videos is about two or three minutes. At the most. Often, I'm bored and ready to click away after thirty seconds. I'd never stopped to think about every video I started watching, whether it was people producing boring material or if my attention span had shrunk to the spark of a lighted match, burning for a few seconds and then dying, craving another flash of fire.

I stood and stretched. I adjusted the blinds and looked out at the street. It was still drizzling. In front of the window was a curved garden area, filled with plants that were almost as tall as me. Large, thick leaves moved gently in the breeze, wet with rain. They provided protection for observing anyone passing by. Even if they glanced that direction, they'd never notice they were being watched.

It was a quiet street, and there weren't a lot of pedestrians, especially on a weekday in the rain. But still I watched, hoping for something interesting. Two magpies landed on the lawn one after the other and began walking around, pecking at the grass. They looked up every minute or so, glaring directly at the office window, giving the impression that even though a human being wouldn't notice me partially obscured by the plants, they were quite aware of my presence.

I felt I was going a teeny bit mad, watching black and white birds hunt for food in my desire to see something outside of the magnificent house that surrounded me on every side. The large, silent house pressed down on my skull, twisting my muscles with backlogged energy that hadn't dissipated, even after sixty minutes of heaving lead plates and bars into the air.

# 33

It took less than fifteen minutes for Sean to complete twenty laps of the pool. The pool was too small for real swimming, it was designed for kiddies to play in and adults to lie around the sides drinking, occasionally hopping in for a game of volleyball. It was a nice pool. Despite the fact he couldn't swim a mile or two without constant turning, he liked the shape and size. Truthfully, he hadn't wanted anything larger. A real lap pool would give the yard the appearance of a public swimming facility. He preferred swimming in the ocean, where there were no concrete walls shaping his connection to the water.

With this group, socializing around the pool didn't seem to be working. Winter coming on in a few weeks didn't help, but they weren't a very sociable crowd. This wasn't what he'd planned when he suggested they share the same living space. He'd thought they would be excited, maybe grateful. Not that he wanted them indebted, but he thought they'd be willing to give up a bit of privacy for the luxurious surroundings and the benefits of a tightly knit team. He thought they'd be eager to develop life-long connections with genuine friendship as a foundation. He'd heard stories of startups where they became so close they were like brothers, and sisters.

There were also stories of startups where the founders had a falling out as the company matured and grew, but he preferred to focus on the positive. Those stories made the news because they were rare. It wouldn't happen to them.

They were off to a rough start, but it could be corrected. He needed to show more leadership. The small size of the company had deluded him into believing he could direct the team without a lot of authoritative behavior, but he'd seen that was wrong.

He'd thought running another company would be easy, now that he was experienced. But it had been four years since the first company, and maybe things had changed more drastically than he'd realized. He had confidence in their skills, their drive...all but Alex. There must be something he was missing.

The moment his eyes met Alex's for the first time, he'd known she was a predator. Tess mocked him for thinking that way, but he knew he was right. He'd met Alex's type before and you could feel it immediately. He wondered if they smelled your blood.

He never would have hired her himself.

He did trust Tess's judgment, and he had no doubt Alex would do a stunning job, but you had to be careful of the people you let into your company, into your life.

It wasn't as if he thought she was after him or Gavin. She wasn't predatory in that way. She seemed cool toward both of them, very aloof and he hadn't caught a hint of her trying to flirt or come on to them.

What was it then?

He climbed out of the pool and shook his hair. He toweled off his back and arms and legs and walked to the covered area of the patio. He needed to give her another chance. She'd seemed intelligent when she was working with the app. Walking into his room uninvited was disturbing, but it wasn't that he'd thought she wanted to steal the statue, or damage it. She hadn't taken anything and there was no evidence she'd gone through his things. Why couldn't he put his finger on it?

He went inside and got a beer. He stood in the kitchen drinking it. He hadn't dried himself fully and water was dripping onto the floor. He dropped the towel from around his neck and let it fall onto the damp tile to soak up the water.

Things had to change if he was going to see his dream of a truly integrated workplace come to fruition. They couldn't be holing up in their bedrooms. It wasn't that he didn't understand the need for time apart. But they knew the ground rules and they were defying his authority by their choice to avoid the common areas except when they were forced out of their caves by hunger.

He put the beer on the counter and picked up the towel. He took out a rag from beneath the sink and swabbed it across the floor. He grabbed his beer and went up to his room.

Some of the pleasure in his sleek, minimalist room had been damaged by Alex. The furniture and carefully made bed, the light coming through precisely angled shutter blades all seemed less serene than they had before she walked around, possessing them with her eyes. He felt her presence in there even now, pawing over his things, her aggressive wanting taking up psychic space. It was entirely possible she would do that to the company as well.

But he'd wanted strong people, the type who would work hard to make TruthTeller a phenomenal success.

He picked up his phone and typed out a message to the other three: *BBQ and beer tonight. Seven. Be there.*

He added emojis of beer steins, a burger, and four

grinning faces. That should be clear. He changed into jeans and a jumper and slid his feet into flip-flops. They needed more beer, he wanted a lot of drinking going on, some loosening of inhibitions. His mind began working through the food — burgers, sausages, some potato salad from the deli, maybe fried cheese — the Americans would get a charge out of that.

When he returned from the food wonderland that was Woolworths, it took him three trips to carry in all the bags of food.

Gavin had responded to the dinner message with an eye-rolling emoji, Tess with a thumbs up, and Alex with a yellow face wearing sunglasses. He'd thought maybe one of the girls would offer to help pull everything together, but after their initial responses, his phone remained dark and silent. It wasn't that he expected it, nothing sexist like that. And he wasn't letting Gavin off the hook because he was a guy, Gavin wasn't one to offer much of anything, his head was always somewhere else. But he'd thought as guests…well, he'd told them this was their home, so he shouldn't expect them to be acting like grateful houseguests.

He lined up the beer in the fridge, a row of bottles for each of the three brands. He made beef patties and filled bowls with crisps. Once the meal was ready to go, he would put out several kinds of dips, the potato salad, and plates of everything necessary for a good burger — lettuce, grilled onions, tomato, chili mayo, pickled beetroot, pineapple, cheese, and the rest of the usual condiments. Two cooks were required if he wanted to pull off the added topping of a sunny side up egg, so he skipped that.

The smell of sizzling beef and pork sausage drew the

others downstairs. Through the open door of the family room into the entryway, he saw them descend the stairs one after the other, like spirits drifting down in response to a ghostly summons.

Tess was a good sport and popped open a beer along with Gavin. Alex insisted on mixing herself a martini. Sean couldn't imagine drinking a martini with burgers. He couldn't imagine drinking a martini and then switching to beer. Or did she plan to spend the whole evening consuming such high octane drinks? But maybe that would be a good thing. The aloof mask would slip to the side and reveal her true self — good or bad. For all he knew, he'd misjudged her completely and she'd turn out to be sweet and soft and fun. Maybe she was having trouble adjusting to Australia. Although he couldn't imagine why — there was no better place on earth.

By the end of the evening, he knew she was not sweet or soft, but she was definitely fun. As they ate and drank and talked, she joined in. Gone were her two- or three-word answers, gone was the haughty look.

She was a spectacular-looking woman, the type who was aware of that but didn't behave like that meant she deserved extraordinary privilege. She helped serve food and replenish the crisps, and she seemed eagerly interested when he explained that Australians liked more variety on their burgers than Americans. She said she was willing to try the pineapple and beetroot because *when in Rome...*

They drank enough to pleasantly loosen up. The conversation flowed with crazy stories and silly puns and jokes. It was the kind of conversation you felt could go on forever, the kind that made him feel truly connected to other human beings. Maybe his experiment could work after all, and this barbecue was exactly what they'd needed. Their first barbecue had been too soon, they were all strangers, and Alex was still in a jet-lagged stupor. Now, finally, they were getting to know each other, they were talking about things that would give insight during their workday — the things that scared them and excited them and made them laugh or step back in awe.

The only troubling moment came when he told the story of finding a deadly funnel-web spider scurrying over the edge of his blanket and onto the bare skin of his upper arm. He painted a long, detailed picture of the horror of that tiny body, and then his scream. He'd thrashed in the sheets and finally killed it with a bottle of expensive wine he'd taken up to his room for a nightcap. It was the only thing he could think to grab in his confused shock of being ripped out of sleep to see that beast. The bottle broke and wine soaked his mattress. For weeks, he smelled wine and felt regret for the loss. He thought of how close he'd come to a painful alteration in his organ functions as its venom attacked his central nervous system, the certain death if it was a male. He'd wondered what had woken him, if it was some instinctive part of him that sensed the spider, his body taking charge of its life without needing his rational mind.

Alex commented that he'd over-reacted.

He suggested she would be afraid of spiders, certainly those that can kill you with a small, sharp bite.

She'd said she wasn't afraid of anything.

He didn't believe that.

# 34

The tang of pickled beets, which Sean and Gavin insisted on calling beetroot, was not Tess's idea of a delicious hamburger. She wanted to be polite, wanted to be a good sport about Aussie culture, but beets, especially pickled beets, did not go with ketchup and mustard. Every time she thought of it, a quivering sensation ran through her stomach.

Alex had gushed all over Sean about the beets and grilled pineapple. He didn't appear to notice she ate a burger dressed only in tomato, onions, and mustard.

Overall, it was a good evening. It felt so much different from her previous life — a barbecue with copious amounts of beer on a weeknight. She didn't remember doing anything like that since college. Even in grad school, life was too serious, the classes and projects due the following day too important to risk a hangover.

It wasn't that she hadn't had lavish business dinners where she'd consumed the entire day's calories with her entree, and then some of the following day's calories piled on with the alcohol. Usually it was wine, occasionally cocktails and appetizers. With customers and colleagues, she was very conscious of how much she drank, guarding her glass from over-enthusiastic servers and dinner companions.

Drinking with co-workers could be useful or dangerous. This evening, they'd stayed well on the useful side of the line. It wasn't healthy to view drinking as the center, a critical component, of social activity. Any expert in alcoholism would warn that it's a sign of trouble to believe alcohol is what connects people to each other. Sports had the potential to form strong bonds, but most people like the easy friendship and minimal effort of a few drinks rather than arranging dates and locations and clothing and equipment and people for team sports or even a round of golf.

It was probably an indictment of the human race that people needed chemical relief from their personalities, lubrication in order to reveal more of themselves, to listen to less-than-interesting stories, to laugh easily. Was there something very wrong with the way children were raised that so many people wound up so self-contained and cautious and self-protected that alcohol seemed like a requirement?

When the evening wound down, Gavin and Alex cleaned up the kitchen and put the food away. Sean and Tess lounged on the family room couch, sipping beer, watching.

There was something unnatural about the way Alex and Gavin moved around each other in the kitchen. As if they were magnets with two south poles — coming near to each other then moving quickly away, one repelling the other by an invisible force. They didn't speak, which wasn't that unusual since Gavin rarely said much. Alex had been right about her initial observation that he was socially awkward. Even after four beers and in the midst of telling stories from their high school years, he only had one story to the others' five or six, and it had been brief.

*My older sister put peanut butter in my sneakers.*

That was the entire story! Nine words. Still, he seemed content to be eating dinner with them, didn't smile a lot, but kept a pleasant expression on his face. She couldn't figure out if he didn't have much to say or didn't like saying it. Surely his mind wasn't empty most of the time. Maybe it was filled with the details of his work and he knew she and Alex wouldn't be interested in the technical problems he faced, the triumph of re-writing a line of code. They wouldn't understand even if they tried to pretend interest.

The counter was empty, wiped clean and buffed dry with a towel.

Gavin raised one hand toward Seth and Tess. "Good dinner. G'night." He left the room.

Tess finished her beer and stood. "Me too. I'm tired."

Alex was standing in the center of the kitchen, watching her as she carried the bottle to the recycling bin. Tess dropped the bottle inside where it clattered against the other glass. She pushed the container back along the rails, tucking it beneath the counter. She said good-night to Sean and thanked him for the food. He waved her away and said no thanks required, which made her feel she should be offering to cook dinner. Next week. She'd think about it then.

Since the presentation of her marketing plan wasn't until Friday, tomorrow was relatively free and she could sleep in. And call the slacker detective.

Alex had practically begged to make the call, as if she had some tremendous advantage over Tess in her ability to influence. Or just wanted to make Tess feel obsessed with Steve, making too much of the relationship that was long over by the time Steve died. Alex seemed to take pleasure in describing the obsession. It felt as if she was trying to shame Tess into forgetting about him.

Remembering a suddenly deceased colleague that you'd had a relationship with was not an obsession. Neither was wanting to be sure his reputation stayed intact. She just wanted to do the right thing. Why did everyone find that so difficult to understand? She shouldn't have to explain why she wanted him remembered truthfully and with the respect he deserved, despite his flaws. It should be obvious to any human being. And yet, it wasn't.

Together, she and Alex climbed the stairs. Now that she'd started up the stairs, she was suddenly exhausted. It was the beer. Not just the dulling effect of the alcohol, but the bloat and lethargy that came with beer.

Alex seemed as perky as ever. After three martinis. Tess couldn't believe she moved so quickly, seemed so relaxed and open but not at all tipsy. Tess would be flat on her back.

At the landing, Alex turned toward her room.

Still a few steps below, Tess paused. "Wait."

Alex took two more steps away from the stairs.

Tess climbed to the landing. "Did you call Detective Gorman?"

Alex laughed. "Good food and beer and lots of laughs and you're still obsessed with him?"

Tess wasn't going to argue the finer points of obsession. "Did you call?"

"Not yet. And I'm not going to do it right now."

"Never mind, then. I'll call him myself."

"You're making a mistake." Alex moved closer and lowered her voice. "If you want the best shot at getting him to do more investigating, you should wait for me to call him."

"But you're not doing it."

"I will."

"What's the holdup? It's a simple phone call."

"There's no holdup. I'm just not obsessed with it. Thinking about him when I'm supposed to be partying and enjoying life instead of thinking about dead guys."

"Don't say it like that. You're making him sound like a statistic. And I'm not obsessed. I just want them to take action and your suggestion seemed like a good one. But if I'm going to have to nag you…"

"You don't have to nag." Alex seemed to lean on the word *have*.

It was odd that Alex was procrastinating when it had been her idea. She'd just call him herself. If Alex did it too, all the better. She smiled and walked toward her bedroom.

Inside, she kicked off her sandals and stretched out on the bed, feeling the lumps of twisted sheets and bunched up sections of the comforter pressing against her bones. Tomorrow she'd make the bed properly. Tomorrow she'd straighten her room, open the doors to air it out, call the detective, and lift weights for an hour, followed by thirty minutes of yoga. The swampy feeling of this place was getting to her, and it wasn't just the beer.

# 35

Although John was turning out not to be the complete creep I'd thought, I still didn't want to encounter him and have to wrestle away from his insistent presence during my run. He was mildly disturbing, despite his apology. Yanking out my earbuds was borderline assault. It was insulting and crossing a boundary and territorial all in one swift motion.

Leaving the house at quarter to five in the morning didn't bother me. It's easy for me to wake up before the sun. I like watching it advance silently and without hesitation, up over the trees and houses. I like the illusion of having the world to myself.

While my housemates slept off their beer, I ran for an hour and twenty minutes. The air was cooler than the day before, which helped me keep a good pace. It's harder when I'm overtaken by sweat and the heavy feeling that comes with running in full sun, rays beating down on my head and back, sending heat up off the pavement until I feel like my body is melting into the consistency of liquid tar.

Even at that early hour, I expected to see John as I rounded the corner headed back toward Sean's, but when his house and Sean's came into view, he wasn't there. Instead, a woman stood on the sidewalk in front of the house on the other side of John's. This was the older style construction — red brick with a sloped shingle roof. It was a very good looking house. Stately. As large as the modern ones beside it, although not as big as a few of the near-mansions across the street that had been built around the same time period.

The woman zipped her jacket and turned toward me.

I slowed to a walk. When we were a few feet apart, I said *hi.*

She greeted me, but her smile was brief and seemed to require a huge effort. Her blonde hair was streaked with brown and cut to her shoulders, a single length all the way around. She wore dark glasses even though the sun was only now starting to spread pale light onto the edges of the sky. She wore a navy blue jacket, leggings, and a hip-length top that hung below the jacket hem.

Even with the large dark glasses, it was obvious that her face was beautiful. She was slim with the kind of breasts that make men look longer than they should, risking being caught in the act because they can't not take a second or third look. She had long legs and, like the dark glasses, her loose top and jacket couldn't hide her body. She seemed unaware of how she looked. There was something meek and uncertain about her.

I pointed toward Sean's. "I'm Alex. I just moved in, two houses down."

"That's nice. Welcome."

She said her name was Lisa. I asked how long she'd lived there — five years — and how she liked it, what the neighborhood was like. She gave short answers, one or two words. She seemed to want to get away from me. Wanting it badly, not as if she was missing her walk or might be late to work, but as if she didn't want to talk to me no matter how much time she had.

"It's good to meet you. I haven't met anyone else except John."

"Such a sweet man. A great neighbor."

I stared at her, looking for the hint of a sarcastic smile. "You don't think so?" she said.

"He's very aggressive. He yanked my earbuds out when I was running."

She shrugged. "It must have been an accident."

"No."

She smiled. "He looks out for his neighbors."

"What's his wife like?"

"Quiet. She's visiting their children in America. He gets lonely, I think."

"Lonely?"

She nodded. She fiddled with her zipper, sliding it down a few inches, then back up again. "But such a sweet man. So many people nowadays don't care much about their neighbors. He makes our street feel safe."

"I didn't realize it was dangerous."

"There's not a lot of crime, but you never know when someone living right next door to you might turn out to be... cruel, violent. A drug dealer. Gang members. We just need more people to be caring, don't you think?"

"It never hurts."

She tipped her head and unzipped her jacket halfway. She zipped it up again. "Like the older lady over there." She pointed at the house diagonally across from hers. "He helps her carry in groceries every week. And he checks on her if he doesn't see her come out all day." She shoved her hands in her pockets and hunched up her shoulders. "Sometimes I feel like he can see into my soul."

There was no way to respond to that bit of crazy. Something about all this caring didn't fit with my impression of an early-retirement-with-a-boatload-of-money kind of guy. An executive relaxing in Australia after battling the world in the vicious upper echelons of a major corporation. But maybe that's a stereotype.

"I'll head out for my walk now, good to know ya," she said.

"Same here."

She smiled as if my inelegant response was the highlight of her day, and she already knew, at six in the morning, that her day wouldn't get any better. She turned and began walking quickly.

I went into the house, took a shower, and went down to the kitchen. I drank some orange juice, grabbed a muffin out of a covered tin and went back to my room. I sat on the balcony and ate the muffin. It was so moist I didn't mind not having coffee with it. I considered it an entire meal since it was filled with pieces of walnut and strawberry. I didn't miss butter either. I'd eaten one the day before and during my run, I'd spent the last quarter mile thinking about how good they were, longing for another one, hoping they hadn't all been eaten.

I opened my tablet and read news of thunderstorms in Queensland. I read about goings on with the Australian government which seemed quirky and friendly compared with the US federal government. Maybe that was only because I was an outsider.

The conversation with Lisa drifted across my mind. I closed my eyes and tried to picture her expression when she told me that John was such a good person. She'd seemed very devoted to him, as if she considered him her protector. Her comments that he watched out for his neighbors sounded as if she counted on him for that. I hadn't had the impression Sydney was riddled with crime, but maybe all those bloodlines descended from criminals still lurked in the dark corners.

My gut, without the assistance of an app, insisted John was someone to keep my distance from. Maybe that very looking out for his neighbors was overdone and that's what made him creepy. Who asked him to look out for anyone? Still, I was intrigued by the telescope and curious to look at the sky from the Southern Hemisphere. He'd made it sound so interesting — thrilling, almost. I'd never thought much about the night sky except what I could see with my own eyes. Seeing it up close might be a lot more remarkable.

But there was that edginess I felt around him — grabbing at my earbuds, the unbuttoned shirt. Was it a mistake to go over there at night? I could take Tess with me. Or, the whole gang — it could be a team-building event.

The idea was actually very good. I would look like a team player, and since Tess and Sean were so concerned with that, they wouldn't be able to turn down the offer. I should ask John, but what would he do if we all showed up at his door at ten at night? He wasn't going to send three of the four people home. That would just be rude.

# 36

*Los Angeles*

The tiny dorm room where I'd be spending the next year towered above the earth, compared to the second-floor bedroom where I'd grown up. It was surrounded by hundreds of identical cubbyholes. The sounds of freshman moving into their new homes echoed down the narrow corridors but was muffled inside my room. My mother had shut the door to keep our conversation private. She must have known what was coming. Her expression had changed — her face was pale, even her lips had lost their color. She hardly blinked, staring at me, but not focusing, looking past me, maybe seeing something from another realm. She was hoping I wasn't going to break my father's heart, destroy our family, ruin my future, cut them out of my life, or enrage my father, causing him to yank me back home until I repented once and for all.

She might have thought back to my forced baptism, the near-drowning as I was compelled to repent physically if not mentally. I never had repented and she knew it. They all knew it, but that didn't stop my father from trying to drag me into the kingdom of god. He continued to believe he could break my defiant, stubborn spirit and pummel it into the malleable putty he longed to see inside all of his children's minds.

"Yes, there was a place on the form to mark your religion," I said. "I checked atheist."

He sat down suddenly, almost falling onto my roommate's bare mattress. He put his elbows on his knees and rested his face in his cupped hands. An enormous sigh eased out of him.

"You don't really mean that." My mother smiled. "I think you mean agnostic. That means you're not sure. And you are a very opinionated girl, you need everything proven." She smiled even harder. "You're an agnostic. God will have to do something amazing and dramatic in your life. Something you can't ignore, so you'll see His wonder and power."

"I know what atheist means. I know what agnostic means. I put atheist."

"How can you say that?" My mother's voice was panicked. "After all the testimonies you've heard in church? Your entire life? How can you say that? God will hear you."

"Shh." My father took his head out of his hands. "Stop talking, Hannah." He stood and went to the window.

My mother moved back toward the door, as if she wanted to slip out of the room without him.

After looking out at the other buildings, the park-like setting in between, he turned. The light behind him put his face in shadow and I couldn't read his expression. It didn't matter. I didn't have to.

"I'll still pay for your education," he said.

"Thank you."

"I can't condemn your truthfulness."

"She doesn't really mean it." My mother nodded, giving me a look that said, *please don't do this. Change it to agnostic, don't upset him. Don't upset me. Why are you like this?*

"Yes, she does." My father crossed the room and stood beside my mother. He put his hand on her shoulder. "Good-bye, Alexandra. We'll see you at Thanksgiving." He straightened his back. "Even though she is faithless, he remains faithful." He opened the door and went out.

My mother took a few steps toward me, hugged me with a tight squeeze, and followed my father out of the room without speaking.

His paraphrase of the Bible was rather distorted. The faithfulness mentioned was attributed to god. I didn't sit in church and Sunday school for eighteen years without learning what the Bible says. Quite a few people who throw that book in your face should think about re-reading parts of it. Like my father's, words get shifted around, changing the meaning slightly or quite a lot. I suppose the passages that move people the most overshadow the others. They cling to a few key ideas and pretty soon it's a one-note song. And that goes for all religions, not just those drenched in the Bible. I just happen to be familiar with that religion and that holy book.

I hung my skirts and dresses in the closet. I lifted my sweaters out of one of the boxes we'd shipped ahead. Between my sweaters and jeans was a small box wrapped in pink paper with a white satin ribbon tied around it. A tiny card was tucked beneath the ribbon that went around the box. I opened the card.

*We love you Alexandra. Be good. Do what the Lord asks of you.*

It was signed by *Mom* and *Dad* in my mother's large, loopy cursive. I untied the ribbon and tore off the paper. Inside the box was a silver cross on a well-crafted chain. I took it out and saw the card from the store. The cross wasn't silver, it was platinum. I held it up by the clasp and let it spin on the chain.

Did they believe I would wear this, sending a message to

boys that I was off limits? Did they think having a cross hanging from my throat would stop me from saying what I pleased? Did they think the expensive, precious metal would provide more of the protections they were looking for? I had no idea. I don't think it was to chastise me or create guilt. I think they truly believed…something. I'm not sure what. That I would wear it because it was nice looking and it would keep me both safe and pure.

I finished putting my clothes away. I tucked the box with its expensive contents into a drawer, burying it beneath a bunch of socks and tights. I made my bed and stretched out on my back. I stared at the ceiling. It was in need of paint and a few slender cracks ran out from the wall near the head of my bed. I thought about the girls who had slept in this bed before me.

Did they love it here? Did they feel free for the first time in their lives? What did they think about? School? Sex? Making friends? The future for which I was there to prepare? It seemed very far away.

# 37

*Sydney*

Everyone was still sleeping, or so it seemed, when I finished the muffin. As tasty as it was, I wanted something more after all. I returned to the kitchen and made a latte while I tried to decide what I was in the mood for.

Scrambling eggs was too much effort, given a belly half full of muffin. I wasn't starving, just not quite satisfied. I dug through the fridge drawers. A package of sausages meant for a barbecue were wrapped in plastic, two of the original four already eaten. They weren't breakfast sausages, but they were the very thing my body was craving.

I cut them into disks and cooked them in a pan with a spot of oil, slicing up part of a yellow bell pepper to give them some color and contrasting flavor. I sat at the bar and began eating. They were spicy — pork with lots of garlic and some flakes of red pepper. I sipped my latte, thinking about Lisa.

As I put a bite of sausage looped with a string of blackened bell pepper into my mouth, Gavin walked into the kitchen. He took the basket out of the espresso machine, dumped the wet grounds, and started a fresh cup. He wiped off the steam wand with a damp towel and washed and dried the stainless steel milk pitcher.

"I was going to do that," I said.

"No worries."

"Did you have a good sleep?"

He didn't answer. He took eggs and tomatoes and cheese out of the fridge and placed them on the counter near the stove.

I ate a few more bites of sausage, giving him thinking room.

After a minute or two, I set my fork on my plate and picked up my coffee mug. "You didn't talk much last night."

He said nothing.

I changed direction. "How many of the neighbors have you met?"

"Four."

I waited for the rest of the answer. When none came, I realized he'd answered precisely the question I'd asked. "Which ones?"

He shrugged.

"The guy next door?"

"John, yes."

"On the other side of us?"

He shook his head.

"Lisa, next door to John?"

He nodded.

"Who else?"

"Don't recall the names. Old guy across from us, the husband of the family two doors down from him."

"Is this the kind of place that has block parties?"

"Can't answer that."

"How long did you live here before I moved in?"

"Two months."

I supposed four neighbors in two months wasn't bad. It wasn't as if his move had all the surrounding activity that tends to bring neighbors out of their fortresses, and provides reasons and opportunities for introductions to the new kids on the block. Moving into someone's already established household hardly causes a ripple.

I ate some more sausage. He didn't volunteer any additional thoughts.

"Have you seen John's telescope?"

"No."

"It's in that second story patio that looks like a box. It's a sort of observatory."

"Sounds good."

I couldn't figure out if he was speaking even less than usual, trying to communicate in his non-verbal way that our kiss had been a one-time event, and not to be assumed to represent a relationship of any kind. I ate the last of the sausage and finished my latte.

Gavin moved out of the way when I went around the counter to put my plate in the dishwasher. Sweaty as I was, another kiss was out of the question. I needed to figure out what the next step might be. If there was to be one. I needed there to be one, if for no other reason than I needed to see his bedroom.

That, and this itch for a man that had grown much larger than any mere prickling of skin. I'm not even sure why that word is used — *itch*. There's nothing itchy about it. Rather, it's a sensation of your mind drifting constantly, repeatedly off to the body of any man you come in visual contact with, and there's the warm, soft ache inside of you. "He invited me to look through the telescope. He knows a lot about the night sky. It's pretty interesting."

"Good."

"Do you want to go with me? He was very casual about it, so I'm sure he won't mind. I thought about asking everyone, but you're here." I smiled.

"Convenient."

"Yes, very."

He took out a glass bowl and began cracking eggs on the edge, letting the insides fall into a thick pile of yolks, each added yolk forcing the others to move, as if they were jockeying for position. He took a whisk out of the drawer and tipped the bowl at a slight angle. The flash of the whisk and the sound of liquid splashing and gulping, the wires tapping against the bowl, muffled by the dense yolks, was mesmerizing. I waited for him to finish. And to speak.

He rested the whisk handle on the side of the bowl. He added shredded white cheese and moved the whisk around, burying the strips of cheese in the yellow goop. He chopped onion and tomato and put a pat of butter into the pan. He turned on the gas.

After a few more minutes of utter silence except the faint sound of the flame, he poured in the egg mixture.

"So does that sound interesting?" I said.

"It does."

"That means you want to go?"

"I don't think so. I said it's interesting."

I was suddenly tired. He wasn't the only good-looking guy in the house, and certainly not in Sydney. Trying to read him, trying to carry on even a simple conversation was too much work. "If you change your mind, let me know." I started toward the hallway.

"I won't."

I ran up the stairs. I trotted down the hallway and tried his bedroom door. Locked.

# 38

The upside of being sequestered in the house was that my running had taken a major uptick. In Tess's San Francisco condo, trying not to be observed by the sister and daughter of two people I'd killed, and avoiding being seen by the detectives lurking around the building next door, running had been hit and miss, mostly miss.

I loved being back at it. My endurance was improving again. I'd had no chance for a cigarette since I'd arrived, so that was probably helping my fitness level. Not that it meant I'd give up smoking completely, but it did feel pretty good running faster each day, more and longer sprints woven in.

With that thought in mind, I decided to take a different route, turning wherever it seemed right and choosing the streets that looked interesting, relying on GPS to get me home. It would slow me down for a day or two, but the more I explored, the more the streets would begin to fit themselves together in my mind.

I ran two and a half miles before I stopped to map my way back.

When I returned, I slowed to a walk at the corner, wanting to observe the house from the opposite direction. I walked past Sean's toward John's walkway. He wasn't outside. Obviously he only saw me if I passed in front of his house. Maybe all my future routes would begin by turning left out of Sean's house, although he'd eventually figure it out. Mr. Savior-of-the-street. I laughed.

As I neared the edge of John's property, Lisa's front door opened. It was difficult to see much. Her porch was more secluded than the modern designs. Tall leafy plants crowded the porch and vines gripped the posts, their flowered tendrils spilling outward, moving gently in the breeze. The furniture was hidden in shadows and it would be impossible to see anyone sitting there even during a sunny afternoon.

A moment later, Lisa emerged from the darkness of the porch and walked down the three steps onto the front path and zipped her hoodie. She turned and saw me. She yanked the cord on her hood and took a step forward. Then, she glanced back at the house. She turned and ran up the steps. She disappeared inside.

Between her and Gavin, even Sean, I was beginning to wonder about these chilly Australians who were not responding to me in the way I was used to. Did she really want to avoid me so badly she couldn't even bear to say good morning? I tried to remember our conversation but the only piece that stuck in my mind was her gushing about the caring oversight provided by John North.

The sun was coming up, the air was fresh and clean-smelling. I couldn't imagine skipping a coveted walk just because I wanted to avoid a two-minute greeting with a neighbor.

I returned to Sean's house and did some stretches on the walkway, waiting to see whether she changed her mind.

My entire body was limber, all the muscles relieved of their tightness, and she still hadn't come back outside. I jogged up the walkway to John's house and rang the bell.

He answered immediately, wearing his red running shorts and a dark blue sweatshirt.

"You already had your run?" he said.

"Yes."

"You're an early bird."

I smiled. "I want to take you up on your offer to look through your telescope."

"Splendid."

Splendid? I wasn't sure I'd ever heard anyone use that word in real life. He wasn't that old. It was a word that belonged on the tongue of a seventy-year-old British woman.

"Tonight?" I said.

He nodded. "I'll look forward to it."

"Likewise."

The twist of his lips suggested a victory of some kind. A faint shiver ran through me, wondering whether I was making a mistake. I didn't think he'd assault me, or anything like that. But everything about him — his clothing, his expressions, and half the things he said rang alarms throughout my head. Yet, he'd enticed me with his description of the night sky in the Southern Hemisphere and I very badly wanted to see some planets up close and personal.

Since I was perfectly capable of handling him, I wasn't sure what the alarms were all about. He didn't outweigh me by more than forty or fifty pounds. He was just under six feet, so not an enormous man. And although he was slim and fairly fit, he didn't have a lot of muscle definition. And I know some tricks.

The alarms were just that — to keep my distance, to watch my back. It didn't mean I had to deny myself a chance to see Saturn and the swish of her rings. His interest in the solar system made him seem like a thoughtful kind of person, but still — there was an intermittent squirming in my stomach and occasional prickles along my spine.

I jogged back to the front of Sean's house. John remained on his patio, watching me. Apparently Lisa found that charming, I found it awkward at best. I glanced toward her house. The overgrown porch and its secluded nature took on a sinister appearance, if I let my imagination wander over the possibilities. She wasn't outside. I didn't think she'd left her house again while I was accepting the invite, I would have seen her from the corner of my eye. And I hadn't been talking to John for more than a few minutes.

I walked slowly toward the front door, my thoughts on Lisa's abrupt termination of her walk, my eye on her porch, and John's eyes on me.

# 39

Tess presented the marketing plan at nine o'clock. We sat around the dining room table in this suddenly hybrid corporate environment with Tess's laptop, a small projector, and a large screen that had materialized out of one of the massive storage closets in the billiards room. The single mirrored wall and the floor-to-ceiling windows looking out on the back garden, the gray-streaked marble floor, the red and blue Persian area rug, the black lacquer table and chairs, provided a bizarre contrast to the props for a business meeting.

Sean loved Tess's plan, including her detailed description of my social media strategy. It was slightly unjust that she was the one presenting my ideas, but it was just another trail of blood spilling out of corporate America — chain of command and all that. It was clear that our barely functioning hothouse environment could turn quickly into something very much like the world we were all supposedly escaping.

Business is business. If you're going to launch and manage a company and generate a profit to support four employees as well as future product development, some things become default requirements. What's always worked in the business world is what works now, no sense changing it.

There are proven principles and techniques. A balance sheet was the same no matter what, and the product development cycle didn't change because you were small or independent or sharing a house, the bedroom of your CEO thirty feet from yours.

Tess displayed screenshots to demonstrate what I'd created so far on Facebook. No one said a word about my hat and dark glasses alongside their very naked faces.

When she finished, we discussed deadlines for the product announcement. Gavin gave an update on his bug fixes, and Sean informed us everything was in good shape with the device manufacturer. He still didn't seem bothered that this device was required for the app to function. Eventually he wanted to work with major companies to integrate the app with smart watches and possibly fitness wrist bands, but for now, the device was necessary because it had more functionality than those things offered at this point in time.

In my mind, the device was a huge hindrance to the easy sale of the app. I hoped they'd factored that into their business plan. He was funding the initial phase of the company himself, so I assumed he had enough resources to not worry about the longer and slower ramp time. Tess had emphasized this expectation of a slow ramp in her plan, but Sean was unconcerned.

When the conversation wound down, Gavin slipped out of his chair and left the room with nothing but a lift of his hand in a good-bye gesture. His shoulders were straight and his stride easy. He didn't seem like a man escaping, and he didn't seem annoyed, stomping out in a huff. He was just finished and he stood and left as quickly and easily as possible.

It puzzled and irritated me that with all Sean's togetherness desires, he never called Gavin on his aloofness. It was possible he'd done it during their private technical review meetings, but since Gavin never adjusted his behavior, I really didn't think Sean had said a word. I was told to be charming and friendly, and Gavin could live in his own world, hoarding his words like a miser with his gold coins. Again, no different from a corporation — technical people have more freedom. Without them, the venture is dead. Without me... well, children can manage Facebook pages.

I stood and edged toward the hallway.

Sean held up his hand. "Wait. Let's talk more about your strategy, Alex."

"Tess covered it."

"I want to hear it from you."

There was no information I could provide that Tess hadn't already talked about, and the smug look on his face suggested he knew that. Apparently he wanted to watch me like a performing monkey.

"I'm hungry. I'm going to grab something to eat."

"I've noticed you're hungry quite often. You're probably dehydrated." He smiled. "Have some water." He pushed the water pitcher in my direction.

"Water isn't what I need."

"I want to talk some more. What's the rush?"

"I'll be back in five minutes."

"Where are you really headed? Thinking you can take a quick run up the stairs and poke around in my bedroom again while I'm finishing up with Tess?"

"No."

"What?" Tess turned and looked at me.

"Alex seems to think the house belongs to her." He smiled.

"You said we should consider it our home."

No one spoke. Tess continued staring at me. "Alex?"

I felt like I was back home with my parents, both of them glaring at me, demanding that I explain myself.

"You went into his room?" Tess said. "Why would you do that?"

"Just curious. I told you the layout of the house confused me, with half of it shut off."

"It's two rooms. Not half the house," she said.

"It bothered me." I smiled, quite a charming expression I thought, but their glares continued unabated. I moved toward the doorway again. "So, we're finished."

"Your strategy looks good. You have a formidable task," Sean said.

"I do, but I'm up for the challenge."

"Good. Good."

Tess was still glaring at me.

Sean pushed out his chair and stood. He placed his hands on the back of the chair. "I thought everything should be out in the open. Don't you agree?"

I smiled.

"We're all equals here. But key to that is treating each other with respect. Respect is important to me."

"That's good to know."

He waited for me to say more. When I didn't, he pushed in the chair and walked out of the room.

I truly was hungry, but the rage burning in my gut was pushing the hunger aside.

People who claim everyone is equal are usually quite a few steps, if not several hundred feet, higher on the food chain. From their position, all looks equal. They see themselves being generous and don't realize the indebtedness they foster outside their range of vision. They fervently believe that those without power truly feel as if they're free to speak their minds.

There is no equality in a work environment. There's the boss and the employees, the subordinates. There is no equality when you own a multi-million-dollar home that you offer to share with a bunch of strangers. This was his house, these were his rules, and these were his quirks setting the agenda. For everything. From the swimming pool to the beets and pineapple on the hamburger. Tess ate them to be polite, I could see the way she pulled back slightly before each bite. That's not equality.

It was illustrated by his decision to *get everything out in the open*. Asking me whether I agreed was an obvious power play. He knew I wouldn't disagree.

But maybe I didn't think everything belonged out in the open. Maybe no one held that opinion. Gavin, with his locked door, certainly didn't.

# 40

"Why would you do that?" Tess said.

"I told you." I walked to the doorway.

"Don't leave. We need to talk."

"I'm starving."

She closed her laptop and followed me to the kitchen.

While I rummaged in the fridge, she continued repeating her question — *Why would you? Why would you?*

I took a plastic-wrapped hamburger out of the fridge. I grabbed an egg and some halloumi. I'd never eaten halloumi before I arrived in Australia, but was quickly growing fond of it. The cheese comes from Cyprus and has a high melting point, so it's often fried, which was very tasty. I straightened and closed the fridge door. "I already told you, why do you keep asking me?"

"I think I'm in shock. I can't believe you'd betray me like this."

"I didn't betray you."

"I told you not to do it. I'm trying to make a good impression here. I want Sean to value you. It seems to me you could care less what he thinks."

"I'm not going to cow-tow and quiver in the corners."

"Going into his room is so wrong. I shouldn't even have to point that out."

"He should have given us a tour. It's weird to live in a house and not know what the whole place looks like. It feels like Bluebeard's closet."

"Oh for God's sake."

"It does. Think about it. What's so damn private? Doesn't it give you the creeps that Gavin's door is always locked?"

"Makes perfect sense now that I know there's a predator living here," Tess said.

I laughed. I beat the egg. I crumbled hamburger into the liquid, put the pan on the stove, and turned on the gas.

"You should have asked him, if you're so determined to see it."

"Maybe."

"Not maybe. You should have. What if he went into your room? Wouldn't you feel violated?"

"First of all, I keep the door open sometimes when I'm not in there, so he can see how it looks whenever he wants. And second, how do I know he hasn't?"

She came close to where I was standing, thrusting her face toward mine. "Because people don't do that."

"Yes they do."

"Not mature people. Not adults. Not people who have boundaries and respect for those around them."

"Maybe I don't respect him all that much."

"Why not?"

"What has he done to earn my respect?"

"Human beings deserve respect and consideration because they're human."

"I didn't snoop in his closet or bathroom drawers. I just wanted to see the room. I don't think it's all that disrespectful." I poured the egg and hamburger into the pan. It sizzled and spit. I stirred it with a wooden spoon, turning over the egg, making sure the hamburger touched the pan so it browned and got nice and hot.

"That's a weird breakfast," Tess said.

I smiled. I turned the egg over again and began breaking it into pieces. I dropped in cubes of halloumi and splashed on some hot chili sauce.

"People in authority, co-workers, your boss's boss, in case you forgot, deserve respect. Because of their role."

"I don't agree. I can think of quite a few political figures who don't deserve respect, no matter what their role is. You have to earn respect."

"I'm not talking about politicians. And I think Sean has earned yours."

"How?"

"By hiring you. Paying you a very nice salary. Offering you free run of his home. Inviting you into his exciting venture."

"Yes. But then he wasn't a very good host. He didn't offer a tour."

She sighed.

I turned off the gas and scraped my breakfast onto a plate. I carried it to the bar and sat down.

"I hope you haven't irreparably damaged your position here."

"He said my social media strategy was good, so I think everything is fine."

She put her hands in her pockets. "It's kind of embarrassing for me, did you think of that?"

"It has nothing to do with you."

"I vouched for you. I put my judgment on the line, assuring him you'd be an asset."

"I still am."

"I hope so." She moved toward the open space between

the bar and the breakfast nook. "Did you call Detective Gorman?"

"I will."

"When?"

"Hopefully today."

"Hopefully?"

"We'll see how it goes. Right now my mind is focused on getting the Twitter thing going. I'm thinking I can drive people to the Facebook page through Twitter, get an audience established before we even launch."

"I know. I presented your strategy, remember?" She didn't smile, or cringe as she acknowledged that she'd been center stage presenting my ideas.

"I'll call him," I said.

"He's going to be moving on to other cases."

"I'll call him, okay?"

She started walking.

"Don't you want to know?"

She turned. "Know what?"

"Don't you want to know what his room is like?"

"No."

"He has a gorgeous statue — a wood carving of a nude woman."

Her nose turned slightly pink and she looked away from me.

"It's hard to describe. You have to touch it to really comprehend how exquisite it is. Although it's also stunning to look at."

"And I suppose you did. Touch it."

I smiled.

She walked away.

I continued eating, still hungry, wishing I'd made some toast. But once I settled down, this would probably satisfy me, I just needed to give my body time to absorb it. I planned to spend the rest of the morning playing with Twitter and then relax on a chaise lounge in the sun.

After a few days of rain and drizzle, the sun was pushing most of the clouds toward the horizon. It was expected to be in the low seventies by mid-afternoon. Getting a light tan is easier in cooler weather. Once spring came and the hot tropical air settled over everything, it would be impossible to lie about in the sun, so I figured I needed a head start, even though spring was a very long way off.

Despite all the rough patches, I was sure I'd still be here in the summer. The product was due to launch in July, so they definitely needed me until then, even if I was disrespectful. And although I didn't have much respect for him, I was pretty sure Sean respected me in a strange, irritated, angry, possibly envious sort of way. Most people do respect someone who goes after what she wants, even if it means invading the space of others.

# 41

Before I put on my black bikini, I spread sunscreen over my entire body. Applying lotion while I'm naked ensures I don't miss little strips of skin around my straps and the edges of the bottoms, ending up with a red stripe that eventually turns a darker brown than everything else.

It's considered a terrible risk to lie in the sun for no other reason than turning your skin brown. The risk of cancer is horrific, at least if you believe the brochures in doctors' offices. They're filled with colorful photographs of pink and red lesions and bubbled skin and black scabs. But I've read about people who got skin cancer on parts of their bodies that never saw the sun, and I've heard stories of cancer springing up uninvited in every single organ of your body — lung cancer in baby pink lungs that never breathed a thread of smoke, and liver cancer in teetotalers.

Cancer is out to devour us, but I'm not going to hide in a closet and eat nothing but kale until I die. Life is deadly. Australia is deadly, with its venomous spiders and paralyzing jellyfish and fast-moving crocodiles. There are amoebas that crawl into your nose and eat your brain and you don't even know they entered your body.

I'm not in denial about the reality of death. I'm fully aware I'll die at some point. I have no idea from what, but in the meantime, I'm going to enjoy the ride without biting my nails and trying to hide from all the demons that want to deliver premature death.

By the time I made it out to the backyard, the clouds had re-captured half the sky. The sun was moving behind them and re-emerging every few minutes. It was still pleasant enough for sun tanning, but I hoped it would clear completely in time for the stargazing later that night.

I put a beach towel on one of the lounge chairs, and pulled it out from under the patio roof, leaving it at the farthest point possible from the shallow end of the pool. I stretched out on my back and closed my eyes. I pushed thoughts of social media out of my head. I pushed Sean and Tess out of my head. I allowed Gavin to traipse around in there for a few minutes, replaying the feel of his mouth on mine, and then I pushed him to the side as well.

Eventually, I think I drifted to sleep, or at least to that strange netherworld where your thoughts turn into nonsense and you feel you're asleep even though the sounds around you are still audible, and the temperature of the sun and the breeze on your skin is still sharp and clear.

A splash in the pool, followed quickly by another, startled me back to full consciousness.

I opened my eyes without shifting my position, to avoid giving any indication I was alert. My dark glasses prevented them from seeing I was watching, if they could see my eyes at all from that distance.

Gavin and Sean were splashing about, half-heartedly swimming laps. Every few strokes they dove beneath the surface where the angle of my chair and the sides of the pool prevented me from seeing them.

They surfaced and Gavin chased Sean, swimming like dolphins, to the deep end of the pool. Once there, they wrestled, arms thrashing, legs cycling to keep their heads above water. Sean shoved Gavin's face into the water and pushed him deeper. Gavin twisted away and resurfaced. He grabbed Sean's neck in an armlock and pulled him down. As they burst up, laughing and coughing, a few drops of water landed on my thigh. I brushed them away

They kept on like this for several minutes. I closed my eyes and concentrated on the sun warming my toes and spreading across my belly. I felt like a dinner roll, slowly turning brown, my insides growing hot and soft.

A few drops of water landed on my arms and legs. A moment later, a droplet struck the left lens of my glasses. I took them off and polished them on the towel, which mostly smeared the water. I put them back on and closed my eyes. Hopefully, they'd get tired of playing soon.

The sounds from the pool dimmed and I started thinking about the stargazing, trying to figure out how John managed to make my skin crawl at the same time his description of the night sky caused my mind to quiver with excitement.

The pool was suddenly quiet. I hoped they hadn't drowned each other.

A few seconds later, a shadow fell across my thighs and hips, cooling my skin. I opened my eyes, expecting more clouds.

Gavin and Sean were standing at my left.

"Come on," Sean said. "We gotta do it. Like it's an initiation."

"Girls hate that," Gavin said.

"She's a good sport."

I sat up slightly. "You're blocking the sun."

"She speaks," Sean said.

"Would you move, please?"

Neither one moved.

"I'm trying to get some sun."

Gavin took a few steps away from me.

Sean laughed. "Don't chicken out now."

"Not a good idea," Gavin said.

"We have to. She's asking for it."

A shiver ran down my spine. I settled back down, expecting Sean to follow Gavin's lead, expecting him to show a little respect, since it was so important to him.

"Why wear a swimsuit if you're not going to swim?"

Gavin said nothing.

"She's been trespassing. We have to punish her, don't you think?" He laughed, trying to prove he was teasing.

"I don't think she knows how to swim," Gavin said.

"You believe that?" Sean laughed.

A moment later, I felt his hands. One slid quickly beneath my shoulders and the other behind my knees. Before I could take a second breath, he'd lifted me off the lounge chair and was turning toward the pool.

"Put me down."

"Be a sport."

"What about all your bullshit regarding respect?"

"Aren't you going to scream? You're no fun." He took a few more steps and dropped me into the water.

My glasses lifted away from my face as I went under. I coughed and choked, swallowing water. I tried moving my arms to put myself on my feet but the knowledge that water was washing over my entire body, pressing into my nostrils and mouth and ears, kept me from thinking clearly. I couldn't get my feet cemented to that dark concrete that looked so close but felt like it was as far away as the planets, unseen above us in the daytime sky.

Through water-clogged ears, I heard a dull splash. A moment later Gavin was beside me. He put his arm around my shoulders and pulled me up so my head was above the surface. I coughed, gasping for air, blinking the water away from my eyes. I coughed again.

"You asshole. She said she can't swim."

Gavin moved my body slightly until my feet were touching the bottom. He plucked my sunglasses out of the water and handed them to me.

"It sounded like a joke to me," Sean said.

I walked to the steps and climbed out of the pool. I felt them watching me as I walked to the lounge chair and picked up my towel.

"Sorry," Sean said. "I can't imagine someone not knowing how to swim."

I turned toward the pool where Gavin stood. "Thanks."

He nodded once.

I wrapped the towel around me and went into the house, not caring that my hair and swimsuit were dripping water all over the tile. I climbed the stairs and walked down the hallway with equal disregard for my wet footprints on the carpet.

In my bathroom, I stripped off my suit and stepped into the shower. As I stood under the water, careful as always to keep my face out of the stream, I decided my next venture, after stargazing, would be an extended time enjoying the statue in Sean's bedroom. Followed by a careful look through his cabinets and drawers and all the hidden crevices.

It was past time to get the upper hand with him. Tess had made him out to be a laid back Aussie who worshipped nature.

That might all be true when he was floating around the Great Barrier Reef, but this was something different.

# 42

*Los Angeles*

**M**oira Davidson swept into our tiny dorm room as if it were the Ritz Carlton and paparazzi were lining the red carpet that protected her feet from touching concrete soiled by lesser women. She looked at the bare mattress and simple wood frame of the unoccupied bed.

"You should have waited for me before picking a bed," she said.

"They're exactly the same."

"This one is closer to the door."

"So?"

"You'll walk past my bed if you come in late."

I stood. "I'm Alexandra."

"Moira. But don't change the subject."

"I just thought we could get to know each other, before we argue about beds."

"This needs to be resolved first."

"I'm not going to wake you up."

"You can't possibly know that."

"I'll try not to wake you." I'd looked forward to meeting my roommate, confident we'd have a few things in common, eager for my first exposure to college life, living with a stranger. No more siblings to fight with. Just me and a new person to hang out with — no drama.

She gave me a solid stare and dropped her purse and

duffle bag on the empty bed. "If you do, we'll need to change beds."

I smiled.

She seemed to take this as agreement.

Her parents burst through the open door, faces red, her father carrying boxes, her mother pulling suitcases. They looked oddly like my parents — interchangeable parental figures. Although in my case, I'd carried a few boxes. Moira waited for them to make several trips up and down the elevator, which took nearly an hour since people were moving into every floor and the elevator had to wait for occupants to struggle in and out with their cargo.

Moira and her parents got busy discussing the logistics of unpacking.

I put on earphones and listened to classic rock on my portable player. I laid on my side and watched them as if it were live theater with a Pink Floyd soundtrack. It was quite entertaining, especially the line about not getting pudding if you didn't eat your dinner. Not laughing was difficult. The song seemed to be written for Moira and her parents.

Finally, the parents left and Moira became slightly less chilly. We walked to the dining hall and exchanged personal information. She was from Ohio. UCLA had been her first choice. We talked about high school and plans for our first year of college, more social plans than academic.

Things went along relatively smoothly for the first few days, mostly because I didn't come into our room late and wake her. When I left to go running along the empty campus pathways early in the morning, I crept out in bare feet. I sat in the lounge area a few doors down from our room and put on my socks and shoes.

Then I began to notice something far worse than her original haughty attitude.

She was a slob.

Her clothes were everywhere — clean and dirty, even discarded underwear dotted the floor. I had to use my ruler to push things to her side of the room.

She had allergies that filled fifteen or twenty tissues a day. She left the tissues scattered on the floor near her bed and across the nightstand and the top of her dresser. While she sat on her bed studying, she ate ice cream from takeout cups, popsicles and candy bars and potato chips. The crumbs and drops of lime popsicle wound up on her sheets and the floor without her seeming to notice. Candy bar wrappers lay among the wadded up tissues on her nightstand.

I asked when she was planning to pick up her trash. She stared at me as if I'd asked her when she was planning to shave off her long, thick brown hair. Possibly her eyebrows as well.

Finally, during the second week of school, I came home from class to an unoccupied dorm room. I filled the trashcan with her discarded wrappers. I used a clean tissue to pick up her dirty ones. I took the trashcan into the bathroom shared by ten of us and emptied it. I got the vacuum cleaner from the closet in the lounge and sucked up chips and cookie crumbs. I couldn't do anything about the popsicle drops.

When she arrived back at the dorm, she flopped on her bed and opened her laptop. She shoved it up toward her pillow. Lying on her stomach, she opened her European History text book. She reached into her backpack and pulled out a pink highlighter and a Three Musketeers bar. It amazed me that she could eat a seemingly endless supply of sickly sweet candy and never feel queasy and never gain an ounce on her long, lean legs or around her narrow waist.

"You're welcome," I said.

She looked up, chewing chocolate and fluffy light brown filling that's mostly artificial but has a divine taste and texture. "What?"

"I picked up your trash."

"I didn't ask you to do that."

"It was gross."

"It wasn't hurting you."

"I have to look at it. And live with the germs."

She turned her head and uncapped her highlighter. She placed it along the spine of her book and took another bite of the candy bar.

"Were you just going to let it pile up until we couldn't see the floor?"

"The point of college is to not listen to your mother nag you anymore."

"I'm not nagging you."

She raised her voice into a high-pitched imitation of no one's actual voice. "Clean up this pigsty. This isn't a slum. No prom if you don't clean that room. Pick up your crap in the bathroom, I'm not asking you again." She laughed and took another bite of her candy bar.

"But this is your own place, don't you want it to be nice?"

"It's not my place. It's a dumpy little room with cinderblock walls. Like a prison."

"We can make it nice."

"Knock yourself out."

"Do you want to go to the mall this weekend and get some posters?"

"Not really. But feel free. As long as they're on your side of the room."

"If we both decorate, we'll be more motivated to keep it nice."

"It's a prison cell. Look around you. There isn't any *nice.*"

"But it's ours. And I don't want to live in a bunch of garbage."

She turned on her side, facing the wall. She dug around in her backpack and pulled out her iPod and earphones. A moment later she was moving her head to whatever was pumping in there. Or maybe just trying to piss me off.

After that, her allergies seemed to get worse. She went through a box of tissues every two days or so. They piled up on the floor around her bed. They decorated the nightstand like little white birds.

Unlike beautiful white birds, they made me nauseous.

# 43

*Sydney*

Tess opened her laptop. She took a sip of espresso from her fourth cup of the day. It needed to be her last. She hoped she didn't plunge too quickly into irritability if the Detective was unwilling to listen to her concerns. Pissing him off would not achieve her goal. The police always had the advantage. They could do as they pleased in a lot of ways. If you pushed, they put up an impenetrable wall and pushed back harder, and if you stepped over any line they drew, they won.

She opened a browser and typed in *San Francisco Police*. There was a number for the narcotics division but of course they didn't list detective's names like a corporation might. She'd gotten Detective Gorman's name from Cynthia, but Cynthia didn't have his first name. It was probably just as well. He might not react well to being treated like a peer.

She picked up her phone and attached the bluetooth device to her ear. If it turned out to be a lengthy conversation, which she hoped, she wanted her hands unencumbered to write down what he said. It was as if she was building a case of her own, one of police indifference to a victim of…what? Was she going to suggest Steve had been murdered? At least some sort of negligence must be involved. Wasn't that manslaughter? But jumping to an inflammatory word didn't seem like a good way to start. Too aggressive and too likely he would immediately counter with defensive moves. He might feel his skill or integrity was being challenged.

Best to start with questions. Maybe thank him for taking her call, if he did.

She dialed the number and was tossed into a voicemail tree. After several tries, she landed on a path that rang through to a real person. A miracle, really. A man answered.

"May I speak to Detective Gorman, please?"

"He's out right now. Can I take a message?"

Tess sighed. How likely was he to call her back at an international number? Not at all. "I'm calling about the Steve Montgomery case."

"I can't discuss cases."

"I'm a friend of Steve's. Was."

"Can I take your name and number?"

"I'm out of the country. It's easier for me to call him. Do you know when he'll be in?"

"Try back just before eight."

She thanked him and hung up. Only an hour and a half until eight in the evening San Francisco time. She took her espresso out to the balcony. The sky was clearing. The street was silent, no birds in sight. She leaned back and took a sip of coffee. The ninety minutes would drag if she did nothing but suck down strong, dark caffeine.

She returned to her room, picked up her phone, and opened an audio book about marketing and branding during the infant phase of a startup. She put on her noise cancelling headphones and began listening. The ninety minutes went quickly.

This time, a woman answered the phone. She asked Tess to hold while she located the detective.

According to Tess's phone, it was six minutes and twenty-four seconds before he picked up the line. "Gorman here."

"Hi. My name is Tess Turner. I worked at CoastalCreative and was a colleague of Steve Montgomery."

"Yes?"

"You investigated his death?"

"Yes. Heroin overdose. I'm sorry for your loss."

"Thank you. I just wondered, how do you decide when it's an overdose?"

He started talking before she could correct the rather obvious way she'd phrased the question.

"Dope on the dresser, dope in his blood, no stroke, no aneurism, no etc. Overdose."

"What did you think of a man like him using heroin? Were you surprised?"

"A man like what?"

"Successful, and…"

He laughed, then stopped abruptly. "Dope and addiction don't make class distinctions. What's this about, Ms…"

"Turner." The questions were a mistake. She should have been more direct. He was likely pressed for time, handfuls of cases. "I worked with Steve for years. He wasn't a drug user."

"First time for everything."

"What would make you look into it further?"

"Look into what?"

"I don't believe he died of an overdose."

"The facts are very clear in the autopsy report, and what we found in his room."

"What I mean is, I think someone forced him to take it. Or something like that. He wouldn't…"

"Ms…it wasn't an injection. He snorted it. No one forced

anything. There was no evidence of another person being in his home, except the housekeeper."

"But he wouldn't...why do you assume it was his choice?"

"Because that's how these things go. I know it's difficult to accept an untimely death. The shock. The loss. Brings up your own mortality and all of that..."

"This isn't about my mortality. It's about Steve's reputation."

As if he hadn't heard, he continued. "People can be surprising. Everyone has secrets, dark corners in their lives. We never know about it until something goes wrong."

"Steve didn't use drugs. I was in a relationship with him. I knew him."

As if she were in the same room with the detective, she could feel, across thousands of miles of ocean, the tightening of his expression, the look in his eyes that dismissed her as a grief-stricken lover.

"He died of an overdose. Again, I'm very sorry for your loss. I'm going to have to hang up now."

The line went dead.

She stared at her phone. After a few minutes, the screen faded to black.

She removed the bluetooth. The memo pad app on her laptop was blank. She wasn't sure what she'd planned to write down after all. She closed the app and shut her computer. She returned to the balcony and leaned on the railing, looking out over palm trees and eucalyptus, glimpses of the other equally spacious and well-groomed yards, most of them secluded by the mature trees and enormous shrubs, held together by fences and adobe walls.

Although the people who were close to Steve were shocked by the supposed circumstances of his death, it didn't change how they would remember him. Not really. But she still couldn't let go of it. His body cried out for justice. She laughed. So much melodrama. He was dead, his body burned into a pile of ash and bone, not crying out for anything at all. Possibly he didn't even care how he was remembered. In fact, knowing him, he might laugh that everyone got it wrong. He might find it amusing that he left behind a bit of mystery and confusion.

Her fingers curled around the railing under their own volition. She could not let it go.

# 44

Just before ten p.m., I pulled on a navy blue hoodie over my long-sleeved pale pink t-shirt. It had gotten quite cold after my unplanned dip in the pool. I hadn't seen Sean or Gavin since. Hoping to avoid them further, I'd walked two miles to the pie shop. I should have translated it into kilometers. I couldn't get kilometers or temperatures given in Celsius anchored in my head. There was no frame of reference. I hoped it would sink into me by osmosis at some point.

I bought two meat pies and a bottle of water. I sat at one of the four narrow tables along the window facing the parking lot and ate them slowly, savoring each taste of meat and gravy and flakey, warm pastry.

They filled me up enough that even after the walk back to the house, I didn't feel at all hungry. I stayed in my room, the door closed and locked. I watched a movie on my new laptop, courtesy of TruthTeller. The nice room, the food, the laptop, and the new phone were not going to make me believe I owed anything to Sean but the job I'd been hired for.

Tess thought I needed to be more charming, but Sean could have used a little of that himself. And even though he was the CEO, he didn't get to toss me into the swimming pool like a rubber ball.

Until a year earlier, I'd avoided all water after my dreadful full immersion baptism at the age of seven. I thought I'd faced down my antagonism toward overwhelming quantities of the wet stuff when I deposited two bodies in Soquel

Creek. It hadn't turned out that way — the memory of the baptism was still more intense than the other.

Now, I was considering whether I should learn to swim. I didn't like knowing someone could debilitate me so easily, so quickly. Not that I would be in all kinds of future situations where I'd be tossed into swimming pools, but knowing I had this weak spot nagged at me. Learning to swim would mean dealing with water in my face. It meant memories rushing through me, things I'd rather forget. But it would prevent anyone having the upper hand in that area.

Getting tossed into the water was almost as bad as the baptism. Because I was older, I didn't panic as severely, but I'd felt the same certainty that my life might end suddenly and painfully.

I managed to leave my room, walk down the stairs, and out the front door without seeing any of my roommates.

John was waiting on his patio. He gestured toward his open front door.

In the living room, open to the foyer, he offered me a glass of Zinfandel. We said cheers and took a small sip. He took another sip then led me upstairs to the enclosed patio that ran along the front of his house. The telescope was near the concrete half wall, angled up toward the sky.

He put his wineglass on the nearby table. "Are you warm enough?"

"Yes." I took a sip of wine.

He stepped closer to the telescope. "Take a look, a long look, as much time as you'd like."

I took a few more sips of wine and put my glass beside his. I sat in the chair in front of the telescope.

"I've pointed it so you get a good look at Jupiter first.

There are a lot of magnificent stars, and I can help you find the constellations, but I thought we'd start with something more dramatic."

I pressed my right eye socket against the lens casing. My lashes brushed against the hard ring. I pulled back slightly.

"The bodies strung out near Jupiter are three of her moons. She has sixty-seven that we know of."

Through the telescope, the planet looked like it was made of silk. It was soft with mocha-colored swirls and so close I felt I could reach out and run my finger around the surface.

As if he'd read my mind, or maybe my observation was a common one, John said, "You want to touch it, cup it in your hands and feel the smooth weight of it. The shades of brown and the blue are so soft, so alluring. From this distance, you have no idea what's really there, how uninhabitable it is."

"It is beautiful." I moved away from the scope to look out with my naked eye, comparing the incredible difference between the shimmering dot that stood out among the stars with the planet that was visible through the telescope.

"All those moons. As if they're drawn to the planet and can't ever tear themselves away," he said.

I put my head back to the scope and spent a few more minutes gazing at the mysterious planet, so close, nearly filling the viewing space, yet hundreds of millions of miles away.

"From this distance, all we see is the incredible beauty," he said. "You don't have to think about the hydrogen that would destroy you in a single breath. And the temperature — minus two-hundred-thirty-four degrees Fahrenheit."

"Brr. I guess we won't see anyone planting a flag on Jupiter."

"That, and the surface is more or less liquid, so no. Move

away for a minute and I'll reposition it to Saturn."

I got up from the chair. He sat down and shifted the scope, fiddling with the knobs to make some obscure adjustment that I assumed was accounting for the greater distance.

I sat down again and looked through. Saturn was so unique, it seemed unreal.

"Aren't the rings like something living?" he said.

I nodded, not wanting to speak. It was even more magical than Jupiter. Right there, so huge, so soft. A perfect sphere. The rings were painfully beautiful and so mysterious.

"Knowing what all that is made of but looking at it are two very different experiences, aren't they?"

"Yes."

"The rings are nothing but gas and spinning rock and ice that would slice your head off."

It was a rather gruesome image. "How did you get interested in studying the stars?"

"It's fascinated me all my life. As a kid, my father thought gazing at planets and stars was a foolish waste of time. In high school, I started saving my money for a telescope. He decided my part time job at a hardware store was taking me away from my studies. He wanted to be sure I was accepted at a superior university. And once I was there, and then building my career…it seemed…It was a luxury I didn't have time for."

I couldn't imagine something that rocked your world, like stars seemed to rock his, becoming a luxury you couldn't afford to devote your attention to.

He adjusted the scope again and while I looked at the stars and the patterns of constellations, he explained each one, directing me where in the visible area to focus.

"The solar system was mapped by the ancients and all the constellations carry the same names as they have for centuries. Some stars have burned out so the constellations appear different to us than they did in the past, but the basic pattern is still there."

"I wonder why they believed they needed to name them? Some of the shapes seem like a bit of a stretch. It's more imagination than anything else to see the dipper, or a bear or a lion," I said.

"Mankind wants to control his environment. Naming is part of that."

He was quiet for a few minutes, when he spoke his voice was slow, sounding almost drugged with pleasure. "It's impossible to stop looking at them. All these heavenly bodies, moving through space, flying really, but to us they appear to be standing still. You can't take your eyes off them. You feel grief when they fade with the sunrise. And each evening is a new experience, slightly altered positions, different pieces that stand out against the rest."

He went on to talk about the features of stars and planets, the Solar System and the Milky Way, slowly spreading out to the rest of the universe. He explained that if the solar system were the size of my hand, the Milky Way Galaxy would be the size of North America, and there are billions of galaxies beyond that. He continued with an unbroken flow of information that I'd never remember without doing my own studying.

I moved away from the telescope.

"Had enough?"

"I think so. It's amazing though." I walked to the table

and picked up my neglected glass of wine. I took a few steps and looked out at the sky with my bare eyes. It was framed by the rectangular enclosure where we stood, making it seem slightly unreal.

"Many people don't have the patience for looking out at the exquisite beauty of the universe. Or they don't see the value."

"People are impatient," I said.

"Or blind to what's around them."

"Yes." I didn't consider myself particularly blind, but I got his point. I'm quite aware of what's around me, always. I have an intense instinct that constantly notices what everyone is doing, feeling their slightest movements in any direction. I notice plants and animals. Anything that's naturally beautiful. Especially homes. And now, a few detailed pieces of the endless sky.

He was less neanderthal than he'd seemed, and really quite sensitive. It made me curious again why his lavish home was decorated in such a pedestrian way. He was more artistic, a philosopher in some ways.

We finished our wine, looking out at the sky, not talking.

When I left, he thanked me for coming, which was an odd reversal of the norm.

# 45

Walking the thirty or forty feet back to Sean's house was like re-entering a lesser world. I was truly shocked at the revelation of deeper, more intricate layers within a man who was so aggressive and socially clueless and entitled that he ripped earphones out of a woman's ears and peered out at them from his front windows. There was still something odd about him, but maybe his oddness was his extraordinary passion for the exquisite beauty of the stars and planets.

It was a rather boring hobby. I'd loved looking, and I definitely saw the value in owning a telescope. In fact, I'd added it to my list of requirements for the magnificent home I was building tile by tile in my imagination. But I wouldn't spend hours every single night of the week gazing at enormous rocks either burning hot or bitterly cold, silken-shrouded planets hundreds of millions of miles away.

Some of the things he'd talked about were fascinating, but I didn't need to know the temperature and orbit and specific gas composition of every object in the galaxy. I suppose it could keep you occupied for a lifetime, and maybe that was his plan. Maybe he didn't even notice his wife was gone for months at a time. There was no one talking in his ear while he sat in his open-sided concrete box and pressed his eyeball up to a lens that made the universe more real, more alive, more intimate. Instead of a sprinkling of lights, each one was a living, breathing body.

I unlocked the front door and went inside.

All the rooms were dark except for the living room where a single light gleamed. I walked toward it and saw Gavin stretched out on the couch, feet propped on the coffee table. He wasn't holding a tablet or phone and didn't have a drink beside him. He was simply sitting there. He watched me approach.

"Hi," I said.

"How were the stars?"

"Spectacular."

"I already knew that."

"I saw the rings of Saturn."

"Sweet."

"What are you doing?" I said.

"Nothing."

"It's late," I said.

"After midnight."

I moved into the living room. "Mind if I join you?"

"Your choice."

It was actually also his choice, but he seemed to find that less important. I walked over and sat beside him.

"Do you wonder…" he paused.

Expecting a question about the solar system, I waited for a moment.

"Do you wonder if using social media to get the word out about our app is a bunch of bullshit?"

"No." I actually did wonder the same thing, but I was being paid to believe in the word of mouth power of social media. Despite my treacherous relationship with Sean and uncertain connection to Gavin, I absolutely wanted to stay in Australia for the foreseeable future. Now that I was here, I wanted to explore the country. I was also still determined to keep Tess at a distance from the San Francisco police. And I simply needed a change of scenery. In order to do that, a job was required, so it was best not to trash my own reputation as a social media maven. Besides, maybe Sean had put him up to the question.

"You seem smarter," he said.

"Well you can't advertise in magazines or newspapers because no one under fifty reads them, and everyone tunes out TV and internet commercials. So…it's what we have. Marketing is personal now."

"Okay."

We sat in silence for a few minutes. Him thinking… possibly…about the wasteland of social media, or worrying he'd be required to tweet. Me thinking about his delicious kiss, wondering if I'd be required to make the first move again.

I'm not opposed to being the first mover. It's kind of exciting, and I often get impatient waiting for other people. I'm not a woman who needs a man's overture to reassure me that I'm attractive or desirable. Kissing, sex — it should be mutual. How did the idea evolve that the man is the aggressor? Why do women sit around waiting for that? Half the men I've met don't even know how to do it right. They make a move without considering the timing or looking to gauge whether the woman is equally interested. They charge in and get rejected and decide that women who don't respond are bitches.

I like going first. I like being in charge. At the same time, I also like someone making a move on me. Both are equally exciting. I had no doubt he would respond to the touch of my mouth, but still…maybe he had other things he wanted to talk about. Not that there was much talking going on. Five words seemed to be his maximum allocation. Unless he was telling a story and then it ratcheted up to nine or ten. I laughed softly.

"Something funny?"

"You don't say much."

"And you find that funny?"

"Not really."

"Then why the laugh?"

It was too hard to explain. I turned slightly, reached my arm across, and put my hand on the back of his shoulder. I pulled him toward me and lifted my face to his. I kissed him hard and fast.

When I pulled away his eyelids were lowered slightly, his eyes almost black, and his breath ragged. "You're…"

"Yes, I am." I began kissing him again.

We ran our hands slowly over each other, slowly entwining our legs. I stopped thinking about first moves and social media and the solar system. I shifted lower onto the couch, pulling him half on top of me. I moved my mouth away from his. "We should go to your room." I spoke softly, letting my breath slide across his jaw.

"I don't think so." He sat up.

"Why not?"

"It's not a good idea."

"You seemed…"

"Yes. But all of this is not a good idea."

"Afraid the boss will get pissed?"

He stood.

"I think you want it as much as I do. You want to go to your room as much as I do."

He shook his head. "G'night." He turned and walked out.

I heard his footsteps on the staircase, moving slowly, a heavy tread. At one point, he stopped for nearly half a minute. Then the sound of his feet started up again.

I went into the kitchen and got out the vodka and vermouth. I mixed a martini and added four olives because it was late and I was hungry. I pulled a cigarette and my lighter out of my purse and went out to the backyard. After placing the martini glass and my cigarette and lighter on the table, I dragged a chair out from under the patio cover where I could look up and see the stars and the sliver of a moon.

I settled down, lit my cigarette, and took a long, deep drag.

My body wanted Gavin, but he was a lot of work, at least from a conversational point of view. His desire to hide in his room, and hide within his mind was intriguing, but not so intriguing I felt like spending hours trying to get even a glimpse of what was inside his head.

I did still want to know what was hidden in his room. I took a sip of my martini and tried to settle my mind into nothing. The drink was half gone and my cigarette completely finished before that happened.

# 46

I'd finished my run and was in the weight room doing lat pull-downs. The door opened and Tess stepped inside. Her hair was yanked back in a tight ponytail, still wet from her shower. She wore black leggings and a long loose gray sweater. In the shadowy light of the space just inside the door, her eyes looked black.

I raised the bar, lowering the weight blocks back onto the stack.

She came over and sat on the floor in front of me. She crossed her legs and pulled off her flats. She moved her legs into the lotus position. I was impressed.

Before she spoke, I began my second set, pulling the bars down toward my shoulders.

Ignoring the concentrated look on my face, she spoke. "Did you call the detective?"

"I said..."

"Yes or no."

"Not yet."

"So that's a *no*."

"Very good." I pulled the bars down again.

"Will you please stop doing that for a minute," she said.

"I'm working out. You interrupted."

"You are so rude sometimes."

I smiled. "Everyone is rude, sometimes."

"Why haven't you called him?"

"Haven't had a chance."

"I don't think that's true."

"The time difference, there are only a few hours a day where I have a chance of reaching him."

"There are at least seven hours of overlap time. Please call him as soon as you finish your workout."

"I need to shower."

"No. You said you would call, and the more time passes, the less likely they are to do anything."

"Don't you think it might already be at that point?"

"No. You have to call."

"Why can't you let go of this? It's not good to be so obsessed."

"I don't care what you call it. You offered to do it, and I'm counting on you."

"Maybe I changed my mind."

"Too late."

I started my third set. My breath was getting tight from the effort and I didn't want to talk any more about calling the police. It had been a miscalculation to make that offer. I thought she might forget, which was also a miscalculation. Of course she wasn't going to forget. I needed to get it over with.

It should have made my hands shake, the thought of calling the police to check further into a murder I'd committed. It was the worst thing I could do to call attention to myself. I was confident there was nothing pointing to me, no fingerprints or hairs, but the situation was still unnerving.

I raised the bar and let go of the handles. I stretched my arms overhead.

"Right now. As soon as you're finished. Please."

"I really don't think anything will come of it. Once they

close a case, they don't start second-guessing themselves, do they?"

"We have to try."

"We?"

"You offered to help, so I said *we*. You have to tell them he would never do this. You have to make sure they understand that they might be letting a killer remain loose. They can't take that risk. You have to make it sound ominous, that they're jeopardizing their credibility or something. Maybe make it sound like you're afraid. Maybe…you could act like you think it was a workplace threat…"

"Really?"

"Yes. That would be perfect. I'll sit in the room while you call. You can put him on speaker and I'll write notes to guide you, depending on what he says."

"I'm not doing that."

"Why not?"

"I won't be able to act naturally if you're sitting there listening, second-guessing every word out of my mouth, pushing too hard. If he hears you breathing or senses I'm not alone, he'll write it off as a nuisance call."

She sighed. "Will you do it right now? And you need to say what I suggested."

"Fine. I just have to do curls and abs."

"I'll wait."

"You're hovering. It's not helping me relax into my workout. Can you just leave me alone for twenty minutes and I promise I'll try calling right after that."

"*Try?*" She eased her left ankle off her right shin and the other foot off her thigh.

"He might not be sitting around waiting for a woman

who works in high-tech to tell him out to do his job."

She stood. "You're not telling him how to do his job. And please don't have such a defeatist attitude. It won't get him to take action. You have to push. Hard."

"Absolutely. Push hard." I grinned.

"I'll be in the office. Come find me as soon as you're done. Even if you don't reach him, I want an update."

I smiled, a hard gritting of my teeth, but she didn't notice.

She left and I went to the free weights. I picked up a sixteen pound dumbbell in each hand to do hammer curls. It took all my concentration, keeping my arm straight, not letting the weight pull my forearms out of alignment as I slowly bent my elbow, bringing the weights up close to my shoulders.

During the rest period, I considered this absurd situation. Hopefully, he would dismiss me and that would be the end of it. Unless Tess got so wound up she decided to call the detective's boss. I hoped not. I finished three sets of curls, did a bunch of exercises for my abs and returned to my room.

I dialed the number she'd given me. After a walk through a voice mail menu, a woman answered the phone. I asked for Detective Gorman. He wasn't in, so she took my name and number and the fact I was calling about Steve. I trotted down to the office and gave Tess an update. She told me to try again if I didn't get a call back in two hours.

I went back upstairs, showered and dressed in jeans and a black turtleneck. It made me feel very Silicon Valley, except in a female body. The blue jeans and black turtleneck wearing crowd is mostly male. It's kind of funny because an Apple Computer commercial from the nineteen-eighties mocked IBM's regimented clothing styles. It presented office workers as drones wearing dark suits, white shirts, and narrow ties. The ad labeled them lemmings, cogs in a machine, stripped of individuality and creativity. Then along comes Steve Jobs with the uniform of the nineties and early twenty-first century and suddenly people copied — not always blue jeans, sometimes khaki and the black turtleneck, but lacking individuality and creativity all the same. Lemmings. No one saw the irony.

As I was on the last bit of damp hair, styling it so the waves disappeared, the phone chimed. I picked it up.

"Detective Gorman, calling for Alexandra Mallory."

"Hi. Thanks for returning my call so fast. I…"

"What country am I calling?"

"I'm in Australia, but I worked at CoastalCreative. I'm calling because I'm concerned that Steve Montgomery's death was ruled an overdose. He wasn't a drug user." My voice sounded forced and phony.

"So I've been told."

"It seems too easy to call it an overdose when someone could have…"

"How many times do I have to explain this? There is no other evidence. Nothing to suggest suicide. He OD'd. I know that's hard for you people to accept."

I was supposed to push hard. But would Tess ever know what I'd said to him? If she called him herself, would he pass on the nitty gritty of what I'd said, what he'd said? I didn't think so, but a little push was probably a good idea. She was not letting go and I had no doubt she would call him herself if I didn't get results.

"I'm worried someone is using heroin to go after executives at CoastalCreative."

"Did someone else die of a heroin OD at CoastalCreative?" His voice sounded more alert, firmer.

"No."

"What is this, some kind of campaign to save the reputation of a company hero?"

"It's not a campaign."

"You're the third person to call. Can I expect more?"

"I didn't realize that. I just wanted to see if there's a chance you might look into it further."

"No chance. Anything else?"

"No. Have a wonderful day." I said this without any sarcasm. I was truly pleased with his answer, although obviously he didn't know that, and possibly he saw sarcasm where none existed.

"Good-bye Ms. Mallory."

So, Tess had already called him. And she hadn't told me, trying to push me into following her plan. I don't like it when I'm put up to something without knowing all the facts. She was going to find herself owing me.

# 47

There was no rush to tell Tess I'd spoken to the detective. In fact, I could easily string this out to the next day with a voicemail tag story. After setting me up like she had, I'd do a little setting up of my own. I'd see how frantic she got, whether she lost it enough that she'd call again. Maybe she'd sabotage her own goal by pestering him and I could stop giving brain cells to thinking about her curiosity turning toward the end of my relationship with Steve.

There wasn't a single fiber of worry in my mind, but I still didn't like her poking around asking questions. I didn't like that she was continuing to push the issue and she would surely keep calling, or get someone else to do it, until he stopped taking her calls. She might circle back to the CEO and enlist his help.

My call was the third. Who else wasn't buying it?

Maybe I should be more concerned. I'd cleaned Steve's condo meticulously. The things I'd worn and used were well settled in a landfill by now. But there were those text messages. The messages we'd exchanged before I got the burner phone. The messages that contained streams of conversations I no longer remembered, things I'd written before I decided he needed to die. Besides that, my dummied up messages suggesting I might accuse him of sexual harassment could backfire. What if they looked into harassment, what if they thought that was a possible motive for murder?

A cigarette would calm me, but for now, I wanted to stay in my room, not run into Tess, or Gavin, for that matter. Any of them. And even stepping onto the balcony ran the risk of someone deciding to go for a swim, taking away my solitude. Besides, smoking in the daytime wouldn't work. Sean would be all over me, just to be annoying, even if the smoke didn't bother him. I took a deep breath and opened my laptop.

I went to Twitter and checked the profiles I'd set up years ago. They'd lain dormant while I was in San Francisco. Surprisingly, I'd only lost about thirty or forty followers on my other profiles. That proves how many people aren't tweeting. Their profiles gather dust while they've moved on to other social media or into a real social life.

I opened a new account for TruthT. I abbreviated it because TruthTeller was too cumbersome. If TruthT turned out to be too obscure, I could always get another free email address and set up a second profile.

For the banner photograph, I used the TT PayPal account to purchase a stock photo of two gorgeous cockatoos. The birds would suggest the company was Australian, and give a friendly appearance. At the same time, I was thinking of Damien and how a bird is incapable of being untruthful, it repeats what it hears no matter how upsetting or rude. It seemed appropriate, although subtle to the point that possibly no one would see that. I opened Facebook and replaced the blue whale with the cockatoo image for more consistent branding.

I returned to Twitter and looked through the trending topics. Even though I was seven thousand miles away, and Twitter shows trending topics for your part of the world, the damn orange-haired president of the United States was front and center. He was making crazy again, tweeting to defend his gorgeous but extremely duped daughter against some new criticism. They were a bunch of crybabies. Well, he was most of all, but so were his kids.

He'd tweeted a similar message four times. It seemed to me, he was drawing more attention to the issue rather than letting the criticism quietly die, washed over by tidal waves of news on every topic from every single country in the world. But he's clueless about human behavior. It makes you wonder if he's some sort of mutant — the human race striving to evolve, but getting it wrong. Surely that happens from time to time. A new strand develops and eventually, hopefully, it's unable to survive after all. It had the wrong adaptation.

Also trending was a rap singer, a hashtag about pets, and a new movie release.

This was going to be the problem with marketing TruthTeller via social media. The hot topics were politics, pop culture, and pets. There were other things, of course — the inspirational, the quirky and funny, the heartwarming. But the trifecta was the three P's.

It was smaller by hundreds of thousands, but the inspirational crowd might be a good target for our app. I followed a few who posted pithy quotes about following your own path, marching to your own drum, being true to you. Maybe that fit under pop culture after all.

After following, I was tempted to re-tweet. There's nothing so engaging as honoring a stranger with a RT to get them paying attention to you for a micro second. But I needed to review my plan again and consider what the first ten to fifteen tweets would be about. This was supposed to be strategic.

Of course, who would see those re-tweets, since we currently had no followers? And does anyone really go back in a feed more than a day or two? By the time we got traction and even a sliver of attention, these early tweets would be so buried only the NSA would have the tools to dig them out efficiently.

I re-tweeted the quote about being true to you. It seemed to fit. We would be aiming to persuade people they shouldn't look to friends and family for guidance. They should look into their guts, make contact with their ids, reflected in the biological functions of their bodies.

There was a knock on the door. I jumped up, eager to see which of my quirky roommates it might be. Not just out of curiosity, I needed to write some tweets to have in the queue for release on a consistent schedule, and the best way to think of those would not be sitting and staring at the screen.

Tess stood in the doorway. "Did you get ahold of him?"

Suddenly, I was tired. Too tired to string her along. In fact, stringing her was a mistake. It would simply feed her obsession. If she continued to face slammed doors, she would let go of it sooner, before it mushroomed into something unmanageable. "Yes."

"Can I come in?"

"There's not much to tell you."

She walked into my room. She went to the balcony doors and sat in the armchair facing my bed. "Tell me everything."

"He said there's no chance they'll take another look into Steve's death."

"Did you do what I said? Mention a threat to the company?"

"Yes. He wanted to know who else at CC died from a

heroin overdose."

"What did you tell him?"

"That no one else OD'd."

"You should have played it out."

"What does that mean?"

She narrowed her eyes. She leaned forward slightly, pressing her elbows into her legs. "You should have said you weren't sure, you'd have to check. Asked him to call HR."

I waited, holding her steady gaze.

"What else?" she said.

"That's it. I said — *There's no chance?* And he said *no chance.* That's a direct quote."

She stood abruptly. "That's unacceptable."

"There are some things you can't control."

"This is wrong. It's defamation of Steve's character. It tarnishes his career, his entire life."

"It's not your job to buff up his image."

She glared at me. She walked across the room and out the door, leaving it open.

I stared into the hallway, briefly considering sending an anonymous note to Detective Gorman to let him know that Tess Turner was mentally unstable. In the end, I decided against it. She would dig her own grave with him.

# 48

The weather was cool and breezy. Low dark clouds formed a thick layer over everything, making it seem closer to dusk. It was perfect weather for a mid-day run. Getting farther away from the computer would allow the some of the detailed steps of my tweeting strategy to take shape in the back of my mind.

I turned left from Sean's front walkway, taking the newer route which was slightly longer. One or two more runs and I would have the new route cemented in my mind so my future early morning runs could start away from John's line of sight.

No pedestrians strolled down the middle of the sidewalk, no cars backed out of long driveways, allowing me an obstacle-free first mile. After that, I felt limber enough that I could easily dodge around the few people out walking, veer into the street if a car was leaving home.

I ran for almost two miles then turned back.

When I reached the end of the street, I saw Lisa. She was seated in the middle of her lawn, her butt nestled down as if she didn't feel the cold earth and damp grass. Her head was bent forward, hair falling over the sides of her face. She was cross-legged, wearing jeans with one knee torn open and a brown sweatshirt. A pale gray scarf covered the back of her neck and hung open in the front. Her feet were bare. It wasn't extremely cold, but it wasn't barefoot weather. Something about her whole posture didn't look right, suggesting she wasn't sure where she was.

I slowed to an easy jog as I neared her yard. She didn't look up. I slowed further and then stopped directly across from her. She was only about fifteen feet from me, but didn't appear to notice I was standing there.

"Lisa?"

She didn't move her head or shift her position in any way.

I waited for several minutes. I took a few steps to the left to get a better view of her. She held her hands cupped as if scooping water out of a pond. The backs of her hands rested on her ankles. I raised my voice, on the precipice of a shout, the volume I'd use if I were standing on the opposite side of the wide street. "Hi, Lisa."

Her head moved slightly but not in my direction.

I walked along the stepping stones that led to the front porch. When I was halfway, I turned and cut across the lawn until I was standing a few feet away from her. "Is something wrong?"

Her shoulders heaved. "She never had a chance."

I moved closer and looked at her hands, almost closed over a tiny object. "What is it?"

She spread her hands a few inches. Lying inside the bowl she'd created with her fingers was a baby bird, its mouth partially open, the downy fluff, not even real feathers, of a very young bird. "What kind is it?"

"I don't know." Her voice wavered.

"It happens. They fall out of the nest."

She looked up at me. The skin around her eyes was red. Her face had faint streaks where tears had run down and dried. "There's no tree where it could have fallen."

She was right. If the spot where she was seated was the place where she'd found the bird, there were no trees with branches overhead. The nearest trees were two palms about ten feet away from us.

"It never had a chance. I can't...it's too hard. It's so awful." Her shoulders trembled and tears spilled out of her eyes. She closed her hands as if trying to keep the dead bird warm.

"It's probably not a good idea to hold it."

She looked at me, uncomprehending.

"It might have a disease. If it didn't fall out of a tree, it might have died and..."

"I think the mother dropped it here. She couldn't keep it fed and warm and safe."

"Do birds abandon their babies like that? Maybe they leave them in the nest, but they don't carry them to another location. How would they even do that?"

She raised her voice. "I don't know how, but that's what happened."

"You shouldn't hold it."

"I'm not going to get a disease."

"Why don't you bury it?"

"I can't."

"Why not?"

"It's too hard." Her voice wavered again. She bent over and let her hair fall over her cheeks again, hiding the streaks of tears.

"I can dig the hole if you want."

"I can't put it in the ground. I can't cover her eyes and mouth with dirt. It's so cold, I need to keep her warm."

"You can't do that forever."

She bent her head lower, as if trying to sweep the ends of her hair across the bird's body.

"If you plan to keep holding it, why don't you move to the patio where it's not so damp."

She looked up at me, her eyes blank, staring past me. "Please leave me alone."

"I…"

The sound of a car stopped me from saying more, or maybe I hadn't planned yet what I was going to say. I turned. A Range Rover had pulled into the driveway. The driver's door opened and a tall man climbed out. He had a short dark beard and perfectly clipped dark hair. "Lisa!"

She uncrossed her legs, moving awkwardly as she tried to rise to her feet without using her hands.

The man strode across the lawn. He glanced at me and back at Lisa. "What are you doing?"

She held out her hands, spreading her thumbs to reveal the bird.

"You need to get rid of it and go inside. It's too cold to be sitting around in the yard. It's not healthy."

He glanced at me again. "Have we met?"

I held out my hand. "Alexandra. I live two doors down."

He nodded. "Girlfriend of the long-haired guy?"

"No." I wasn't sure how much Sean wanted our new company talked about in the neighborhood. He hadn't given any guidelines. Maybe there were zoning laws. "Just a bunch of us sharing a house."

"Didn't realize he was strapped for cash."

I didn't answer.

"Well, good to know you, Alexandra. I'm Barry."

"Good to meet you."

I turned to go. Lisa was nowhere in sight.

# 49

Drinking a glass of wine at one-thirty on a weekday afternoon was not Tess's usual style, and might send a wrong signal if Sean or Gavin wandered through the living room, but she sort of didn't care. She wanted a glass of wine. Focusing on work was impossible, so a glass of wine it was.

She couldn't recall feeling so thwarted in years. The more Steve's death was dismissed as the shocking revelation of a secret side of his life, the more she was compelled to do something. But now, she had no idea what that something might be. Any further questions were in the hands of the detective. She certainly couldn't force him to check further, she couldn't seem to persuade him that something was wrong. There was no channel for an appeal, no process for challenging the decision, and no way that she could see to make him listen more carefully.

At this point, he was probably afraid of looking bad for making a determination that might be proven wrong. If she could figure out a way around his ego, she might be able to make progress. The other option was to call his superior officer, but she had no leverage there and unless Gorman was underperforming, it was unlikely his boss would take kindly to an average citizen questioning his skill.

And once she made that call, the option of working around his ego would be off the table. He'd be furious and refuse to talk to her at all.

She took a sip of wine. There had to be something. Ted

had more clout than she did — as CEO, as a male, as Steve's boss… Maybe that was a better avenue. He would listen to her more willingly and she could make her case. But he'd already blown her off. There had to be some little thread of insight that would make him change his view, something that would force him to care. The reputation of the company should concern him. But that was probably why he wanted it to all go away.

She could write a letter to the editor of the San Francisco Chronicle. Sometimes public shaming worked. But that could come across like…

"It's a little early for wine."

She turned at the sound of Sean's voice. He stood at the edge of the foyer, giving the impression he'd been standing there for several minutes. His hair was loose, not tied in the ponytail he wore most of the time when they were working. It looked like he hadn't washed it for two days.

"It is, but I have a lot on my mind."

"Can I put something else on your mind?"

She took another sip of wine. "Sure."

He walked into the room and sat across from her. He turned on the light beside him. The sky was getting darker even though sunset was still a while off. Clouds had been piling on top of each other all day, starting with pale gray this morning and growing increasingly black.

"It's about Alex," he said.

She sighed, trying to hold the sound of her breath inside so he wasn't aware of her frustration. Of course it was about Alex.

"I think she's upset with me."

She put down her glass. "Why?"

"I tossed her in the pool yesterday."

"She doesn't swim."

"So she said. But I didn't know she *can't* swim at all. I thought she just…"

"She'll get over it."

"Has she said anything to you?"

"No." She crossed her legs and wrapped her hands around her kneecap.

"She and I have gotten off on the wrong foot."

"Calling her a predator doesn't help."

"I didn't call her that to her face."

Tess uncrossed her legs, picked up her glass, and took a sip of wine. She settled back into the couch. "You both need to chill out."

"I am sorry. I thought she was telling a fib. I thought she didn't want to join in the fun. She's very aloof most of the time. Cold."

"I don't think that's it at all."

"Well she's cold to me."

"She's not cold. She behaves more like a man — unapologetic. Maybe that's what you don't like. She doesn't couch everything she says in hesitant, uncertain words and meek phrases to make sure she's being appropriately compliant."

"Why do you always defend her?"

"I don't. I'm correcting your biased view. Look at her as you would Gavin, and see if your perception changes."

He shrugged. "Well I'm sorry I tossed her in the water. I honestly thought she'd be a good sport about it. She was wearing a swimsuit."

"So it's okay to toss someone into the water against their

will as long as they're not dressed in nice clothes?"

"It's all in fun."

"Do you do that to other men?"

"All the time." He laughed.

"Maybe you should get to know her better."

"I'm trying. She doesn't make it easy."

"Grabbing her and throwing her into a swimming pool doesn't make it easy for her to get to know you, either."

He nodded. "I said, sorry."

"We have a product to get out the door and into the market. That should be our focus," she said.

"Having fun is part of building a team."

"Not forced fun."

"I'll take that into consideration."

Tess stood and walked to the window. She held her wineglass with both hands and looked out at the trees. Branches and fronds waved and bowed in the increasing wind.

"She holds herself apart," he said.

She remained where she was. He was searching hard to find Alex's flaws and then focusing only on those. For whatever reason, they hadn't hit it off. Smoothing out the rough spots between them was not her job. Although Sean was very laid back, put on a casual air, there was an aggressive undertone. He had very strong, cemented opinions. Of course he and Alex were wary of each other.

"You're fixating on her weaknesses," she said. Alex shouldn't have gone into his room, but maybe she had a point. Why hadn't he given them a tour of the house? It was no big deal, and it felt off balance that he was familiar with their rooms but his and Gavin's were sacrosanct.

"The Facebook photos illustrate my point," he said. "The rest of us are open and smiling and she's hiding behind glasses and a hat, like she doesn't want to be recognized." He laughed. "I don't trust people who hold themselves off from others."

Now Tess saw Alex's point even more clearly — Sean had sealed off part of the house. If they were a team, if this all belonged to all of them in terms of a workplace, why were the men's bedrooms forbidden territory?

# 50

Trying to have a conversation with Tess about Alex had been a waste of time. Sean wasn't sure why he kept pushing it. Tess clearly wanted to shield Alex from even the most constructive criticism. Tess insisted he hadn't given Alex a chance. She implied he was being sexist, but he simply couldn't shake the memory of his visceral reaction the first time she'd shaken his hand.

Alexandra's grip was strong, tightening as their hands moved in a quick uptick. His immediate instinct was to pull away but she held on as if she wanted to make him uncomfortable. At the same time, she shook hands like a woman from decades ago — remaining seated as if she was entitled to deference. And those eyes, staring him down, unafraid to hold his gaze. All the time. During their barbecue, despite the camaraderie, he'd caught her looking at him several times with an iron stare that said she was assessing him and wanted something from him. Something he did not want to give.

A tightly woven team was crucial. He wanted the app to experience mind-blowing success. It had phenomenal potential. For that to happen, he needed the whole team moving in a coordinated effort. He didn't want interpersonal conflicts and he didn't want someone who had an agenda of her own. He had no doubt she wanted something out of the job and their shared living that had nothing to do with the success of TruthTeller.

He put on a jacket and stepped out the front door. He needed to clear his head. She unnerved him, and now he was magnifying all her flaws. Tess had been right about that. Yet he felt if he didn't magnify them, he would be lulled into a state of acceptance that would allow her to take control.

But control of what? It wasn't as if she wanted to own the company. She wasn't capable of running the company. There wasn't a technical thought in her head. No, she had what they liked to call emotional intelligence. She was all about social games and political machinations.

He went down the stone walkway, stopping a few feet from the sidewalk.

Two houses over, he saw Alexandra. Even from this distance, seeing only her back, he knew it was her. She wore a dark blue jumper with a hood and workout clothes. She was kneeling by the Thomson's front steps, bent forward slightly, looking at something.

He waited to see what she'd do.

This was a perfect example of his sense that she had her own agenda. Why was she in the neighbor's yard? Why wasn't she in the office working? Of course, Tess wasn't either — having a drink in the middle of the day. He laughed. Neither was he. They needed more structure, needed to make sure they were moving forward as fast as possible. The only one demonstrating a decent work ethic was Gavin. He lost himself in screens full of code, making adjustments, spending hours studying and tweaking his work, testing for bugs.

What a strange collection of personality types he'd managed to assemble. But that was supposed to be a good thing. They complemented each other, making the organization stronger. He needed to figure out what Alex's strengths were and stop this slightly paranoid train of thought that she had an agenda that might damage the success of their efforts.

He walked past John's house so he could get a better look at what she was up to. Neither of the Thomsons were in the front yard. Barry's SUV sat in the driveway, barely pulled up past the edge of the property, as if he'd been in such a hurry he couldn't be bothered to pull forward parallel with his house, much less drive the car to the back of the lot and into the garage.

Alex stood and turned. She walked alongside the porch and around the side of the house. She disappeared from view. She was on the verge of trespassing. That's all he needed was conflict with his extremely private neighbors. He moved close to the palm trees near the corner where the front path and sidewalk joined, making his presence less obvious.

A few minutes later, Alex walked back around the side of the house carrying a spade. She squatted in front of a shrub with large thick leaves and enormous fuchsia blossoms made of individual nodules that looked something like tiny test tubes filled with blood. She began digging. Every few minutes she glanced over her shoulder, as if she knew someone was watching her. He moved closer to the tree, stepping back so part of the trunk was in front of him. Still she continued checking, looking left one time, right the next. Was she paranoid, always feeling watched? It seemed that way. He had no doubt that if she saw him, she'd come directly up to him.

When there was a pile of damp soil the size of a rugby ball beside her, she stood and wiped her palms on her pants. She returned to the front porch and picked up something, moving carefully as if the object was made of blown glass and the slightest touch against the porch step or the post would shatter it into microscopic fragments.

He couldn't stand it. He stepped away from the trees and walked along the stepping stones to where she stood. "What are you doing?"

She turned without startling at the sound of his voice.

"Burying this." She held out her hand. Lying across her palm and the insides of her knuckles was a dead baby bird.

"Why?"

"It's dead."

"I can see that. Why are you in the neighbors' yard and where did you find the bird and why is it any of your business?"

"Wouldn't you bury a dead creature if you found it?"

"I'm not clear on how you came across a dead bird."

"Lisa had it." She turned and walked to the fresh grave. She knelt and placed the breathless creature inside. She spooned soil on top of it, filling the hole. When she was done, she tapped the spade gently on the loose dirt.

"You shouldn't be in their yard, and you should ask before digging holes in property that doesn't belong to you."

"Lisa had the bird. She was too upset to bury it."

"I see."

She walked up the steps and placed the spade on the porch. Once again, she wiped her hands on her pants, came down the steps, and smiled at him. "There. That's taken care of."

"So instead of working, you're out socializing with the neighborhood? I meant for a casual environment, but we still work business hours, for the most part."

"I'm not socializing with the neighborhood. I know Lisa

and John. That's it. Oh, and I met Barry."

"Very friendly of you. It would help if you would extend that same friendliness to your co-workers at TruthTeller."

"You aren't my co-worker. You're the CEO."

"You understood my point."

She smiled. "It's important to know the people living around you. Did you know John was an expert in astronomy?"

"I didn't."

She began walking along the stepping stones. He followed, thinking about the things Tess had said. One of them had to stop being so combative. He supposed it might as well be him. It was possible he hadn't given her a fair chance. Agenda or not, it was his responsibility to build the team and he hadn't put enough effort into that. A CEO needed to remain impartial, not allow personal feelings to cause him to treat various employees differently.

He moved up beside her. "So John's an expert in astronomy? What did he say about it?"

"He has a very nice telescope. He invited me over and I got to see Jupiter and Saturn. It was spectacular. The rings are so mysterious."

"Nice," he said. "You're into astronomy?"

"Not really. He was very excited about it and I was curious."

"My cousin had a telescope when we were kids," he said.

She didn't respond.

"I don't recall seeing the rings of Saturn," he said.

"I'm sure he'd let you look. He's very eager to share it."

"That would be excellent."

"I'll ask him. We could all go over. A team building

event!" She turned and grinned.

He wasn't sure if she was mocking him or truly wanted to facilitate their bonding over an evening of stargazing.

# 51

It wasn't easy to shake off the suddenly-friendly-eager-to-get-to-know-you presence of Sean. He followed me back over to his house and we went inside. He waited while I took off my shoes and hoodie. He waited while I readjusted my ponytail. Then, he invited me into the kitchen for a glass of wine. Then he tried to start a conversation. First about my education and work experience prior to CC. When I wasn't overly forthcoming, he moved on to the topic of the dead bird and Lisa, but I had nothing more to tell him on that front either.

We remained at the bar, taking large sips of wine. The silence lasted for several minutes. He took his last swallow of wine. He stood and assured me it had been great talking to me, getting to know me better, sharing a glass of wine, seeing how much I cared for the fragile body of the bird.

I waited for him to walk through the entryway toward the offices. I slipped out of the kitchen as fast as I could and ran up the curving staircase and hurried down the hall to my room. Knowing he was at least a few seconds behind me, I was tempted to check out his room, but I couldn't count on him staying down there where he belonged. I needed more time, when he, when all of them, were out of the house. Then I could further investigate his room and relax in his soft, buttery leather chair, enjoying the beautiful curves and polished wood of his statue.

I went out to my balcony. The sky was almost black now,

with tufts of pale gray. I didn't think I'd ever seen a storm that took so very long to build. I stared down at the equally black water of the swimming pool. The wind moved across the surface, rippling it like a crumpled piece of shimmery wrapping paper. The sky was empty of birds. If they were hunkered down in the nearby trees, they weren't making a sound.

A few minutes later, I heard a door open below me.

Gavin emerged from beneath the cover of the patio. He strode toward the pool and dropped his oversized towel on one of the chaise lounges. He returned to the deep end and dove into the water without a moment of hesitation.

His body glided forward a few inches below the surface. The rippled water distorted his form so that his skin and tropical swim trunks looked like plant life and fish moving through the water. He was halfway down the length of the pool before he surfaced. He swam with an easy rhythm, one arm rising out of the water and plunging back as the opposite arm rose. His feet kept up a steady cadence of small kicks. Every few strokes, his head turned to the left and he took in air, then put his face back in the water, unperturbed by all that water covering his skin, cradling his face, pushing against all the openings of his head, trying to make its way inside his mouth and nose and ears. He wasn't battling the water as if it were a monster grabbing him and pulling him down to his death. He acted as if the water was a friendly presence, buoying him along.

How did a person come to such comfortable terms with water? How had he fallen in love with the stuff so that the first thing that came into his mind on a cold, stormy afternoon was diving into the swimming pool?

The impending touch of death that came over me when I was thrown into the pool still gripped my intestines, tearing them into gelatinous strands.

I'd honestly thought I'd faced down the most threatening enemy of my life when I pushed that canoe to the center of Soquel creek and allowed myself to tip into the water. All I'd really accomplished was victory over the initial contact. I'd known the bottom was right there and every other instinct was kept in check by the awareness of my need to rid the earth of those two people. I'd managed because something more compelling drove me.

Learning to swim might be a good thing. I didn't want to live my life with that all-consuming aversion to water dictating my vacations and my social life. I didn't ever want to be in a position again where someone could overcome me and throw me into the arms of death so easily. Next time, there might not be a Gavin there to get me back on my feet.

As long as the water threatened me, it was winning and I was losing. As long as I avoided water, there was something out there that controlled my life more than I did. I was vulnerable to every over-zealous party boy who wanted a bit of fun, any guy who got off hearing the shrieks of a female.

I leaned my forearms on the railing. The metal bar that topped the glass panels dug into my bones, but I pushed the discomfort aside, feeling myself inside of Gavin's elegantly moving body, imagining myself in that pool, conquering the water, knowing how to keep myself afloat, how to propel myself forward, how to breathe easily at the right time.

The mesmerizing passage of his body up and down the pool continued while my mind drifted again to Bluebeard's closet and the parallels with his locked bedroom door. The lock said *stay out*. Possibly even Sean didn't know what was kept inside of that room. Of course it wasn't the heads of wives he'd murdered. I knew that. I laughed, rather loudly, but he didn't hear me with all that water pooling in his ears.

It obviously wasn't something horrifying like that, but he acted as if it were. And I couldn't stop thinking about it, picturing a stack of heads like a pyramid of cannon balls in the corner.

I could care less if any of the others took a peek into my room. Maybe it's because I've done a good job all my life hiding the things I don't want seen.

I also know that making it clear you're hiding something is the best way to stir up curiosity. Like Bluebeard. If he hadn't told his newest wife she could go anywhere in his castle but inside that closet, she wouldn't have gone mad with curiosity to know its secret.

In all likelihood, the room had computer equipment, possibly lots of dirty clothes, maybe some porn magazines, maybe the evidence of jerking off in his bed — soggy tissues and stained towels. Lots of men had things like that in their bedrooms. Why did he feel he had to keep the door locked at all times? He never forgot. I'd developed the habit of checking it multiple times a day, every chance I got. Sometimes I even dashed upstairs when he was eating, or when I had a good sense of where everyone else was located on the first floor.

Accusing Tess of obsession wasn't really fair when I'd developed one of my own.

# 52

*Los Angeles*

**W**hen Moira started leaving blood-soaked tampons in our shared trashcan, not bothering even to wrap them in toilet paper to hide the red-streaked cotton, I had to fight back with more than just a self-preserving daily trash pick-up.

First, I tried talking to her, knowing I was likely to get nowhere, but the rules of social engagement need to be followed before you can move on to something more effective.

She walked in the door, letting her backpack slide onto her bed. I pointed to the trashcan beside her dresser. "This is disgusting. I do not want to live with your stale, stinky blood in my room."

"It doesn't smell. I'll empty it later."

"They belong in the bathroom trash."

"Sometimes I need to change one in a hurry."

"Yuck."

She smiled.

"It's a health hazard," I said.

"No it's not. It's part of the human body."

"So is shit. Is that what's coming next?"

"You can't smell anything. You're just not in tune with your own body, so you're ashamed of its natural functions. Monthly blood is a beautiful thing. Some day, a baby will grow in that blood."

"The idea might be beautiful, but the blood itself is not. Especially like this." I picked up the trash can and tipped it toward her. The motion moved the bloodied plugs with their white string tails close to her face.

She laughed. "You need to lose that shame, girlie!"

"I'm not..."

"I see it in your eyes. A woman's blood is not something dirty. It's beautiful. It's power."

"It's biological waste. Get rid of it and don't do it again."

Moira laughed. "You are so fucking cute." She pinched her nostrils with her thumb and index finger, lifting her other fingers to mock her take on my delicate nature.

Still holding the trashcan, I walked to the side of her bed. I turned it upside down. Two bloody tampons, a bucketful of soggy tissues, and four candy wrappers fell on her books.

"Pick that up!"

"It's beautiful. It's natural. What's the problem?" I put the trashcan beside her bed. I pulled out my desk chair, sat down, and opened my Introduction to Psychology textbook.

"Clean it up."

"It's not my mess."

"It is now. You can't dump shit on my bed."

"The tissues were on the floor around your bed and all over your desk. I already picked them up. They didn't bother you on the desk. So..." I uncapped my highlighter and began reading.

"You're a pain in the ass," Moira said.

I nodded my head without turning.

"You got blood on my book cover."

"I think the blood is mostly dry now."

"I..."

Finally, I think she realized her anger was undermining her own argument.

"I stay out of your stuff, you stay out of *mine*." She began rustling around, scooping the tissues and tampons off her bed and into the trashcan. There was a soft thud as she set the trashcan beside her dresser.

I wanted it emptied, but so far, I had a slight edge. Turning around and speaking would only start the argument up again.

"Why are you such a prude?" she said.

"I'm not."

"You are. You're so afraid of a little mess."

"I like things nice."

She was quiet for several minutes. I continued to feel victorious, but at the same time, she wasn't headed toward the bathroom with her trashcan. In the end, she would regain the upper hand because she would now let it fester there even longer. I probably had a week of disgusting garbage to look forward to before it finally overflowed and she emptied it on her own.

I'd dreamed about my future college roommate, believing all the stories of gal pals in dorm living. I'd imagined parties and getting to know someone like a new-found sister, sharing our hassles with school and studying together, talking about crushes and our plans for the future, hanging out and philosophizing about *Life*.

She was right, I felt like her mother, harping at her to clean up, doing it myself because I couldn't stand the mess, like a parent who didn't know how to enforce the rules. I was surprised we didn't have ants. Or roaches. I suppose our floor was too high up for them to be able to find their way, but surely flies would be coming in through the unscreened windows on hot days.

The bed creaked as she flopped down. I heard the thud of books being re-stacked and more creaking of the bed. I didn't want to have a silent stand-off. It would be a long year if we never spoke to each other. But what she'd done disgusted me. I wasn't sure if she truly believed the praise for shed menstrual blood that she'd spouted or if she was doing all of this to irritate me.

Thick, heavy silence filled the room. I continued reading about the history of psychology, the interest in studying the mind and behavior that dated back to ancient civilizations. As early as the first century, kind treatment of psychiatric patients was advised, including comfortable conditions with light, warm rooms. I was marveling over the fact that people have always known the importance of lovely surroundings, when Moira started blowing her nose, quite loudly, as if to argue with those ancient suggestions for good mental health.

I pictured the wet tissues piling up on the floor. Once I stood up from my desk, I'd have to tiptoe my way through the puffs of white fiber to avoid landing my bare toes in her globs of mucous.

All those years growing up, I'd thought tension in my house was due to my parents' rigid beliefs and their desire to make sure they controlled all of our thoughts as well as the behavior of me and my siblings. Possibly this was the first lesson of college — living with other people is a series of battles and compromises.

# 53

*Sydney*

The storm finally let loose about two minutes after Gavin climbed out of the swimming pool. Almost immediately, his towel was soaked. He ran with sure steps across the wet concrete and disappeared beneath the cover of the patio. Thunder rumbled and a few minutes later, there was a crack of lightning. The sky was so black, I turned on all the lights in my room. I left the glass door open so I could hear the sharp cracks and the rolls of thunder. The balcony was wide enough there was no chance of water coming into the room unless it rained sideways, and even then, it might not reach the carpet.

I took a shower and pulled on leggings and a cropped white sweater with a V-neck. I settled in the armchair and picked up my tablet. There was something about the storm that made me not feel like working.

Or maybe it wasn't only the storm.

There was a growing malaise in the house. Maybe it was Steve's ghost, haunting Tess's thoughts, but no one was working much. I couldn't understand why Sean wasn't cracking the whip, insisting we show up in the offices on a regular schedule.

I was antsy, as if my four-mile run had been days ago instead of a few hours. I thought about the dead bird, soaked in its grave. When I'd finished digging the hole, I'd glanced up at what was presumably the living room window. Lisa stood there, holding the curtain to the side with a single finger. Her expression didn't acknowledge what I was doing or show any sign of what she might be thinking.

Still, I was glad I'd done it. Burying the bird felt like a problem that was solved. Whatever had bothered her so much about it, she could now move away from.

What I still really wanted, and the reason my legs were twitching with the desire to get moving, was to take another look at Sean's bedroom. Despite his effort to make nice, I still sensed a desire to be rid of me, as if he blamed me for the malaise. Maybe the unwanted swim in the pool was his passive-aggressive way of letting me know. How could I work for someone who didn't accept my words as the truth? It was wrong in so many ways, and he thought a simple *sorry* was adequate. It never should have happened, and I didn't want him to think he had some kind of power over me. I needed to pay him back.

His bedroom was so minimalist, I wasn't sure what I thought I'd find there, but everyone has secrets hidden somewhere. Bluebeard came to mind. Again.

I put aside my tablet and went into the hallway. No light came from under any of the doors. I'd told myself to wait until the house was empty, but something about the storm pushed me to make my move now. And if he caught me in there again, so what? If he wanted to fire me, he already would have. He did want to, but his respect for Tess prevented that. Instead, he thought he could intimidate me into resigning.

I walked toward his room, glad that my feet were still bare. Even though shoes would be soundless on the thickly padded Berber carpet, bare feet always seem stealthier. In bare feet, every rough spot is immediately perceived by your body, you move faster, running quietly if necessary. I was simply lighter and better able to maneuver. I was less likely to step too hard on a creaky floorboard, although I hadn't noticed a single creaking board in the well-constructed house.

His door was unlocked. As I pressed down on the handle, I wondered if he was testing me. Had he tried the old movie trick of a thread tucked between the door and the frame? I wouldn't notice it falling, and if I did, I would never be able to return it to the precise spot.

I pushed open the door.

The room was no different from before — spotlessly clean and without a single piece of clutter. The glass doors were closed, but the shutters fully open. Lightning flashed across the sky, filling the room with an eerie glow that made the statue look as if it were coming to life.

I went immediately to his enormous walk-in closet. Below the section for hanging folded pants and shirts were three rows of drawers, five in each row. I opened the first drawer. Inside were socks folded in half, stacked side by side. The next drawer held boxer shorts, followed by drawers with swim trunks, board shorts, and finally, a dish of coins, two small decorative boxes with Asian characters etched on the tops, bottle openers, a handful of matchbooks, and keychains from various tech industry trade shows.

In the second row, all five drawers were filled with t-shirts folded into narrow rectangles. It looked like a department store display. Sean's demeanor was so carefully casual, laid back, right on the edge of scruffy, but his room, and especially his drawers made him out to be one step from a pathological neat freak. Even the so-called junk drawer had a tidy look to it.

The bottom row of drawers contained notebooks and papers. In the fourth drawer was a red expandable file folder designed to hold individual file folders. *GutSay* was scrawled in black permanent marker across the front. It was the temporary name they'd used until Tess came up with TruthTeller. I thought it was a better name. It attracted attention, aroused curiosity. And if you said it casually, the word sounded like *gutsy*. But along with her other concerns, Tess had insisted the word gut, and its metaphorical use, didn't translate well into other languages.

I pulled out the folder. Inside were legal documents regarding the formation of the company, along with employment contracts for Gavin and Tess. I slid both of their three-page contracts out of the folder, slipped them into the waistband of my leggings, pulled down my too-short sweater as best I could, and returned the folder to the drawer.

My original plan had been to sit in the armchair and admire the statue. Once I'd seen it in that surreal light from the storm I was even more captivated, but this was so much better. And I needed to get out of there. The hiding place inside my clothes was awkward and the papers weren't completely concealed. I hurried to the door, checked the hallway, and went out.

Back in my room, I pulled out the papers and placed them on my desk.

I'm not a thief. Besides, as soon as I'd read them, they would be returned, tucked neatly inside the folder. I was just curious. Reading them wouldn't necessarily give me any advantage over the others, but more knowledge is always good. Especially knowledge that other people don't know you possess.

My phone buzzed with a message from Tess that she'd made dinner and I should hurry down. I shoved the papers under the bed and went out. I locked my door with the key I'd been given the day I moved in and tucked the key into my bra.

The four of us ate together, not talking much except to marvel over the heavy rain and wind. Tess had made a stir fry with chicken and shiitake mushrooms, green onions and chili peppers. It was delicious, served over sticky white rice. We shared a bottle of Chardonnay. No one drank more than a glass. Afterwards, everyone retreated to their rooms.

I peeled off my leggings. The storm had turned the air muggy and the fabric clung to me like plastic wrap. I dropped them in my dirty clothes basket. I got a glass out of the bathroom and filled it with an inch of water. I pulled my cigarettes out of my bag and went out to the balcony. I closed the door, sat down, and lit a cigarette. The smoke was sucked away by the strong wind which made a less pleasant smoking experience, but I needed to think and that meant I needed a cigarette.

The lightning and thunder had subsided during dinner, but now both were back in full force, giving a fantastic show — crackling flares of light filled the entire sky.

When my cigarette was gone, I lit another and stood. I leaned on the railing, holding the glass of water and ash in one hand. I couldn't stop watching the flashes of light, feeling the rumble of thunder reverberate through my bones. I wanted it to last all night.

The cracks of lightning lit up the trees and the

surrounding houses, light hitting the windows of John's house that faced the backyard of Sean's. The place looked deserted except for a small disk of light in one bedroom. I closed my eyes for a moment, trying to picture which room I was looking at, but I couldn't figure it out. I opened my eyes and enjoyed the show and the cool wind that swept across my bare legs and up beneath my short, loose sweater.

# 54

The stars were glittering when my alarm woke me at five-thirty the next morning. The shutters were still open and the nearly full moon shone into my room like the soft lighting of a stage set for the opening scene of a play. I slithered out of bed, refreshed from sleep that had been made richer by the pelting rain and fading rumbles as the thunder moved off into the distance. The final flashes of light before I'd fallen asleep were quiet pops rather than the sky-tearing cracks of earlier.

I put on navy blue Capri spandex pants, a white t-shirt, and a white sweatshirt. The Aussie guys called sweatshirts jumpers, and every time they referred to one, I felt my brain do a quick sorting through of images to dismiss the picture of little-girl plaid jumpers over white blouses. How long would it take to get used to their differing words — bin for trash, boot for the trunk of a car, tomato sauce for ketchup? And then there were the half-made-up abbreviations like brekkie and barbie. It was almost like a foreign language. I imagined I'd eventually get used to the new words, and without really noticing, start using them myself, sucked into their culture.

I braided my hair and tucked my phone into its holder.

I picked up my running shoes and a pair of socks and went downstairs and out the front door.

The patio was well-designed for stretching — it was wide and completely dry, and the pillars provided solid support for leaning against while I stood on one foot to stretch the opposite leg. I breathed in the freshly washed plants and grass. The birds were starting to make noises, although it was a while until sunrise.

I ran for over five miles. It was the first time I'd really let loose — stopped consciously thinking about following my route or checking my phone to get my bearings. The streets felt familiar and I didn't hesitate at corners, trying to decide, or remember, which way to turn.

As I neared the end of the loop and drew close to Lisa's house, the sun was coming up. The houses on our side of the street faced east, and just as I reached her property line, the sun popped over the houses across the street and light splashed across her porch.

She sat in a wicker chair holding a coffee mug. As the sun hit her square in the face, she flinched as if she'd been punched. She ducked slightly, trying to escape the piercing rays. She stood and moved her chair, angling it so her back was toward John's house. She sat down and took a sip from her mug.

There was no sign of the SUV, or any car, for that matter. I waved to her. She didn't wave back, but I started up the stepping stones toward the porch anyway. Before I reached the steps, she leaned forward and placed her mug on the ground. She straightened. "What's up?"

"Did you enjoy the storm?"

She shrugged. "It was okay."

I'd reached the bottom of the steps. Her face was splotched with red spots, glaring and harsh on her pale skin. Maybe that's why she was dodging the sunlight.

"We don't get thunderstorms in my part of California, so

it was pretty awesome. I've never seen one with so much lightning, and so close. The whole sky exploded."

She stared at me without changing her expression. She didn't blink or give an indication she had even heard me, much less had an opinion about California's weather.

"Are you okay?" I said.

"Not really."

I put my foot on the first step. "Can I come up?"

"If you want."

I climbed the steps and leaned against the post. She didn't suggest I take the other chair that would have required me to drag it several feet closer to where she sat. "What's going on?"

She waited a long time before she spoke. "He betrayed me."

"That's rough."

"I thought he…well I guess you shouldn't assume things about people."

I wasn't sure if she was talking about her husband. But when someone's opening a door into an area I haven't seen before, I follow their lead instead of flinging questions, rushing too fast where they might not want to go. If they want to say more, they will. I'm not going to reel it out like I'm hauling a fish out of the water, releasing and pulling, playing some sort of game until the other person is exhausted and just spills their guts.

"I thought I knew him."

Those were common enough words, especially with boyfriends and husbands. But they can be true of the entire human race.

"Last night was the worst, and I thought…that's why I

didn't pay much attention to the storm. I do like them, but it was just a lot of background noise." She laughed, a single, sharp cry. "It felt like a horror movie. A corny horror movie. Overdone."

I nodded.

"Thank you for burying the bird."

"No problem."

"I saw you do it."

"I know."

"I don't want children."

It was a strange way to introduce the topic, and a startling change of direction, but she was a rather strange person. She drifted everywhere, not really paying attention, and not completely focused, or something. It's hard to describe.

She leaned forward, wrapping her arms around her ribcage. She bent her head down. Her hair covered her face but her voice was crisp and clear. "I've had three abortions."

"Wow. Is that good for you? Why don't you use…"

She sat up suddenly. "He won't let me. He wants kids. Lots of kids."

"Oh." Clearly they hadn't aligned their desires very well before they got together, before they exchanged rings and vows and merged their finances and set up house. It seemed like a rather significant point to miss.

"Well, not lots. But three. Maybe four."

"That seems like a lot to me. He doesn't know about the…"

She shook her head. Vigorously, hair swinging. "And you can't tell him."

"Why would I?"

"It just needed to be said."

Silence fell between us. She gazed out across her yard, turning her head to look in the direction of the bird's grave.

After a while, I shifted my position. "I should probably get going."

"Absolutely." She didn't look at me. She didn't move.

"It was..." I'd planned to say it was good talking to her, but I hadn't talked at all. And she probably didn't see it as something good, unless she felt unburdened.

"Thank you for burying the bird. It means a lot," she said.

"No problem."

"I just thought...I guess I thought he cared about *me*." She looked up. Her eyes were filled with tears, liquid so thick it turned her irises a washed out hazel. "So thanks."

I had no idea if this thank you was also for the bird or for listening. I smiled. Neither of us said anything else, and I left.

As I walked past John's house, he hurried down the walkway toward me. "Alexandra."

I stopped.

"What were you talking to Lisa about?" He took a step closer and peered into my eyes, his own eyes like tiny spades trying to dig around inside my head.

"Nothing much."

He took a few steps back and shifted his gaze. "Nothing much?"

"Small talk."

"You looked very intense."

"I'm sure I did. I'm a very intense person." I smiled. "I was thinking, what about all of us...my roommates and I... coming over to look at the stars."

"All of you? How many are there?"

"Just the four of us. I told them how cool it was."

He nodded. He ran his hand through his hair slicing the thick, straight strands. They fell back into place as if his hand had never passed through. "When?"

I glanced up at the cloudless sky. "Tonight?"

"Sure. Okay."

"I'll bring some wine."

"Okay. Good."

"See you then." I started walking, quickly, almost running. He called after me. "Ten-thirty."

I waved to let him know I'd heard. Sean would be impressed I was such a team player. And maybe Gavin would speak more than three words. Or, maybe he'd say nothing at all since John would be busy explaining the solar system.

# 55

I took a shower, made a latte, fried some bacon with a handful of leftover boiled red potatoes, and took it all up to my room. I didn't see any of my roommates.

I turned on the ceiling fan to blow out the damp smell of rain which was so lovely outside but was on the verge of stale and swampy inside. I spent the next few hours roving around Twitter, following interesting people — NASA, a guy who tweeted artistic and unusual photographs, The Great Barrier Reef, a bunch of actors and journalists, and a few comedians. I followed a person who tweeted about obscure laws in American towns, such as — It is required by law to carry a shovel in your car when visiting Cape Cod. Crazy human obsessions fascinate me. I can't imagine what caused a group of town leaders to say, *We must regulate this. Those who fail to comply deserve a fine.* You know something bizarre prompted it.

I posted a quote about following your dreams on our Facebook page and uploaded a photo I'd snapped of lightning across the night sky. Then I pulled out the contracts from under the bed and read about the deals struck between Gavin and Sean, Tess and Sean.

Gavin's was similar to mine in all but the salary, which made me wonder why mine wasn't in the folder. Maybe Tess hadn't given it to him yet. His salary was close to thirty-five thousand dollars higher, but I couldn't begrudge that. Software developers are essential and they know it. And if they're good, they can find work anywhere. It still puzzled me why he didn't want to be a principal, but maybe he just didn't like the headaches. Maybe he was more of an artist and it was all about his creative satisfaction, not money, as long as he had enough, whatever *enough* is.

Maybe I'd ask him. The three-word answer would be along the lines of — *That's what I wanted.* But that's four words, four and a half.

Tess's was another story. She owned forty percent of the company. There were no plans to make a public offering, but she was set to collect her percentage of the profits. Her salary was a whopping three-hundred-ten-thousand dollars. Clearly Sean had a lot of confidence in this app. A *lot.* He also had a lot of confidence in a woman he'd met while wearing a bathing suit, offering nearly half his company to her in the space of twelve days.

I had no idea what she'd made at CC, but I doubted it was anywhere near that high. Possibly with the addition of bonuses and stock it came close. It made me wonder what she did that was so remarkable. Was there any part of her job that I couldn't learn? In some ways, she was paid for responsibility, for taking heat when things went wrong, for headaches and pressure. I didn't want any of that, but still…

It was close to eleven when I carried my dishes down to the kitchen.

I found Tess working in the smaller of the two offices. She sat at the desk, head thrust forward toward the computer, not seeming to notice the cockatoo on the other side of the window, sitting five feet from her, studying her as intently as she was peering at the screen.

I knocked on the doorframe, walked in, and pulled out a chair from the conference table.

She turned. "How's it going?"

"Slow."

"That's not good."

"I think the social media should have been started a long time ago. It's going to take weeks to get even a minuscule amount of attention."

She leaned back. "You need to be on it all the time."

"I realize that. But it's Sunday. Tomorrow, I'm going to come up with about forty or fifty things to tweet about and start a regular update. But I need to interact with other people first, and I'm trying to figure out the best candidates for that."

She nodded. "It's been hard to concentrate. Getting acclimated."

I nodded.

"And I haven't been as available as I should have." She closed her eyes and pressed her fingertips to her forehead. "I just can't...Steve is on my mind all the time."

"I thought you were done with that?"

She moved her hand and opened her eyes, swiveled her chair, and looked out the window. The cockatoo had left a minute earlier. She didn't even realize he'd been there.

What was wrong with her? Was she still in love with him? I hadn't thought she was in love with him at all, ever, but now I wasn't sure. She couldn't seem to think about anything else. She wasn't getting paid that astronomical salary to mope over a short-term love affair from her old job, in another country, on the opposite side of the planet.

The detective had made me fairly confident that they weren't planning any further investigation, but if she kept stirring things up, hounding him, asking CC execs to push for a deeper look, constantly talking to me about it, the same questions cycling over and over until a new sliver of light broke through... I needed to find a way to get her off that once and for all.

"You must feel a lot of pressure for TT," I said.

She frowned. She tucked her hair behind her ears. "Not really. Why?"

"Getting visibility for this app is all on you."

"And you." She smiled.

"Maybe you're thinking about Steve because it's easier. Launching and marketing a new product without all the infrastructure of a big company...and knowing how much it might be worth to you if it's successful. Getting paid so much money because he knows you'll make or break things. That's a lot of responsibility."

She gave me a coy smile. "I'm not getting paid that much. And if that's a back door way to find out about my compensation package, it failed."

"Everyone on the ground floor of a new company makes a lot. With any company. Right?"

She shrugged. "Not always." She crossed her legs and pointed her toe slightly. Her shoe slipped off her heel. She flexed her foot, trying to draw the shoe back into place. "But that has nothing to do with Steve. He was a close friend. I need to do right by him."

"Now he's turned into a close friend? I thought you practically hated him?" Why wouldn't she let it go? I took a deep breath and gave her a kind smile. "Are you still in love with him?"

"I was never in love with him. Don't be stupid."

"That's not how it's starting to look."

"Well you're looking wrong. You're misreading. I'm just treating him with respect."

"He didn't treat you with respect."

That seemed to startle her. She blinked. A moment later, she blinked again. "What are you trying to say?"

"I'm saying his reputation, his legacy, whatever you want to call it, is not your responsibility. And having a shocking and untimely death doesn't wipe out his whole career."

She didn't say anything.

"Don't you owe more to Sean, and me?"

She laughed. "What do I owe you?"

"Mentoring. To make sure I get this social media thing right. It is new territory for me, at least doing it for a product is new."

"You're smart and competent. I have no doubt you can find your way to success."

"If I had millions riding on it, I wouldn't be thinking about some guy who died that I can't do anything about."

She frowned. She looked down at her foot where the shoe still hung free of her heel. "What makes you think I have millions riding on it?"

"Like I said, it's the norm, right?"

Again, she said nothing.

"Do you even need the money?"

She looked at me, hard, the spark in her eyes fading as her gaze first held mine, and then wandered somewhere else even though her eyes still looked in my direction.

"Just wondering," I said. "It's hard to get motivated because everyone is drifting around, either working in isolation or not working at all. Maybe it's being in this house instead of an office. There's no energy. And to be blunt, you're acting like you're more connected to CC. That's where your mind is. You can't save Steve and it's going to spoil everything if his ghost hangs over what we're trying to do here."

She was quiet for nearly a minute. She put her hand over her mouth and coughed slightly. "I'll talk to Sean about putting more structure in place. You have a point."

It wasn't the point I wanted to make, but maybe if she felt more pressure, more urgency from Sean about where we were headed, Steve would fade into the horizon.

At least she'd never pushed to find out how my relationship ended with him, whether he'd offered a job, whether I'd fucked him. I'd certainly done that.

# 56

Sounds of Tess working in the other office gave the impression business was moving forward. Sean liked that. It was reassuring to know she was putting in evening hours, fired up with whatever it was that got marketing types enthused. Earlier, Gavin had delivered a new bug fix update, and Sean had spent the hours before dinner on the phone with the device manufacturer. Everything on that front was looking good.

Just before they sat down to eat, Alex had popped into his office insisting that the clear weather demanded they all go to the neighbor's to look at the planets through his state-of-the-art telescope. She went on about how incredible it would be, a team building experience, views of the spectacular night sky they couldn't imagine. She acted as if no one had ever looked into a telescope before. He'd almost asked her whether she had, but then she'd eased her way out of the room, calling back that he needed to make sure Gavin joined them because it would spoil everything if the whole team didn't participate.

Sean couldn't object, although it was odd dropping in on a neighbor he'd only spoken to in passing. Maybe it took a woman to create the glue that moved neighbors from front yard chats to social events. He'd chosen two bottles of Zinfandel from his wine collection to bring as a thank you.

It struck him as contrived that Alex was so enthused. After her standoffish attitude, she now thought socializing was essential, but it had to be on her terms. It almost felt like she had an ulterior motive. But he couldn't imagine any surprises in simply looking at a few stars and getting a closer peek at the rings of Saturn, which she was most wound up about, so maybe it was nothing. He was simply over-sensitive to everything she said or did after that stunt with his room, after the miscommunication in the swimming pool.

For dinner, Gavin went to pick up Thai and they'd eaten together on the patio.

At a few minutes before ten, Alex walked into the game room where he and Gavin were shooting pool and drinking beer.

"Time to put the game away."

"I need to finish this shot," Sean said. He grabbed his bottle and swallowed the rest of his beer.

"We can't be late."

"What's so urgent? The stars aren't going anywhere." He picked up the chalk cube and ground the end of his cue inside, covering it with blue powder. He went to the back corner, lined up his shot, and knocked the red striped ball into the opposite corner pocket, right where Alex was standing.

"Well done," she said. "Now let's go."

"It's the middle of my turn."

"I told him we'd be there at ten-thirty."

He took another shot and missed.

They left the house and walked over to John's in single file, like school children on a field trip. The sky was clear and stars winked and glittered, planets indistinguishable from the rest.

Inside John's house, Sean took a few minutes to get his

equilibrium. The presence of white was overwhelming. Absolutely everything was white — floors, counters, walls. It looked like an indoor snowstorm. None of the others seemed to find it remarkable, but he felt compelled to point it out. "You like white, huh?"

John looked at him. He took the wine bottles Sean held out.

An image filled his mind — the bottles inexplicably sliding out of John's hands, crashing on the white tile, red pouring across the large white rectangles, pooling in the grout, racing along the lines like irrigation channels headed toward the white carpet. So much wine, it splashed on the walls, dripping down, leaving thick wet stains on the living room floor. He turned and looked at the others. They smiled, all consummate neighbors ready for a pleasant evening.

"I'll open this." John raised one of the bottles.

A shiver ran down Sean's arms as John waved the bottle in front of him. He smiled and hoped he looked moderately normal. Getting outside where Alex had said the telescope was located on the second floor deck would be helpful. He needed a gulp of fresh air, that was all. The white, too much white, it made his eyes ache and had played a trick on his brain, that was all.

They walked up the stairs, each holding a large wineglass with a splash of red liquid.

John moved the telescope into place while they sipped wine. He positioned the chair in front of it, and invited Tess to go first.

Very gracious of him to choose a woman. Sean swallowed some wine.

While they took turns sitting in front of the telescope,

squinting and gazing through the small concave lens, John kept up a running commentary on the solar system, the constellations currently visible, the position of the planets, the marvels of the galaxy, and the endless reaches of space that mankind would likely never reach.

When John said *mankind,* Sean glanced at Alex and Tess, expecting them to object to the use of male-dominant terminology. Neither one seemed to react. Sean swallowed the rest of his wine and placed his glass on the table.

"More?" John said.

"Sure."

John went into the house and returned a few minutes later with the second bottle Sean had provided. He refilled all the glasses. John, Gavin, and Sean leaned against the railing, gazing up at the sky with naked eyes.

"So you come out here every night and look at stars?" Sean took a sip of wine. "They don't change much, I think it would get stale." Sean tried to make out which of the lights were planets, which were merely stars.

"It never gets old," John said. "They seduce. Their beauty takes over your mind. You can't stop looking. The feelings they stir up — it's almost impossible to describe. Most days, I'm counting the hours until dark. When it's cloudy, I hardly know what to do with myself."

No one spoke. John sounded like a nut case. There was no point to it. Studying for a stated purpose, as part of some organization, to advance scientific understanding made sense, but this was beyond comprehension. Except for seasonal shifts, the solar system never changed. The stars just sat there. And with a telescope for home viewing, you didn't really see all that much detail. Compared to the naked eye, sure. But not enough to really dig into the intricate features of the planets.

Diving, on the other hand, was different every time you went down. Not a second passed that the undersea world didn't shift. The current was always flowing, thousands of varieties of sea life, the corral…growth and decay and the hunt for food. New life, the fight for dominance. The colors were infinite, the movement sublime.

Why spend every damn night of your life looking at something that only shifted a few millimeters each day? And even with that, you couldn't really tell it had changed. He took another sip of wine.

Alex started going on again about the mystery of it all, the vastness, the beauty.

Sean finished his wine and walked to the table. He refilled his glass, pouring a healthy amount.

For nearly an hour, they took turns looking through the telescope. The conversation drifted over one thing and another. John went inside and returned with two more bottles of wine.

Sean's consumption was well ahead of the others. He had a slight buzz going. It might be the strain of staring at all those lights, tipping his head up, or low blood sugar from not eating enough meat in their veggie-heavy Thai meal, but the wine was hitting him harder than usual. He was annoyed and somewhat irritated with all of them. "If I had a scope like yours, I might use it to look at the neighbors. Is that what you're really doing up here every fucking night of the year, Johnny? Watching your female neighbors undress? Maybe more?"

Tess laughed. Gavin joined her.

Alex was quiet, staring up at the sky, her face in a state of rapture.

"Had enough to drink, mate?" John said.

Sean laughed. He hated it when Americans called him mate. Maybe he'd ask around with a few of the neighbors, find out more about this guy. That guy across the street, Chet. He said he'd met John's wife once. And where was his wife? The house was silent, John obviously its only occupant.

Sean swallowed the rest of his wine. "Right you are. We should let you get on with your evening. Thanks for the view."

When they left, John grinned and patted Sean's back with a hearty slap. Sean was curious. He didn't seem offended by what Sean had said. It wasn't possible to be so in love with the stars that you spent your whole life looking at them. Maybe the guy was off balance, rattling around in that big white cloud of a house, it could twist your brain into something unrecognizable.

# 57

I thought I'd won the tampon war. The day after our standoff, Moira emptied her trash. For the next week, she was friendly enough and she stopped leaving hazardous waste all over her desk and bed and the floor. I was quite pleased with myself and I tried to be extra interested in her life and what was going on in her classes, letting her know there were no hard feelings.

On the following Saturday night, Moira went to a party. I was tired and I had a paper due the following Monday. A twenty-page paper that had been assigned three weeks earlier. I hadn't started it.

I skimmed the first of the two rather short books required as background material for the paper and went to sleep at eleven-thirty. I didn't hear Moira come into the room.

At quarter to one, the violent creaking of her bed woke me. There were no lights on, just a dim glow of outdoor lighting coming through the thick white window shade, and a small fat candle burning across the room on her dresser.

I turned on my side.

Moira was sitting up, naked. Her head was tipped back, her hair streaming across her shoulders and down her back, gleaming almost white. Her skin had a silver cast from the strange lighting. Beneath her was a guy who was holding her breasts in both hands, breathing loudly through his mouth.

Moira slowly moved up and down, letting out tiny squeaks of pleasure.

I sat up and switched on the light attached to my headboard. "Are you kidding me?"

Moira laughed briefly and carried on, the bed squeaking more loudly now, if that were possible. The guy grunted. His hands stopped massaging her breasts. "Uh, Moira. Maybe we should, uh…"

"No way," she said. "I'm almost there. Stop talking."

"But your roommate's awake."

I fell back on my bed and closed my eyes. "This is so fucked up," I said.

Moira moaned softly. "Stop talking. Everyone stop talking, you're killing it."

The guy tried to shove himself up onto his elbows.

She pushed him back. "Hey, don't collapse on me."

"Sorry," he said. "But she wrecked the mood, I can't…"

"I wrecked the mood? What mood? This isn't a dog park," I said.

Moira stopped. She twisted toward me. "Go back to sleep."

"I can't, I'll have nightmares," I said.

The guy put his hands on Moira's hips and tried to move her to the side.

"Jason. Don't. We can't stop now."

"C'mon. Let's go to my room."

"I don't want to get dressed and walk all the way over there."

"Well this isn't…"

"If she would just go to sleep again and stop being such a voyeur, we'd be…"

I laughed, more of a shriek, drowning out whatever she planned to say. "A voyeur is someone who *likes* to watch. I'm a prisoner."

Moira smiled as if I'd given her a compliment. In the flicker of the candlelight, backed by the glow through the window shade, her teeth glistened. Her hair had fallen over her brow and eyes but she didn't brush it away.

Jason tried again to lift her hips off of his.

"Stop doing that. I mean it." She turned to face him. She bent over and brushed her lips across his mouth. She flicked her tongue across his lower lip. She straightened and began moving up and down, bracing her hands on his shoulders. "Pretend she's not here."

Jason tried to sit up. She pushed him back. "She can go back to sleep. Usually she sleeps like a fuckin' log."

That gave me a chill. Had she been watching me while I slept? Tried to wake me and failed so she determined I was a deep sleeper? It made me feel as if part of my life had taken place while I was absent. I didn't like the thought of her observing me when I was unaware.

Jason pushed her off him. Her shoulder thudded against the wall. He leaned over the side of the bed, patting his hand on the floor. He plucked a pair of boxers out of a pile of clothes. He sat up, swung his legs over the side of the bed, banging his knee into Moira's chin in the process, and yanked on his shorts. He stood and pulled them quickly into place.

"C'mon, Jason. You can't leave now."

"This is weird. I told you it was weird before we started." He picked up his jeans and pulled them on. He grabbed a t-shirt and yanked it over his head. When he was fully dressed, including athletic shoes, the untied laces dragging along the floor, he started toward the door.

"I can't believe you can just stop cold like this," Moira said.

"Talk later." He opened the door and went out.

Moira turned to me as the door closed. "Why did you have to disrupt everything?" She scrambled around for her clothes. She put on a thong and bra. She kicked the rest of her things toward her dresser.

"I didn't disrupt anything."

"You should have faked that you were still sleeping."

"Why should I do that?"

"It's the polite thing to do. You turn over and pretend you're asleep. It's the roommate pact."

I turned my back to her and tugged my pillow under my neck.

"So you fuck up my night and *now* you're going back to sleep? Nice."

I ignored her.

She continued talking, telling me how badly she felt that Jason had left, how it was my fault, how any normal person would pretend she was asleep and not embarrass a guy and insert herself in the middle of another girl's sex life.

The drone of her voice became a hum and my brain drifted away, covering itself with a foggy softness, distorting everything until her words sounded like something out of Alice In Wonderland.

When I woke the next morning, she was gone. Her bed was unmade, lingerie twisted in with the sheets. Two condoms sat beside her pillow. There was a note on my desk. *I'm bringing Jason back tonight. Please go stay with one of your friends.*

I crumpled it up and dropped it in the trash. I walked to

my closet and stared at the things hanging there, trying to decide what I wanted to wear. I thought about Moira and tried to figure out how her brain had become so twisted around she considered me the intruder.

Living with soggy tissues and candy wrappers and used tampons was not how I wanted to spend my first year in a dorm, but I wasn't the type to complain to the RA. You get labeled difficult, and a snitch. Then no one wants to room with you in your Sophomore year. I didn't want to watch other people having sex. I didn't even want to hear it. I wanted a roommate who was fun and a little compatible and interesting.

Clearly she'd lied on her application when she said she was tidy and considerate.

# 58

Figuring out how to get the contracts back into Sean's drawer before he discovered they were missing consumed my thoughts. The morning after our stargazing, which hadn't turned into much of a team building event at all, not that I know what one of those things is supposed to accomplish anyway, Sean had decreed we would all be working in the offices from eight until six every day. *More or less.* We could take time away to swim or play badminton or shoot pool. We would conduct casual brainstorming sessions over pool or drinks at least two evenings a week, and those would be scheduled ahead of time. We needed structure. We needed to provide oversight for each other — brainstorming would include ideas for additional features in the app, suggestions for social media success, PR stunts, and the like. Structure was important. Teamwork was essential.

It was impossible to disagree.

Entering Sean's room when he was right downstairs had been risky. The next time, I had to make myself wait until he left the house. If Tess was also occupied, it would allow me to make sure the papers were put away neatly and provide a little one-on-one time with that gorgeous statue.

Although I understood why he liked having it in his room, why he wanted it in a prominent place where he could study it every morning, there was a disturbing element as well. There was something desperate and sexually frustrated about a man lying in his bed and gazing at the unyielding wood curves of an anonymous woman. Not only from his bed, but the way the chair was positioned, it was clear he sat there and relished her beauty.

Of course, I couldn't know that for sure. He might sit in the chair and read his tablet and only glance up occasionally. I wondered how long he'd owned it, what made him buy it, whether Gavin had seen it. So many questions.

My chance came three days after our stargazing event. We were all dutifully working in the offices, foolishly paired into a female office and a male office, although I suppose it was really a marketing office and a technical office, which made some sense. I had the impression Tess's and my arrangement was working better than theirs. Sean seemed to want to have his solitary space to enhance his position as CEO, and Gavin apparently liked to work without any disturbance, even the breathing and heartbeat of another human being. The silence and the resistance seeped from their office like a tangible substance.

Every time I went to the kitchen for a glass of water or a cup of tea or an afternoon espresso, it seemed as if one of them was hanging out in the family room or lounging on the patio, avoiding the office altogether.

Sean cracked before Gavin.

That morning, he let us know he was headed to downtown Sydney. He needed to meet with the guy who did the finances for our venture, and make the best use of his time by also having a meeting with the rep from the company manufacturing the bio feedback device. There were other things that needed taking care of. He was vague about what those *things* were.

He would be gone for the entire day, home in time for

dinner. The moment his SUV rolled out of the driveway, Gavin closed the office door. Half an hour later when I walked outside for a breath of fresh air, I saw that he'd closed all the shutters, blocking out the world in the same way he did from his bedroom.

I told Tess I had a headache and was going to take some pain relievers and lie down for an hour. She nodded, barely noticing I was leaving the room.

In the upstairs hall, I stepped into my room and grabbed the papers. I made my usual stop at Gavin's door. Locked. I continued on toward Sean's room, the papers rustling inside the waist of my jeans. I probably could have carried them, I was confident the others were occupied, but the extra precaution seemed worthwhile.

Sean's room looked the same, the shutters angled, letting late morning light draw stripes across the carpet. I stepped into the walk-in closet and opened the bottom drawer that contained the red file folder. I put the documents on top of the drawers and did my best to smooth them out from the crumpling effects of my waistband. I picked up the file folder, slipped the papers inside, straightened the edges so everything was aligned, and returned the folder to its place.

I went into the bedroom and settled in the chair facing the statue.

The dark honey oak with its black-streaked veins stood out brilliantly against the pale carpet and walls. The sun fell on the floor in front of her, but no light touched the wood. He'd arranged it perfectly. I didn't think wood faded, but it looked nicer without the bleaching effect of sunlight.

For fifteen or twenty minutes, I studied the carving, thinking about the artist, the model, and art lovers.

My thoughts drifted to Sean's desire for a stripped down environment. I admired that about him, appreciated his aesthetic sense. We were the same in that way and it made me wonder why we bristled against each other.

I thought about his jumpy behavior when we'd gone stargazing, his in-your-face comment to John that he used the telescope to spy on neighbors. I stood and went out to the balcony. The angle of John's house allowed a clear view of Sean's back wall, but I hadn't spent enough time in John's house to get a sense of which rooms faced Sean's. The night of the thunderstorm, I'd stood half naked on the balcony, smoking and watching the lightning. Had John turned his telescope on me? There was that strange disk of light coming from one of his rooms, but otherwise, the windows had been dark.

I returned to the bedroom.

It was a little surprising that Sean hadn't locked his room after catching me that first time. Maybe he was a trusting guy, although the comment to John suggested he was more distrustful than most.

I honestly didn't care if he came into my room, I had nothing there that I needed to hide, now that the papers were returned. I had nothing to hide from John, either, if he got a kick out of watching me smoke in my lace and silk underpants and a midriff-baring sweater.

Gavin was another matter.

The drawer of key rings and coins flashed across my mind. I dashed into the closet and opened the junk drawer. Why hadn't I focused on it the last time? Not all of the key rings were simple tchotchkes from trade shows. Two of them had a few keys on the rings. Did I dare take them? It seemed much more likely that Sean would go looking for a key and discover them missing than it was that he'd look for employment contracts.

I grabbed both rings of keys and hurried out of the room.

I stood in front of Gavin's door, my fingers in my pocket, feeling the keys. It was dangerous to go in. More dangerous to unlock a door than to simply open one that didn't demonstrate such extreme concern over intruders. It was dangerous to do it right now when I had no idea how long Gavin would continue working, when he might run up to his room for...whatever.

But he'd kept me out for too long. I couldn't contain my curiosity any longer. I had to know what was so private. I had to know if my Bluebeard fantasy was an extreme case of imagination or if there was something disturbing inside his room.

I pulled out the first set of keys.

# 59

The third key on the first ring of five unlocked Gavin's door. I pressed the handle down and stepped inside, carefully closing the door behind me.

One wall was filled with floor-to-ceiling built-in bookcases. Among all those books were four shelves devoted to small action figures from Star Wars and Harry Potter. It was a cute and rather incongruous combination, suggesting he was still a kid, a nerdy, thirty-year-old kid. One section of the shelving unit had a fold-out piece of wood that functioned as a desk. His laptop sat on that, closed, and a small desk chair was pushed up so the back touched the edge of the desk.

The adjacent wall had folding glass doors covered by shutters, like mine. Unlike mine, the shutters were closed tight, as I'd seen every time I looked up from the backyard. The bathroom and walk-in closet opened off the next wall. The closet had no door, none of the ensuite closets did — they were designed as clothing alcoves off the main room, with built-in drawers and cabinets.

His bed was against the same wall as the door. The headboard was simple oak and the bed was covered with a pale blue comforter. Three large pillows in dark blue cases without any additional covering were squashed in a wrinkled heap against the headboard. A book was tucked under them, but not enough was exposed for me to see the title.

I approached the bookcases. There were three entire

shelves of paperback science fiction novels, the next two shelves were lined with equally worn fantasy novels, and above that were several shelves containing books about computers and software languages. Based on my name-recognition-only of software languages, some of them looked like they dated back to the nineteen-nineties.

The rest of the shelves were stuffed with an eclectic mix of paperbacks — old classics like *Moby Dick* and modern classics like *The Catcher In the Rye* occupied a few shelves, followed by rows of Agatha Christie novels. There were quite a few books I'd never heard of and I assumed they were Australian and British literature. I saw the distinctive black and bright yellow cover of *French for Dummies* and a tattered copy of *Little Women*. There was a shelf of books on Australian history and a handful of American political commentary books.

This guy was more interesting than I'd realized. I wondered if his aversion to speaking was the fact that he much preferred sitting in a room by himself reading books.

I went into the closet and looked through his drawers. They were filled with clothes and swimsuits. Two drawers contained the required junk-with-no-home — coins, rubber bands, computer cords and plugs, ticket stubs and receipts. The bathroom contents were standard — no prescription drugs indicating a secret, shameful disease. Nothing for obscene rashes or infections. There were a few condoms in the drawer with his hairbrush.

Finally tired of looking at everything, searching for something that would explain his paranoia, I moved back toward the entrance. Maybe he didn't trust Sean. Maybe that's why he didn't want a stake in the company. Although the minute that thought passed through my mind, it was clear it made no sense. Being a principal wouldn't hurt him. There was nothing to lose. Either it made money or it didn't. Was he worried about liability from the app? It had crossed my mind that if you tell people they're getting solid guidance for making decisions and one of those app-led decisions doesn't pan out...I had no doubt someone might try to sue over that.

I sat on the bed and looked around the room. I got up and knelt down and lifted the comforter where it hung over the sides. Underneath the bed, near the top, was a small box of molded plastic — the kind of material that coolers are made of. I pulled it out. A metal clasp secured it. I popped it open and looked inside. I swallowed hard and closed it, unable to believe what I'd seen. I opened it again, just to be sure. I closed it quickly, snapped the clasp, and slid it under the bed.

No wonder his room was locked. I felt slightly ill. I stood quickly and walked around the bed, trying to put my mind onto something else.

I glanced at the shutters and then up toward the ceiling, following the dust motes that rose on sharp slivers of light that had managed to seep through microscopic spaces between shutter panels. A tiny white ball was attached to the corner where the walls joined the ceiling. The front had a dark lens. At first I thought it was a speaker. I think my mind wanted it to be a speaker. But it wasn't. A camera was watching me.

The constantly locked door wasn't the only protection for his privacy, he had a webcam. Every touch of my finger on his toys and along the spines of his books, every drawer pulled open, and possibly even my search through his bathroom had been fed into his phone via WiFi. And finally, my peek inside that small box…He'd seen me in a live stream, or would be watching me soon as he checked his recorded footage.

Locking your door twenty-four-seven and recording the empty space confused me. Despite what I'd found, I didn't understand the camera. No one could get into his room, what the hell was he recording? His own activities? His sleep patterns? Maybe it was some updated, super high-tech way to monitor your wakeful and deep sleep periods. Instead of keeping a wrist band record of your tossing and turning, you recorded every muscle twitch. You studied your facial response to your dreams.

Or, he distrusted Sean even more than I'd imagined. Sean had access whenever he pleased. Did Gavin think Sean was using the spare key to enter his room? Did he imagine Sean opening drawers, checking the closet, looking for documentation that Gavin was selling his ideas elsewhere, undercutting Sean and his brainchild? But if Gavin did have some side deal going, wouldn't all those records be on his laptop, protected with one of those fifteen-character passwords filled with upper and lower case, symbols and numbers?

Or, did he simply imagine Sean looking under the bed?

None of that was important right now. The absurdity of filming activity in a locked room wasn't relevant. Whatever the answers to those questions, I was screwed.

# 60

For several days, Alex's comment had eaten at Tess's stomach. She was never in love with Steve. Listening to Alex try to persuade her to let go of her concern over Steve's reputation had left Tess feeling humiliated. She liked having the upper hand with Alex, she liked Alex looking up to her, admiring her. She considered herself Alex's mentor, and apparently Alex had the same view, even though they'd never had a formal discussion about it. Knowing that Alex was disgusted with her behavior was hard to take. But it didn't stop her from the overwhelming need to set things right, to get someone, anyone, to recognize Steve had not died of a self-inflicted overdose. No matter what anyone said, she didn't believe he'd gone down the heroin rabbit hole under his own volition.

She wouldn't discuss it with Alex, but she wasn't going to stop pushing for further investigation.

If Alex thought Steve's ghost had followed them to the other side of the world, that was in Alex's mind. Maybe Alex was the one who was obsessed with him. He'd flattered her into believing she would make a boatload of money and find a lot more satisfaction working for him. Then, he'd gone and died on her. Not to mention Alex's rush to change the subject when Tess asked whether they'd had sex. Who knew what had been going on with those two. If anyone was haunted, it was Alex.

Trying to make sure he wasn't remembered as a doper

was the decent thing to do. The right thing to do. And Alex didn't have to know any more about it. She would believe Tess had dropped it, as long as she stopped looking to Alex for advice. Why had she ever done that? If she saw herself as Alex's mentor, seeking advice was the last thing she should do.

It had become a habit. Alex had good instincts, and she was blunt. She loved to give advice, even when she wasn't asked. It was time to disrupt that pattern. Alex was no longer in a supportive role. She had results to deliver and it was important to hold her to that, not confide and share secrets, weakening the boss-employee structure.

This was the tricky part of Sean's vision for the perfect working environment. Camaraderie was good, shared experiences were good, team activities were good. But lines of authority were still important or they'd have chaos. In the end, that would damage the success of the product because they'd lose focus.

She picked up her phone. It was mid-day in the U.S. She placed a call to Cynthia.

After they'd spent nearly ten minutes on pleasantries and small talk, it became clear Cynthia wasn't going to offer up any information about her pursuit of Ted.

"So…" Tess said. "What happened with your request to Hutchins? Regarding the investigation into Steve's death?"

"He blew me off."

"What did you ask him?"

"I told him your concerns."

"*Our* concerns," Tess said.

"Right, yes."

"And he doesn't see how this could negatively impact CC?"

"He did. He mentioned that. In fact I didn't even have to suggest it."

"Good."

"But in the end, he said there's nothing we can do. It's unfortunate, and obviously none of Steve's peers, or the executive team, knew him well at all. Ted feels badly about that."

"I'm sure he does."

"He's right. We didn't know him," Cynthia said. Her voice was low, tinged with regret.

Tess crossed the room and stepped out onto the balcony. It was so peaceful here. She was suddenly tired. Maybe sometimes you did have to let go. Every step she took, a door slammed in her face. Did she know for a fact that Steve never experimented with drugs? Was it possible he'd gone off the edge after their split? Maybe he and Alex had gotten together and Alex cut him loose, devastating his ego. Anything was possible.

"Are you still there?" Cynthia said.

"I am. I guess there's nothing else I can do."

"I don't think there is. You did your best."

Tess heard the smile in Cynthia's voice.

"It's time to let his ghost rest, right?" Cynthia laughed softly.

"That's pretty much what Alex said."

"Oh."

The chill that rippled through Cynthia's voice wiped out her smile and the gentle laugh, and the image of Steve's ghost drifting on to wherever a person's essence fled to after it left the body.

"I hope you're watching your back with her," Cynthia said.

"We get along well." Tess leaned her hip against the railing.

"That's not what I mean."

"I don't really want to talk about her. You've made your opinion clear, multiple times."

"Just trying to be a friend. That woman will eat you alive if you're not careful."

"So you've said. And I don't even know what that means."

"It means she's hungry — for money, power, sex. You name it."

Tess laughed. "Aren't we all? She just doesn't try to hide it."

"She won't let anything or anyone get in her way. Trust me on this. Watch your back."

"Duly noted."

While Cynthia went on about the people in Tess's former organization, giving her latest assessment of the new marketing VP, Tess's mind wandered back to Alex. She found herself only half listening to Cynthia. When the call ended, she sat down and looked out at the lush yard, feeling the soothing presence of enough greenery to wrap itself completely around her body in a living, breathing cocoon. She closed her eyes.

Could that be part of the problem with their failure, so far, to work together as an efficient, unified machine? They were four adults, none of whom had an active sex life, as far as she knew. Alex wasn't the only one hungry for sex. Surely

Sean's plan wasn't for them to become celibate in devotion to their app and its launch into the marketplace. But that wasn't a topic she wanted to broach with him. It wasn't as if they were forbidden to go out. The group was so small, going out felt like abandoning the others and their mission.

Was an underlying need for sex that they all seemed to be denying causing the lethargic atmosphere? In the past, she might have bounced that question off Alex.

Had Alex and Steve ever hooked up? It had seemed they were headed in that direction. Maybe Alex had a thing for older men. Steve was easily ten years older. And now this guy next door — he was good looking. Charming. That would explain Alex's insane fascination with stargazing.

She tucked her phone into her pocket. She pressed her fingers against her forehead. Too many questions rattling through her mind, too many thoughts scattering in opposite directions. One thing was clear — she needed to cut her connection to her old life, at least for now. No more chats with Cynthia and no more trying to rescue a dead man.

# 61

After I escaped the eye of Gavin's camera, I returned to my room. Not caring if Sean got pissed, I went onto the balcony, closed the doors, and lit a cigarette. I took a long slow drag and released the smoke slowly in a thin, tight stream.

How long until Gavin viewed the image of me prowling through his room? A better question was, how had I not seen that camera the minute I stepped through the doorway? It must have been the enormous bookcase. An entire wall of books, accompanied by colorful plastic figurines, had completely captured my attention. I never looked up. I never expected surveillance inside a bedroom. Unlike most multi-million-dollar homes in the U.S., Sean's house didn't have the simplest alarm much less video cameras.

It wasn't that Australia was free of crime, far from it. But after their crime-ridden start, they seemed to be managing it better than the Americans. Maybe it was the sheer quantity of people in the U.S. More likely, it was the minimal presence of guns in Australia.

Any moment, there would be a knock on my door and I'd be facing...what would I face? Anger, for sure. But how much anger? Would he insist that Sean fire me? Would he complain to Tess? I wasn't sure I could manage her anger.

I smoked two and a half cigarettes and was considering going downstairs to make a martini when the expected knock occurred. I put out my cigarette and went into the room.

Gavin didn't ask to be invited inside, he pushed past me

and nudged the door closed with the side of his foot. Someone else might say he kicked it closed, but I was trying not to dramatize. He crossed the room and sat in the armchair. "Why would you do that?"

This must be about my intrusion, but I didn't know that for sure. No sense giving it up too soon. "What?"

He twisted in the chair and looked behind him. "It smells like smoke in here."

"I was having a cigarette."

"Sean doesn't like smoking. Well, not tobacco."

"He didn't mention it."

"I'm sure he did. He feels quite strongly about the subject."

I waited, fascinated at hearing more than his usual ration of words. His voice was a lovely tenor, and that accent was something that made the muscles in my legs turn to liquid. I smiled.

"You aren't much for rules," he said.

"No."

"There are rules of human decency."

"I know."

"Entering someone's room, going through another person's private things is wrong. Surely you know that?"

"I do, but you were so intense about keeping everyone out, my curiosity got the best of me."

"That's not an excuse."

"It's not meant to be."

"I don't want anyone in my room."

"I get that."

"Then why…"

"I told you." I turned the desk chair around to face him

and sat down. I put my right ankle on my left knee, mirroring his posture. He didn't seem to notice.

"It's very disturbing. I don't know how I'll sleep. I don't know if I can stay here. Sean won't be happy about this. Not happy at all. Plus, the smoke."

I said nothing. There really wasn't anything to say. Of course he was right, but it was too late now. I'd thought he might try to be rid of me, but it sounded like he was more inclined to remove himself from our little group. "What are you so afraid of?"

His eyes darted toward my bed. His face took on a very different look, as if I'd cornered him. He'd come here to...to do what? Make me feel guilty? That doesn't work with me. To try frightening me about my job? It no longer seemed that way. Besides, I was pretty sure it could be worked out, once everyone got over their upset feelings.

"I'm not," he said.

"You're not afraid?"

"I don't..."

"Do you not trust Sean?"

"It's not about trust." He gripped his ankle, as if he were trying to hold his leg in place. His shoulders hunched slightly and the color drained out of his face.

I stood and walked across the room. I moved behind the chair and put my hands on his shoulders. I massaged the muscles, pushing my fingertips up the lower part of his neck, pressing hard, feeling through the twisted cords of tension.

"Don't do that," he said.

"You looked tense."

"Because you broke into my room. That's why I'm *tense*. How did you even get in there?"

I moved my thumbs lower, digging into the muscle between his shoulder blades.

He groaned, but I could feel that he regretted allowing the sound to escape.

"Why all the security measures?"

"I'm just…" He sighed. "I don't like people in my room. I don't like people…"

"You don't like people?"

"That's not what I was going to say. It's different talking to you, not seeing your face."

"Doesn't that make it easier?"

He bent his head to the left and I rubbed along the muscle up to the base of his skull.

"It does, actually. That feels good."

"Being on a keyboard for most of your waking hours wrecks your neck and shoulders. Not to mention hands and arms."

"I like writing code."

"So what are you afraid of?"

"I'm not afraid. I just want my privacy."

"But why?" I thought of the thing under the bed. Did he know I'd seen it?

"It's hard to talk about."

He was silent for a few seconds while I continued massaging.

He sighed. "My sister. My older sister."

I waited, continuing to work the muscles in his neck, feeling them soften ever so slightly under the pressure of my thumbs.

"She came into my room all the time. She moved my things, she was always messing around in there. She borrowed books and clothes without asking. She…."

"Your sister borrowed your clothes?"

"Things that don't have a sex."

I laughed. "Do clothes have sex?"

He laughed but not as if he really meant it. "Sweatshirts, t-shirts. She wore my favorite t-shirts to bed."

That didn't sound too terrible, but I could imagine it might be hard on a little kid. "How old were you?"

"Six. Seven. When I told my parents, or did anything she didn't like, she would take something to see how long before I noticed it was missing."

"Sounds irritating."

"She came into my room at night and watched me sleep." He shuddered. "I would wake and she'd be sitting in a chair right beside me. She had this little smile on her face, like she knew what I was dreaming. It freaked me out. I had nightmares about her watching me sleep. I can't explain it, why I hated it so much. But that made her even more excited."

"I can see why that would be creepy."

"My parents laughed it off, they said I was fussy and too self-conscious. They said she wasn't hurting me and went on to tell me stories of *real* bullies, in their words."

I made a sympathetic sound, waiting for him to continue.

"She kept doing it. For years. When I was a teenager, I tried locking my door, but my dad said it wasn't safe if there was a fire. Finally, he removed the lock. She even watched me when…when…" He tipped his head to the right, cracking his neck with a loud pop. "When I had wet dreams, I'd wake up and she was there. With that smile." His shoulders stiffened. "Anyway. It sounds ridiculous, like it's no big deal. I don't ever want someone watching me when I'm asleep. I can't. I guess it's become a bit of a fetish — making sure I'm alone — if you want to call it that. And making sure no one goes in my room. Ever."

I continued massaging, waiting.

"It's hard for me to sleep. I have night terrors a couple of times a week. Not always about her, just dreams of someone watching me. All the time."

It wasn't the right time to ask about that box under his bed. Not yet. Since he hadn't mentioned it, I was certain he hadn't watched the entire recording, rushing to my room the minute he realized I'd been inside of his. That box — it wasn't at all like Bluebeard's closet, but it reminded me of that guy all the same.

Slowly, he relaxed and let me give him a proper massage.

I moved my hands lower, rubbing his shoulder blades and upper arms, stroking his back along his spine. I eased off the pressure until it was no longer a massage. I explored the wiry strength and shape of his body. I slid my hands down his sides and leaned against him, placing soft kisses on the side of his neck.

He pulled away, stood, and stepped around the chair. He put one arm around my waist and pulled me close. With the other hand he held my jaw lightly and turned my face to his. We kissed, plunging into each other. All my thoughts dissolved into him and the feel of his hands and mouth, the sensation of his body against mine.

We moved slowly, and surprisingly gracefully toward the bed and laid down. He unbuttoned my jeans and I did the same to his. It took quite a while for us to get completely naked, but the long journey to that point was rapturous. I thought of nothing but him and now, his economic use of words became quite perfect as we silently touched each other.

As we moved toward the peak, I wondered whether I was inviting a man into my body and my life who might be a little off center. But he was already in my life. And it felt so good. It had been so, so long. My body hummed, and then sank into utter relaxation. We fell into a deep sleep.

At least I did, possibly his sleep was filled with nightmares.

# 62

It was all out war with me and Moira, at least on my side. I had no idea what was going through her head. But when I'm ready to draw a line in the sand, I hold back. Even then, I knew that was important.

I didn't let her know how done I was with her bullshit. I waited, studying her habits and schedule. I didn't complain about tissues filled with strings and clots of mucous, or the things in her trash can, or her ever-flowing candy wrappers, often smeared with half-melted chocolate. I smiled and invited her to join me in the dining hall, although I always roped in a few other girls to be sure I wasn't stuck having to be super charming to Moira.

It was two weeks before I got my chance.

There was a party on our floor, and within twenty minutes of arriving, I saw Moira making out with Jason. They were getting very intense, very quickly. Both of them were three beers into it and Moira was letting him move his hands aggressively inside her shirt. It was clear they'd be showing up in our room at some point, waking me up while they went at it with bed-squeaking, nightmare-inducing gusto.

It wasn't that I was a prude. It wasn't my rigid religious upbringing suddenly making an appearance. It's just there's nothing erotic about hearing two people thrash around. It's like listening to a cat fight, it's like watching someone catch a fish and wrestle it to shore. That's not the image that first comes to mind for most people, but it was my thought after seeing Moira's thin, pale body made silvery by the diffused moonlight and the weak candle flame. When Matt shifted, trying to extract himself from beneath her anxiously moving hips, he looked exactly like a man wrestling a large fish.

Before I slipped away from the party, I made sure they both saw me — popping a jello shot in my mouth, laughing loudly. They would assume they had time before the interfering roommate showed up. I returned to my room and stripped off my jeans and top. I brushed my hair vigorously and flipped my upper body forward, then back to make my hair fan out across my shoulders in a wild silken cloud. I changed the black bra and underpants I'd been wearing for a sheer red bra with a front closure and a red thong with rhinestones along the top edge. I lit Moira's candle. I turned the light on my headboard to the wall and switched it on. It was still too bright, so I tossed a semi sheer nightgown over it, hoping the filmy fabric didn't drift close to the recessed bulb.

Borrowing Moira's pillows and adding them to my own stack, I arranged them along the headboard in a comfortable, jumbled pile.

The scene I'd set was drawing out my playful side. I opened my dresser drawer and took out a pack of cigarettes. I put one in my mouth, unlit, and studied myself in the mirror. I put the cigarette on my dresser and added a thick layer of burgundy-tinted lipgloss. I darkened my eye liner and added another coat of mascara.

I stretched out on my bed, the cigarette nestled between my moist lips. My heart was thumping, eager for Moira's appearance, hoping Jason was willing to try it again in her dorm room, despite his hurried escape the last time. I was counting on beer and desire to trump his most vivid memories.

The cigarette filter grew soft and damp between my lips as I waited. My neck was getting stiff and I hoped I hadn't called it wrong. If they went to his place, at least I wouldn't be bothered again, but now I was more thrilled about getting revenge than I was about stopping them from having sex while I tried to sleep.

Finally, the door opened and they stumbled into the room. Their shadows were awkward and erratic as they pulled off shirts while trying to keep their mouths locked together. Jason grabbed Moira's butt and hoisted her up. She wrapped her legs around his waist and they lurched toward her bed.

I reached behind me and pulled the nightgown off my light, sending a bright glare up over the wall behind my headboard. I removed the cigarette and spoke. "You're finally here." I put it back between my lips and unhooked my bra just as Jason let go of Moira's hips and they both turned.

"What the fuck?" Moira said.

Jason stared at me, not speaking. A soggy smile spread across his lips. "She isn't such a pain in the ass after all." He turned to Moira. "Did you arrange this for me?" He grinned and gently pinched her butt.

"Put your clothes on," Moira said.

I smiled.

"Don't get shy now." Jason gave her a sloppy kiss and tugged her toward my bed.

She twisted away from his grasp and turned her face toward me. "What are you trying to do?" Her voice was loud and bitter.

"I thought you wanted me to join you. Why else would you do it right there while I'm in the room?"

"You thought wrong," Moira said. "Get dressed."

"Why?"

"Because you're…" She glanced at Jason. "Stop staring at her."

He sat on my bed and put his hand on my lower leg. "You're kind of fun."

"She's not. She's a germaphobe and a….She needs to put her clothes on and leave us alone. I thought you were still at the party."

"This seemed like more fun."

Moira crossed the room and flicked on the overhead light. She picked up her shirt and pulled it over her head. It was inside out, but she didn't notice. "Let's go." She opened the door.

Jason turned, still holding my leg. "But I thought you planned this."

"Nope. Come on. We'll go to your room."

He didn't move.

"Jason! Get your hand off her leg and get your shirt." She plucked it off the floor and held it out as if she was offering a treat to a dog.

"So we're not gonna…" He jerked his head toward me. He smiled hopefully, glancing back and forth between us.

"Rip that thought out of your head right now or you won't be getting anything."

His hand slid off my leg and he stood. He followed her out the door with a quick glance back. His shoulders drooped slightly, making me think again of a dog, sadly following its master after a reprimand and the denial of a treat.

When they were gone, I opened the window. I lit the cigarette. I leaned out the window so most of the smoke drifted up into the cold night air, seeming to drag a soft cloud across the hard, glittering stars.

Two weeks later, Moira informed me she was moving to another building. Someone had dropped out of school, freeing up a space.

After my tennis class the following day, I returned to my room. When I opened the door, Moira's bare mattress sat on the bed frame. The top of her dresser was empty, the small closet door open, revealing nothing but two wire hangers. The trashcan was full of tissues and candy wrappers and some dirty discarded socks and underwear, and a single tampon, damp but bloodless. The trashcan was sitting in the center of my bed, leaning to the right, on the verge of tipping over.

I took the trashcan to the bathroom and emptied it. I washed it out with hot water and cleanser and dried it.

Back in my room, I settled onto my bed and gazed at the wall, trying to think about what kind of artwork I wanted to put up.

I was alone in the room for the remainder of my freshman year.

# 63

*Sydney*

When Gavin and I woke from our post-sex nap, the sun was going down, shining directly into my room, light slicing across our bodies. The glare is probably what woke us within seconds of each other.

Despite the flow of information about the torment he'd suffered from his sister, he maintained his minimalist speaking style that he'd returned to while our bodies were wrapped around each other. He kissed me, got up, and put on his clothes without saying anything beyond, *I should go.*

He brushed his lips across my cheek again and left, closing the door softly behind him.

I took a shower and put on leggings and a sweater. I touched up my toenail polish and grabbed Sean's keys out of the bedside drawer. Returning them would be quick, and I assumed he was still making his way through commuter traffic back to the house.

Each time I entered Sean's room, it seemed as if I noticed for the first time how stunning the carved woman was. Just inside the door, I paused and gazed at her. She dominated the room, and now that I studied her from the perspective of the doorway, all the furniture drew your eyes to her as it echoed the rich wood grain displayed in her body. I closed the door, went into the closet, and dropped the keys in the drawer.

It was such a simple effort, less than twenty seconds.

There was plenty of time to sit and gaze at the statue for a minute or two. I took the leather chair and settled down, crossing my left leg over my right and resting my forearms lightly on the armrests of the chair.

She gazed back at me, her eyes wide open. They had a vacant quality since there was no detail to the surface of her eyeballs. I tried to picture Sean sitting in this chair, tried to imagine his thoughts as he studied her perfectly sculpted, perfectly symmetrical figure.

Like all artists, sculptors control and shape their material. They have the right to create perfection where they want to see it, but what does that say about flesh and blood women whose breasts are not proportional, who have moles and scars and curls of hair marring the surface of their skin, and noses that are slightly large for their faces or not quite straight? What about lopsided smiles and crooked ears and hands with large knuckles? What does that say about the entire female population and the almost infinite number of flaws and imperfections? Of course the same is true of male carvings. And the same is true of paintings — breathtaking landscapes, not a weed in sight, and crashing waves free from tangles of rotting kelp and decayed fish, or snow unspoiled by mud and leaves.

We all long for perfection, and I suppose it's the artist's job to capture that longing. They delve into that longing and give us as near to perfection as they're capable of.

But did sitting and staring at this piece of art in his celibate bedroom mean Sean only desired perfection in a woman's body?

I stood. I was making too much of it. Art strives for the perfection we desire, that's all. Looking at beautiful works of art doesn't mean we reject the real thing.

I walked toward the statue. I put my hands on her shoulders as if I meant to give her a serious piece of advice.

The door opened. I took my hands away and briefly wondered why I'd pushed my luck.

"Are you shitting me?" Sean walked into the room and closed the door.

"It's so beautiful, I just had to see it again. The wood is so polished, so soft, I can't keep my hands off." I smiled with a touch of coyness. "Don't you feel the same?"

"How I feel, is that you have no respect for me."

"That's a bit extreme."

"Is it?"

I walked toward him. "I'm admiring your taste in art, that has to count for something."

He took a few steps back.

I ran my fingers through my hair, lifting it away from my face. "Why do you like to sit in the chair and stare at her?"

"As you said, it's a nice piece of art." He folded his arms. "I'm so disappointed. It looks like I have to start locking my door."

"If you think that's necessary."

He glared at me.

"What do you think about when you're admiring her?"

"You talk as if it's a living being. It's a piece of wood, I don't think of it as a *her*."

"But you like admiring it. The craftsmanship."

"Yes."

I smiled. "You really should move her, *it*, downstairs, so we can all enjoy it."

"You're trying to tell me how to decorate my house?"

"Just a suggestion."

He moved farther away and leaned against the wall. "I already explained my thoughts. I want a professional working environment."

"Is that why you threw me in the pool, to keep a *professional environment?*"

"That's not what I mean."

"I don't understand how art prevents it from being a professional environment."

"As I already told you, I'm sensitive to the concerns of women."

"Is that right?"

"Yes. We're all equals here, women are respected."

"Does beautiful art disrespect women?"

"That's not what I meant. Did you not listen to anything I said? I don't want you and Tess to think Gav and I are imagining you naked, or anything like that." A faint tinge of pink spread across his cheeks. He put his hand on his jaw, rubbing it slightly.

"Don't worry, Tess and I don't compare ourselves to wood carvings. So you don't need to hold onto some deluded belief that it means anything sexual. Unless it does in your mind, and that's always your first thought."

The tip of his nose turned red. He grabbed his hair and held his ponytail inside his fist.

"Besides, whatever is in your heads, we can't do anything about that."

His entire nose was red now. "You're making it sound like something it's not. I respect women."

"Good to know." I smiled and walked toward him. I put my hand on the arm that wasn't clutching his hair as if looking for a safety line. "I guess you want to keep her to yourself. Enjoy your time in your room, looking at her, thinking whatever it is that you think about."

He let go of his hair. He stared at me with a slight look of terror around his eyes. "It's not like that. You've turned this all around into some story you're creating in your head. You're not going to divert me from how I feel about you trespassing?"

"Maybe you're a voyeur," I said. "That's why you accused John of looking at the neighbors — takes one to know one."

"I'm nothing of the kind." He folded his arms. "This is art. John's a freak and he has nothing to do with me. His wife isn't visiting any children in America. She left him and went back to America for good. They don't even have kids. If you're worried about voyeurs, you should be watching yourself around him. You definitely should not be going into his house alone at night."

I moved toward the doorway.

"Don't come in here again. I mean it."

"Got it."

"Do you?"

I nodded. I glanced back at the statue. It was breathtaking, still luring me to touch the polished, silken surface, feeling the curve and weight of the wood.

"I'm sorry I threw you into the pool. I didn't realize you had a phobia."

"It's not a phobia."

"If you say so." He smiled, looking suddenly confident, as if he'd won.

# 64

My state of mind the next morning was not pristine. Instead of running for the pure freedom, I had an agenda that poked at my brain for the entire three-and-four-tenths miles. I still got the surge of energy, the feel-good endorphins charging through my blood. I still experienced the smoothing out of my nerve endings as if they'd been swabbed with melted butter, although I suppose that's not a very appropriate image. Of course, butter doesn't actually touch your nerve endings, but it does have a reputation for adhering to the inside of your blood vessels like cooked on grease to a stovetop. That image made me push myself to a full sprint.

I shoved the thoughts of butter aside, hoping I would see Lisa on her front porch, or sitting in her yard, or whatever new and rather lost position she chose to take up this time.

She had such a lofty view of John, the patron saint of the neighborhood, to hear her tell it. After talking to Sean, John watching out for his neighbors had taken on a different connotation. And was John doing what he'd been accused of, or was Sean simply trying to get me off track and out of his room. But Sean had called him a voyeur right to the man's face.

Thinking back on it, we all took it as a joke. But Sean's voice had that sharp tone that creeps into the words and shifts the atmosphere so you know it's a criticism trying to hide inside of a joke, but not doing a very good job. People can tell when a joke is meant as something else. When the person doesn't quite have the guts to tell the truth, so they fake it with a joke. It doesn't really work.

It's as if they're testing the atmosphere, trying to read the audience. And then, if there are objections, it gets pushed aside — *I was kidding. Can't you take a joke?*

It was plausible he might be using his telescope to look at earthly bodies. He was a very strange man, his only admirable quality in my experience was his adoration and knowledge of the solar system. The things he'd said about the planets — *you want to touch them...so alluring...you can't take your eyes off them* — all of those comments could apply equally to looking at a woman taking off her clothes.

If he was a voyeur, did Lisa realize that? It wasn't possible, not with her flattering, admiring comments about him.

About eight blocks from Sean's street, I saw Lisa up ahead, walking quickly, bent forward slightly, hands shoved in the pockets of her hoodie. It wasn't that cold — sixty-five degrees or so — and there was no breeze, but she looked like she was shivering.

I slowed to steady my breath so I'd be ready to talk without sounding frantic.

I called out to her, hoping not to jolt her. I would have thought she'd heard my shoes pounding the pavement, but she hadn't turned. Maybe she'd disappeared inside her head, completely closed off from her surroundings, lost inside a place that was chilling and so cold it sent tremors through her body.

I called out again, raising my voice.

She stopped and turned. She smiled, un-perturbed, as if she'd known I was there all along.

"Mind if I walk with you?" I said.

"I guess."

"If you'd rather be alone, I can keep running."

"No. It's okay."

Not exactly a red-carpet welcome, but I stayed beside her. "How are things?"

She shrugged.

As I opened my mouth to ask about John, she spoke.

"Awful, actually."

"What's wrong?"

"A lot of things. I'm pregnant. Again." Her jaw trembled. "Barry knows. I must be the most fertile woman on earth. All these women who want babies and can't have them, and me, I keep getting them growing inside me and I can't give them a life."

I stopped and took hold of her shoulder, not unlike the way I'd taken the shoulders of the statue. I turned her to face me. "What's going on?"

"Barry does...he likes..."

"What?"

"He likes sex."

I laughed. "Of course he does. Don't you?"

"A lot. Like five times a day."

"That is a lot." I laughed. It didn't sound too awful, although I suppose it could lose its charm if it became as common as drinking a glass of water.

"I get so worn out. So sore. But he won't let me say no."

"Won't let you? What does that mean?"

"He ties me to our bed."

Again, could be fun, but only if someone is into that.

Tears began trickling down her face. "I shouldn't be

telling you. He'll be so pissed, if he finds out. Furious. I guess...he's been paying attention to when I have my period, and he figured out it's been two months. When he asked, I tried to fake it, but my face didn't cooperate, I guess. He's so excited. But I can't have a child in that house. Not with what he does. Tying me to the bed for hours, sometimes, so I'll be *where he wants me* when he gets home. He thinks it's cute, or sexy. Exciting. He winks when he says it." She wiped her face. She reached into her pocket and pulled out a damp tissue. She blew her nose and stuffed it back in her pocket. She wiped her face again.

She was crying more. "I'm so tired. So, so tired. I write about it in my journal, but it doesn't help. At first it did, but now it almost makes me feel worse."

"Why..."

"And I'm so upset. That he betrayed me!"

"By tracking your period?"

"Not Barry. John."

"What?"

"He knows. And I thought...I thought he cared about his neighbors. And I thought he would do something."

"I'm not following you."

"He watches us. Barry and me. With his telescope. He's seen me tied to the bed, seen us fucking, seen me after. Seen me bleeding, even. After an abortion. And I thought he would...I don't know, it sounds stupid saying it out loud." Her voice rose to a shriek. "I thought he would do something to help! I thought that's why he was watching, but I guess he just likes watching."

A fresh flood of tears filled her eyes and poured down her cheeks, running along her jaw. She looked around, jerking her head in both directions. "I shouldn't be telling you, shouldn't be talking about it."

I pointed to a bench under a trellis in the yard we were approaching. "We could sit there."

"What if Barry sees?"

"Does he drive around looking for you?" I meant it as a joke, but maybe it wasn't really a joke, one of those truths that tries to masquerade as a joke.

"Sometimes."

"The vines cover most of it."

"But the owner."

"It's early. We'll be okay for a few minutes."

We walked to the bench and sat beside each other.

"I know it's dumb. Barry's right, I'm not very smart. But I thought John would tell someone. That someone might help me, that he would help me."

"Why on earth do you stay with him?"

She gestured toward the palatial houses lining the street. "Look at this."

"It's not worth it. So not worth it."

"That's not what I mean. He has money, I don't. I don't have anything, really. My parents are dead. I don't have brothers or sisters or a Nanna. When we got married, Barry said he was my knight in shining armor. He rescued me from a dull life, from high school. It's not like I know how to do anything. Except fuck and cook dinner. I don't even know where I'd go, if I did think about leaving, which I don't. It's my lot in life, I guess. But now…I never thought he'd figure it out." Her eyes filled with another bucket of tears and she looked away from me, trying to hide them as they spilled over and ran down her cheeks that were now swollen, her lips an angry red that was almost the color of the single rose, left from summer, growing a few feet away from us.

"You can't live like that. Surely Australia has shelters, support programs, or people who help…"

"Help with what?" She raised her voice and her skin was suddenly blanched to a sickly white. "Those places are for women who are abused."

"Women like you."

"I'm not abused. He doesn't beat me. I've never had a black eye or a broken nose, or anything like that. He rescued me, I told you that."

"He ties you to the bed and rapes you."

"He's my husband. He can't rape me."

I didn't say anything.

"I thought John was my new knight…"

I still didn't speak. There was nothing to say.

# 65

It wasn't me. I wish it had been, although I can't say why.

Tess came into the kitchen, sobbing. I'd never seen her cry, and that alone stopped me from what I was doing — grating mozzarella and cheddar cheese for a quesadilla. I stared at her face, almost in shock at seeing her eyes filled with tears, her glossy red nose, and her lips contorted into a ragged tear.

She fell against the counter, pressing her palms on it to steady herself. "Oh. Oh my god. We have to...I texted Sean..." She sobbed with a choking sound.

I let go of the grater. "What happened?"

"Sean said he'd go out there and wait. And especially because it made sense since he's the homeowner. And I'm from out of the country."

I moved toward her. "What's going on?"

"I went for a run. Not very long, a little less than two miles. Oh what's wrong with me, why am I talking about bullshit trivia? I was walking the last block home and I saw her."

"Saw who?"

"That woman two doors down. She was...her body. The blood, all that blood!"

I put my hand to my neck. I swallowed, feeling my Adam's apple sliding up behind my fingers, moving down again, like something coming to life in my throat.

"There was so much, you have no idea. Her clothes were

soaked, it was running off the stepping stone, turning the grass this dark color, so dark. Not even red. Black."

I washed my hands and left the cheese standing in a soft pile. I started toward the couch where my phone was sitting. "We need to call the paramedics. How do I do that? What are the numbers?"

"I texted Sean. He already called. They're coming now. Sean said he'd go out there."

The wobbling sound of a siren started, growing louder as the vehicle drew closer to our street, closer to Lisa's house, closer to... "Was she breathing? Did you check?"

Tess shook her head. "No. I think she'd been there awhile, bleeding."

"Did she fall?"

"I don't think so." Her voice was a sudden whisper. "Her pants were soaked with blood. I think..."

Her abortion. I hadn't seen her for days. She must have gone and done it, even though he knew. She must have left the clinic too soon...but they wouldn't allow that...A sick feeling came over me as my mind raced to logical assumptions. She was bleeding, maybe hemorrhaging. He left her alone. Maybe she'd come out looking for help, maybe she was on her way to our house.

I started toward the entryway.

"Where are you going? You can't go out there. They don't want people looking."

"You don't know that." I ran out the front door, leaving it open for Tess to follow.

A white ambulance with bright green and blue swaths of color and a police car were parked haphazardly in front of Lisa's house. As I started toward her yard, another police car arrived. It pulled partially onto the sidewalk, blocking my way. A woman stepped out from the driver's side. She nodded at me and held out her hand to indicate I shouldn't go any closer. I edged around to the back of her car while she walked quickly across the front yard to where two paramedics and two cops surrounded what I assumed was Lisa's body. I couldn't see anything, not even the blood, which I was glad about.

Sean was standing a distance away, leaning against one of the palm trees near the front of the property. He was looking at his phone and didn't seem to notice me.

I waited for a few minutes. I glanced back at Sean's house. Tess stood near the end of the walkway, her arms folded tightly around her waist. She looked thin and small and very unlike herself.

For once, John wasn't looking out his window, bursting through the front door, eager for a chat or a run. His so-called *watching out* for the neighborhood disgusted me. Did he realize Lisa was dead? Did he realize he was responsible for that in a rather significant way? I wondered how many terrible things he'd witnessed through his telescope and never said a word to anyone.

I was glad he wasn't coming out, pretending shock or concern. I was glad I didn't have to see him or speak to him yet. There would be plenty of time for him later. His fate, which had rested quietly in my mind for several days, was taking shape.

We stood in our isolated positions for nearly an hour. Sean by the tree, me watching from behind the police car, and Tess, huddled into herself. The police moved around, in and out of the house, talking in voices pitched to prevent us from overhearing. They didn't actually push me away, but they made sure to always be in the right place to block me if I took even a few steps around the car.

Across the street, a few other neighbors had come outside. They talked among themselves but none of them crossed over to ask what was happening. It felt like a scene from a silent movie, lots of activity but so much silence. Even the birds were keeping their thoughts to themselves.

After a while, the group of people separated and I saw a gurney with Lisa's body enclosed inside a heavy black bag. Two paramedics pushed the gurney forward. It bumped across the lawn, the wheels and bed and cargo jittering in a horrible manner. They put her inside a white van and closed the door.

It seemed as if there was nothing else to see, but leaving was like turning my back on Lisa, not staying to witness the efforts of police to find out what happened. The non-stop trips in and out of the house continued. Now, they were all inside the house.

A paramedic came out of the house, walking backwards. He lifted a gurney with a similar black bag over the threshold and onto the porch. Another paramedic stood at the foot of it. They carried it down the stairs.

When I looked back at Tess, she'd disappeared.

I looked at the spot where Sean had been standing, he was also gone. I hadn't seen him walk past me, but maybe I'd lost touch with my surroundings for several minutes, or longer. I continued waiting until the van and the paramedic truck started up, pulled away from the curb, and crept toward the end of the street. The cops remained inside the house.

I walked slowly back toward Sean's, trying to imagine

what had happened to Barry, the likely candidate in the second black bag. My guess was that he'd killed himself. But why did he have to take her with him? Why do people who don't want to live insist on taking other people with them? I suppose they want to punish the person, or people, who they blame for making their lives miserable. It's so selfish, the ultimate act of blaming someone else for what went wrong, for all the misery in your own world. Most of the time, that world is the one inside your own head. A world half-created by that unhappy person.

Lisa was sadly naive. She didn't seem to have much of a place in the world. Rather, she didn't think she deserved a place. How she came to believe the things Barry did to her were his right, and the only thing in her own power was the ability to make sure no children came into that house, was beyond me.

And the entire time, John stood behind his telescope and watched her raped and degraded and bleeding. He turned it into his private entertainment. I couldn't help Lisa, but I certainly could make sure he didn't get to spend another moment gazing at whatever luscious sights stirred his fancy.

I can't bear the sight of blood flowing out of the human body, but even so, I do wish I'd been the one to find her. I'm not sure why.

# 66

Tess and Alex were sitting on the living room couch, turned slightly, looking out at the backyard. A wine bottle sat open on the table in front of them. Two glasses were beside it, both partially filled, looking as if they hadn't been drunk from.

Sean stepped into the room. Neither one of the women turned. They were either too lost in their own thoughts, or his footsteps had been softer than he realized. He was hesitant to get their attention, knowing what would come next.

It was a horror story — Lisa and Barry. He felt cold as their names ran through his mind. He wasn't up to talking about it, but the minute Tess and Alex realized he was here, they would fire questions at him.

He'd chosen this neighborhood because of its tranquility, the quiet friendliness of everyone who lived here. Solid, genuine people. No one he'd met was arrogant or rude or entitled as a result of their money. They were just nice people. Solid, that was definitely the right word.

Lisa and Barry had seemed the same. They kept to themselves, but they were pleasant when you passed by their house as they were getting out of their SUV. How could so much animosity, hatred really, something sick and perverted, been festering fifty meters away from where he lived and he'd had no clue? They always waved when they saw him. He'd spoken to Barry a few times about lawn care and the inadequate pickup schedule for the yard waste bins. Once, he'd asked Barry if he liked his SUV. Barry had said he wouldn't purchase that model again, in fact he was thinking of replacing it soon. And now he'd hung himself?

How did a guy go from wanting a less repair-prone SUV to deciding he didn't want to live? Sean couldn't imagine ever being in that position. And that guy had it all — money, a satisfying career in finance, or so he'd said, and a beautiful wife. They were planning to have children, or so he'd said. Apparently, only Barry had been planning on that.

He shivered. What Barry had done sickened him at the deepest level. He felt ill every time the imagined scenes passed through his mind.

Tess leaned forward and picked up her wineglass. She didn't turn far enough to see him standing there. He should tell them. He needed to tell them. They had a right to know. But it seemed salacious, talking about such intimate things, pieced together from a journal Lisa kept hidden between the mattress and boxspring. Additional information had been provided in a blame-filled, five-page letter from Barry.

He walked into the living room and took one of the armchairs facing the couch.

Tess and Alex resembled a work of art. They sat about two feet apart from each other on the cream colored leather couch. Both wore black leggings and shoes that looked like something a ballet dancer would wear.

Tess's shirt was a crisp white button down, the tails out. The white made her hair even darker, and her skin's pallor did the same. Usually she wore a lot of makeup, but right now, she had nothing on her face or coloring her eyes. Alex's top was a black sweater with a V-neck. She wore a single pearl on a chain that hung in the center of the V. Her streaked brown and blonde hair was tucked behind her ears. Her skin was also free of makeup.

Both pairs of eyes gazed at him, both hiding so many things. He would give his next three meals to know what they were thinking as they looked at him, waiting.

"The guy I told you about, my mate from high school whose brother is a cop, gave me a few details. If you want to hear them."

As they studied him with those naked eyes, more alluring for their natural state, he told them what he'd learned.

The marriage between Barry and Lisa resembled a prison. Barry had an over-active sex drive and essentially treated Lisa like his sex slave. Her journal told stories of being tied to the bed naked or wearing lingerie, sometimes for an entire day. He raped her countless times, although she never used that word. She described lying on the covers naked, unable to pull a blanket over her body, her hands and feet bound. After work, he gleefully climbed on top of her cold, exhausted, hungry body.

According to what she'd written, he never believed she didn't enjoy it. He thought it was all a thrilling game. He viewed it as the kind of seduction women craved. He was sure her objections were typical for women — never sure of or able to express their desires, ashamed of admitting they liked being taken by force, yielding to a man's strength.

She'd written a lot about her daydreams of being rescued. As if she waited for some kind of prince charming. The police seemed to think it was a fantasy she'd begun to develop to cope with what was going on in her life. Nearly every day for the past three weeks she'd written nothing but — *I know he's coming for me. Soon.*

There was one entry among those repeated lines that mentioned a pregnancy and her plans for another abortion.

"The preliminary report from the coroner suggests Barry punched her in the stomach. She'd gone for the abortion and was bleeding…uhm, she was bleeding quite a lot. And he punched her multiple times. She collapsed in the front yard and he left her there. He went inside, scribbled his letter, tied the rope to a beam, and hung himself while she bled out. So on some level, he did know what he truly was."

Sean's face grew warm. It was awkward telling this to women, made more difficult because they were women who worked for him. It was so sordid, something they would never talk about if it hadn't happened right next door. There was an overwhelming desire pressing against his ribs from the inside, a desire to tell them he wasn't like that! Men weren't like that.

But they didn't need his reassurance. They would likely be offended if he made it about them. It took all his energy to keep his comments focused on what had happened, to not editorialize and comfort and explain. But explain what? That some men are freaks. Predators. He felt unbearably guilty for having used that term for Alex. No wonder Tess objected. It was too strong, it made Alex's aggressive personality into something sinister. He never should have said that.

It was uncomfortable being a man, having to talk about this, knowing he couldn't defend it or…of course he couldn't defend it. He shouldn't even be thinking in those terms. There was no defense. There was no explanation. A monster. That was the only explanation. Somehow, when things like this happened, aberrations of the human race, those aberrations were predominantly male, and it fell on all men to apologize, to make it better. Which was impossible.

He was tired of thinking about it.

"It's shocking, horrifying," Tess said. "So unbelievably sad."

He nodded.

Alex picked up her glass and sipped her wine. She said nothing.

What was happening inside her head? Was she too upset and angry to talk about it? Her face gave away nothing.

# 67

Tess and I didn't speak after Sean finished talking about the degradation Lisa had endured, most of which I already knew. He seemed pleased to be the one telling the story. He was slightly reluctant to mention the details and at the same time, eager to make sure we understood his revulsion toward Barry. I think he was a little disappointed that we didn't talk much, give our reactions to what she'd lived with, ask questions. But what was there to ask? Any questions we had were speculation, not a search for additional facts. They were questions no one could answer, certainly not Sean.

*Why on earth did she stay with him?*

*How did a woman come to believe that a man has total ownership of his wife's body and soul?*

*Why didn't she tell anyone? Was she that friendless?*

I only had two questions that mattered now. What kind of subterranean beast was John North? And how would I stomach charming and seducing that beast?

The next day, I went for my run just as the sun was coming up, counting on his vigilant presence.

Before I'd gone half a block, he was running beside me, seeming to appear out of nowhere. He tapped my arm and I pulled the bud out of my left ear.

He laughed. "I didn't yank them out this time."

"Good for you." I turned slightly and gave him a half smile.

"I'm guessing you'd like company. After what happened," he said.

"That's quite a guess."

His feet were heavier on the pavement than mine, but he moved with a good rhythm. At least he wasn't slowing me down.

"So sad. And so upsetting, what happened," he said.

I slowed my pace since as he began to sound as though he was breathing harder than necessary. "I can't believe it," I said.

"Such a beautiful woman. It was hard to take your eyes off her."

My stomach lurched. I took a few deep breaths before answering. "Beautiful or not, it's terrible to hear about a woman tormented like she was."

"True," he said.

"I'm sick about it."

"You were close to her?"

"No, but knowing what she went through…"

"I suppose it would be hard for a woman to hear that, worrying it could happen to you."

"It would never happen to me. Not in a hundred million years."

"I can see that. And I can…don't take this the wrong way…but I can see why a man might want to make sure a woman like Lisa was…that she stayed close to home."

I wanted to vomit. I needed to take care of him quickly before I suddenly lost my distaste for blood and stabbed him to death right on the street in the middle of a sunny morning. "Let's not talk about it."

"That's all anyone around here is talking about," he said.

"What are they saying?"

"It's a tragedy. So sad that no one knew what she was suffering. How beautiful she was."

"Really? That's what people focus on? Her appearance?"

"Well maybe most of them don't, but I can't help thinking about it."

We ran for two blocks without talking. Finally, he said, "There's so much unappreciated beauty around us."

"Like the planet?"

"Yes. I'm glad you feel the same way. You look and you see the perfect curves and the shimmer of light, and it's absolutely breathtaking."

"I'd like to look at them again."

"Would you? I'd be honored."

I truly did want to stab him.

"And it's okay if you smoke in my house. I don't mind."

For the past mile, my body had been warming nicely. Now, a chill shot through me, from my scalp to my toes in half a step. "What makes you think I smoke?"

He hesitated for several long minutes, realizing his mistake. "I smelled it once, coming from their yard. After you moved in. And I know the guys living there aren't smokers, except for weed."

"I see."

He coughed. "Anyway, it's not a problem."

"I'll bring some wine."

"That sounds terrific. And your roommates?"

"Oh, I think that was too much, the last time." I softened my voice. "I didn't like sharing. I think it's better with just you and me."

"If you want."

Despite his overbearing push to run with me, his invitations into his house, and the leering that burned just below the surface of his skin, I wasn't sure he was all that interested in me. If he wasn't, it would be tricky. Perhaps the looking was all he wanted. Maybe he didn't care at all about being with a flesh and blood woman with all her quirks and opinions and flaws. Maybe he was fully satisfied by lust from a distance.

At the one and a quarter mile point, I turned back. He didn't object. In front of his house, we said goodbye.

During my shower, I worked out the final details of what I had mentally prepared for him. I'd decided that going shopping for my usual supplies would attract too much attention from my housemates. There would be questions about where I was going, why Tess couldn't come with me. The simple break in routine might rouse their curiosity. I also didn't have a secure source for roofies, so I'd be all on my own. All I had was my ability to seduce, some scarves and belts, a few bottles of wine, and a plastic garbage bag. It was enough. It had to be enough.

The other challenge would be leaving the house and returning without being seen. Once John's body was discovered, which might take a day or two, possibly more, my roommates would obviously remember me going over there.

Dealing with them and their curiosity would start before dinner.

At four, I went to the door of the office shared by Gavin and Sean. "I'm sure you've noticed, I'm a huge fan of martinis." I studied their expectant faces. "I've been told my martinis are the best. I thought we'd quit early and I'll make some for all of us."

They stared at me. I wasn't sure whether the blank looks were due to my sudden friendliness, or because they hated martinis.

"Vodka," I said. "They're not as harsh as gin martinis."

They nodded.

"I saw some steaks in the fridge, so I'm going to fire up the *barbie.*" I leaned on the word *barbie* so I didn't sound too ridiculous adopting their slang. "I'll make Caesar salad. Sound good?"

Now they looked as though their eyeballs were going to fall out of their heads. I smiled like a college girl at her first party.

They smiled and nodded.

I delivered the same message to Tess. She grinned like a proud mother, happy that her duckling was following instructions and joining in with the rest of the group… joining their reindeer games, not to go overboard mixing up comparisons to the animal kingdom.

I ran up the stairs and brushed my hair. I put on an extraordinary amount of dark eye makeup, ready for my visit to John's. I'd already dressed in black satin lingerie before putting on jeans and a camisole, covered by jeans and a blousy button-down shirt. I pulled a large leather bag out of the closet. I tucked a trash can liner, four scarves, and two belts inside. I had more supplies than necessary, but it was possible John was stronger than he looked. I needed to be prepared.

On top of the other things, I placed two bottles of wine I'd taken from Sean's supply. I tucked in a joint I'd bummed off Gavin earlier that day. I told him I was edgy and needed a night alone on the balcony, letting my head unwind from all my social media activity.

They downed their pre-dinner martinis while I took tiny sips from mine. They remarked on how good they were but couldn't say whether they were the best. I made a second batch while the steaks grilled. I opened three bottles of wine for dinner, hoping the alcohol would be enough to make them sleepy, especially after a long day working. The plan had its weaknesses, but I was optimistic. The guys were used to beer, and Tess stuck mostly to wine, so the martinis should have them well on their way.

I thought about a third batch of martinis, but that would be pushing my luck, and they might not drink them or the wine. Better to lead them slowly through all the wine.

Dinner was delicious, they all said so. I entertained them with overly long, minutely detailed stories from my childhood, steadily refilling their glasses. When I suggested a movie, they all nodded sluggishly.

I cleaned up the kitchen and made hot cocoa. That would surely push them over the edge into sleep.

# 68

John was standing in the open doorway when I turned onto his walkway. He stepped away from the opening and I walked inside. The house was as blindingly white as I remembered. I smiled, trying not to squint. "I'm really looking forward to this." I pulled the wine out of my bag and handed the bottles to him.

While both of his hands were full, I turned my shoulder toward him and closed the zipper on the bag. I followed him to the kitchen where he opened the first bottle. We toasted the heavenly bodies and took generous sips of our wine. I took a second, very small sip, hoping he'd follow my lead. He did.

We went upstairs to the boxed-in patio where the telescope stood ready, pointing into the darkness.

"It's cold," I said.

"I'll get a heat lamp."

He went into the house and returned with a portable heat lamp. He turned on the gas and it hissed to life.

"It's still a little cold. You can't get a good view through a window?"

"It takes a minute. Be patient." He smiled and took a sip of wine before putting his glass on the table. "It's better out here."

"I guess."

He adjusted the scope and gestured to the chair. I put my wineglass beside his and sat down.

"I can't get enough of this," I said.

"I'm pleased you share my enthusiasm."

"It's so beautiful."

"Yes, breathtaking. Such perfect spheres and seductive colors."

For several minutes I stared through the lens, enjoying the mystery of the rings surrounding Saturn. John began explaining the alphabetical naming of the rings. I had no idea there were so many or that they'd been named as they were discovered. There was so much information about their size and shape and relationship to each other, I'd never remember it all, but I liked hearing about the complexity.

He talked about the history of their discovery. After a few minutes, I wanted him to stop. I wanted to enjoy the magic of it without the sound of his voice. The formation of something that no one truly understood took my breath away — the perfect symmetry, the way dust and rock and ice particles could form rings that were smooth and symmetrical when viewed from a great distance.

This would be my last time looking through his telescope. It wasn't that I'd never have a chance to look through a telescope again, but not for the foreseeable future. Still, I could look forward to hundreds of nights sitting on my balcony, smoking a cigarette, looking at the sparkling canopy over me and remembering how it had looked up close, relatively speaking.

For now, I needed to put all the romantic desire out of my head and focus on getting John into a numbed state. I needed to see if I could attract his attention at all.

I was starting to wonder if I hadn't planned carefully enough. I'd been too impatient. I should have taken time to locate a roofie supply.

When I'd first met him, I was sure he was hitting on me. His effort to insert himself into my running routine, grabbing at me, some of his comments, suggested a man who wanted to make you his. But once I told him I was interested in his hobby, he'd changed. Quite suddenly.

I moved away from the telescope. "Do you want to look?"

I thought he'd say no. After all, he had every clear night of the year to gaze up at the sky. But he moved toward me and when I stood, he took the seat.

He looked in silence for a few minutes, then murmured softly.

"What did you say?"

"So lovely."

"Yes."

He sighed. "You want to reach out and touch them, but of course, that's impossible."

I looked at our wineglasses. I wanted a sip of mine, but I had to restrain myself. "Do you want some wine?"

He didn't answer, his brow bone glued to the telescope.

I took a few steps toward him. "You know what would be cool?"

"Hmm?" He didn't look up or sound all that interested.

"I brought a joint. Want to smoke it with me?"

He still didn't respond. This was going to be a lot more difficult than I'd realized. I longed for the ease of a roofie. Slipped into even the smallest amount of wine, it did its job and I didn't have to work so hard to push someone in the right direction. Not to mention the fact that he hadn't even brushed his hand past mine or touched my shoulder when I sat in front of the telescope. He was completely disinterested.

I stood watching him watch, trying to think. I didn't want to be there all night, standing around in the increasing cold while he stared silently at the sky, or went into another college-level lecture.

I walked over to where he was seated and put my hand on his shoulder. He stiffened slightly but didn't pull back from the lens. "What do you like, besides the stars?" I said.

"Isn't that enough?"

"Not for most people."

"I enjoy looking at beautiful things."

"Like your house? It's gorgeous."

"Yes." He still hadn't moved.

"Why is your house all white?"

"I like things to be clean. Pure."

"The furniture…"

"It needs replacing. My wife chose it. She has no imagination. None."

"You'll replace it with all white? That would be amazing."

"You and I are kindred spirits," he said, still keeping his eye close to the lens. His voice had a dreamy, slow quality, addressing someone else, someone far away.

"Why is that?"

"We like beautiful things. Pure things."

He was accurate in his assessment and I wasn't sure how he'd seen that much about me. It was a little unsettling. I returned my thoughts to mental images of Lisa, tortured in her own bedroom while John watched. Without even trying, my voice grew hard and icy cold on its own. "I do love looking at the stars. It's very trippy, and I want to get high because that would really be amazing. I'll go get the joint." I turned toward the door.

"If you want," he said.

"We're alike, as you said. Trust me on this."

I went downstairs and got my bag. I carried it up and put it on the couch in the lounge. John didn't appear to have moved while I was gone. I slipped out of the lounge and hurried down the hall to the master bedroom to refresh my memory of the furniture and layout. His headboard consisted of two posts with a curved panel between, which would allow me to secure the scarves. I returned to the lounge and got out the joint and a lighter.

John was still staring through the telescope. He'd moved it slightly, studying a different part of the sky. I suppose he'd grown bored with Saturn and needed something fresh. The same way he needed a break from watching Lisa's torment and turned his telescope in the direction of my balcony. It was possible he knew I smoked because he'd smelled it coming from Sean's backyard the one night I'd gone out there, but I didn't think so. There was the flicker of his eyelids when I asked how he knew, the long pause, the cough at the end.

I stood behind him again and massaged his neck gently.

He moved away from the telescope but didn't turn to look at me.

After a few minutes of kneading the muscles in his neck, I let go and fired up the lighter. I held the flame to the tip of the joint and took some smoke into my mouth without inhaling it. I let it out a moment later, coughing slightly to give the impression it had traveled into my lungs, pinching them until they contracted.

"Ever tried pot?" I said.

He stood. "A few times."

I grinned. "Good. The way you reacted when I suggested it, I was worried you're too old for this sort of thing."

"I'm not too old." He smirked, then held out his hand and took the joint.

We leaned against the railing and smoked, handing the joint back and forth. When it was my turn, I touched it to my lips and mimed taking a hit, not allowing it to burn down much, ensuring that most of it went into his lungs.

The conversation drifted lazily, as pot conversations do, skimming over trivia and nonsense, abruptly changing direction from being an American in Australia to the planets, from black holes to his plans to replace all the art in his house — also chosen by his *unimaginative* wife. He never mentioned she was his former wife, carrying on the charade that she was only in the States for a few months, fluttering around with her non-existent girls.

He looked nicely looped when the joint was gone.

"I'll go get some more wine. I'm thirsty," I said.

He nodded slowly.

"And hungry. Do you have any chips?"

"In the cupboard."

He said this as if I would know exactly which cupboard, but they wouldn't be too hard to find, just a matter of opening doors.

When I returned, he was leaning on the railing, slumped over, his head tipped forward, suggesting he'd nodded off on his feet. I opened the new bottle, ate some chips, and refilled his glass. "Should we go inside?"

He didn't answer.

"John?"

"Hmm? I feel a little…"

"Let's go inside." I took his wrist and tugged it gently. I went inside and put the wine on the table in front of the couch. A candle sat near one corner in a ceramic dish. I pulled out my lighter and touched the flame to the fresh, waxy wick.

A moment later, he joined me on the couch.

He drank wine and I kept his glass constantly topped off while I talked about my previous job. I used the dullest voice I could muster, hoping to make him drowsier still. His eyes were half closed, but he seemed to be following me fairly well.

I leaned against him and put my hand on his thigh.

He moved to the left. "What are you doing?"

"Warming you up."

"For what?"

I sighed. "Whatever you need warming for."

"I'm not really…" He took a sip of wine.

"Are you worried about your wife?"

"No. I just…"

What was wrong with him? I had to get him into some sort of weakened state and I wasn't sure he was there yet. If he didn't want to have sex, it would be much more difficult leading him to the point where I could tie his wrists and ankles. "You're not into women?"

"I am."

"Okay. Not your wife, not that you prefer men. So what…I don't get it."

He sighed. "Can't we just enjoy the wine and the stars and leave it at that?"

"I'm curious. And now, I feel kind of insulted." I pouted

with a tiny smile.

"It's not you."

"You don't think I'm good looking?"

"Oh, yes. You are." He took a gulp of wine. "You're beautiful."

"You seemed very flirty with me, the first few times we met."

"Did I?"

"Grabbing me like you did."

"I never grabbed you."

"My earphones."

He laughed softly. "Oh, that. I apologized."

"Yes, but still…"

"In fact, that reminded me of how you are," he said.

"How am I?"

"Women."

"How is that?"

He took another swallow of wine and picked up a handful of potato chips. He stuffed them into his mouth. "I forgot how this stuff makes you hungry."

"How are women?"

"Spectacular. From a distance."

"You like to look but that's all?"

"Pretty much. I like things clean. Pure." He slurred the last word and went on, "Women up close are filthy and flawed, just like the planets, the entire solar system. Women are difficult and selfish and, for the most part, silly."

I swallowed my bile and put down my wineglass. "Why don't we go into your room. I could strip for you. I bet you'd like that. From a distance."

He put his glass on the table and looked at me, his eyes

glazed and hungry. His lips parted but it was several seconds before he spoke. "Okay." He licked his lips.

After that, things moved quickly. I wanted to be done with him, back home in my bed where I could get a good night's sleep. I didn't want to think about how a longing so pure and magnificent as admiration and awe for the universe, and such perverted views of women, and such cruel neglect of human decency could exist inside the same brain.

I took my bag into the bedroom and shoved it beside the bed while he settled on top of the comforter, stacking up the pillows behind him. I pulled up Bailando on my phone and began dancing. I unbuttoned my blouse easing each tiny disk out of its slot with tender care, dancing for a while in my camisole and bra. I unbuttoned my jeans and slowly lowered the zipper. I moved toward the bed and reached for my bag. I pulled out three scarves and held them up. "It's more exciting if you *can't* touch."

He shrugged.

I tied his wrists with one scarf and looped the other through the tie and around the bedpost.

I danced a bit more, awkwardly sliding out of my jeans. I'd only done this a few times before and wasn't all that good at it. Especially wearing skinny jeans. It's impossible to look seductive peeling those off your legs.

He was enjoying it, but battling sleep. He wasn't quite as young as he thought he was. A bottle of wine and most of a joint were too much for him. Finally. I wrapped a thick belt around his ankles several times and buckled it. He protested, but not with a lot of effort.

I sat on his thighs, digging my knees into the bed. I leaned over and pulled out the trash bag, put it over his head and tied it in place. I secured the last scarf around the bag to be sure it was as snug as possible, but not tight enough to leave a mark.

He fought me, but there wasn't anywhere for him to go, as he twisted and thrashed from side to side. The fighting made him breathe harder. It wasn't long before he lost consciousness.

When he was dead, I did my usual cleaning — wiping down tables and chairs, vacuuming to make sure there were no skin cells and hairs, and washing the wineglasses and chip bowl. I polished the telescope and removed the scarves and belt from his wrists. I pulled off the plastic bag and moved him slightly, pulling the blankets up over the lower half of his body.

Given that he seemed to be quite the loner, it was possible his body wouldn't be discovered for days, maybe even weeks. It was going to be tense, waiting for all of that to unfold, but I wasn't worried. It was actually a little more worrisome that Tess couldn't stop thinking about the unlikely circumstances around Steve's death. His death pointed to me a lot more clearly than John's.

Making my way quietly back to Sean's house took forever. It was two-forty in the morning when I finally closed my bedroom door. I took off my clothes and climbed into bed. I was asleep before I could take more than two or three breaths.

# 69

Sean stood on the track where the paneled doors opened to join the great room and patio. It would be a glorious sun-washed day. The sky was filling with light, but there was a persistent darkness in the corners of his eyes, seeping throughout his body and brain.

The bad karma of a suicide and two murders in the houses beside his was terrifying. He hadn't slept well for the past week, the image of Lisa's blood-soaked body waking him every few hours. Of course it wasn't actually karma. That was the result of your own actions. Nothing he'd done had caused those awful deaths. Energy…that was it. There was bad energy flooding their street, finding its way among the lovely palms and gum trees, hovering there, waiting to strike again. How had this happened? It was an excellent neighborhood. No one wanted for any of the necessities or even the luxuries of life. They should have been happy, their lives filled with affirming relationships and satisfying work.

Now, he feared that darkness taking over his own house. He loved this house, wanted to share its beauty with the people who worked with him. He wanted this venture infused with good karma, good energy. He wanted a team that supported and respected each other. The creative spirit would decay if they remained closed off to possibility, if they refused to brainstorm and play and revel in the good things of life.

The human race wasn't meant to have their lives

compartmentalized. Work and play, love and spirituality, sex and friendship should be integrated. The creatures in the ocean didn't have these boxes — *my* office, *my* car, *my* house. Under water, they swam and ate and reproduced in an all-encompassing environment. Of course, he didn't expect sex to actually enter the workplace, so his theory was flawed in that way, but the rest…It mattered to him. He wanted a different kind of company.

Life on the planet needed to evolve or the human race would self destruct, taking the animal kingdom with it.

His three colleagues faced him, all of them sitting on one side of the long patio table. They looked like convicts before a firing squad. He closed his eyes. Where had that image come from?

He opened his eyes and smiled. "So. I thought, with everything that's happened, we need to regroup."

They stared at him. Their expressions were unformed, telling him nothing.

"I'll just plunge in here." He turned and took a few steps toward the barbecue, doing it to avoid their stares, if he was honest. "You all know my vision for this company, and for our work environment. I've made my home yours. It belongs to all of you and I want you to enjoy it to its fullest. We have an opportunity to be a prototype for other small companies, to introduce a new way of working and living to the world. Well, not really new. It's the old way. It's how ancient people lived — work shouldn't be a separate thing. A job. We're designed to enjoy work, we need work, and it should be pleasurable." He turned to face them. None of their expressions had changed.

Fine. He would deliver his piece and they could either

adopt it or find some other venture to pursue. He took a deep breath. He wasn't going to make them prisoners. This wasn't the right energy. He needed to stay centered and calm.

"I know it's taken some getting used to, but I think we've worked out some of the kinks. Of course these horrific deaths have been a setback, but we don't need to dwell on that. We can't hold grudges for past mistakes. We need to move forward with a fresh attitude."

A smile flitted across Alexandra's face. Good, he was having an effect after all. Funny that she was the first to give a hint of her reaction.

"We're going to cook as a team and eat dinner together every night. We're going to get out of here once in a while, beautiful as it is. Go hiking. To the beach. To museums. We're going to invite others in to join us from time to time, for lectures and dinner parties. My point is, we need a re-set. We've all had a terrible shock from the things that have happened. And I think we needed some time to get to know each other a bit, to understand boundaries. But we're past all that. As of today, we'll move forward behaving with integrity, treating each other with respect…" His gaze darted toward Alex. Her smile was gone, but her expression was still pleasant. He let out a deep breath. "We're going to forget the past. It's a new day. That's why I called this meeting for daybreak." He grinned.

"We can't let these horrors get us down. We can't fixate on John's murder. It was most likely someone he knew. That's what the police are saying, as you know. It means we don't need to have unnecessary fears on that front. But we can't get sucked into that. We need to let the police carry on with their business, and we need to focus on our mission and building this team into something kick-ass! Am I right?"

He didn't feel the enthusiasm in his words. On one level he did, but it was as if he was speaking to himself as much as to them. His tone sounded forced. Hopefully they didn't hear the tremor, deep in his throat. Hopefully they didn't see him blinking too frequently, trying to clear the darkness from the corners of his vision.

# 70

It was raining again, but no thunder and lightning this time. The water came down in sheets. In California, a storm like this would only happen during an El Niño — when the warming surface of the ocean near the equator brought an extra gush of water pouring down from the clouds. Here, torrential rain was the norm. The cascading water added to Tess's growing claustrophobia. Despite the enormous house — nearly ten thousand square feet — her world had shrunk to the office and bedroom, spacious as they were, with occasional forays into the great room or out to the patio.

Although the patio was designed to remain dry even during heavy rain, it was too cold, at least for her taste. Sean and Gavin continued using the pool even in the chilling rain. The pool water was heated to a lovely twenty-four degrees Celsius, which was about seventy-five Fahrenheit, but the idea of swimming seemed like pure misery to her. And with thunderstorms a regular threat, it seemed rather unsafe. They were unfazed by that as well.

After thinking over the messages in Sean's little speech, she'd decided to approach him again. They needed to get out of this house, not just as a group, but away from each other. It was too much and he needed to acknowledge that boundaries were required or they'd end up killing each other. She shivered, remembering Lisa's body and the thick, pooling blood. That's what came of restraining another human being. She went into her closet and picked out a long cashmere cardigan. She put it on and felt instant comfort and warmth. She shoved her feet into her Ugg boots and went downstairs.

Gavin and Sean were, of course, swimming. She shivered and pulled the sweater more tightly around her. She went back upstairs and knocked on Alex's door.

Alex opened the door about four or five inches.

"How about a glass of wine?" Tess said. "I'm hoping it will warm me up. I could make baked brie."

"Oh, yum. I'll be right there." Alex closed the door quickly, as if someone else was in the room and she was trying to hide that fact.

Tess went downstairs. She turned on the oven and unwrapped the brie. She took out the thin pastry she'd bought a few days earlier and peeled off a sheet, folding it over the cheese. When the cheese was completely covered she put it on a cookie sheet and slid it into the oven. She opened a bottle of Zinfandel.

They settled on the couch and each scooped a cracker through the warm pastry and oozing cheese before they made a toast.

"To a fresh start," Alex said.

"Let's hope so." Tess touched her glass against Alex's and took a sip.

"You know, you never really gave me a straight answer," Tess said. "Or maybe I never actually asked."

"What's that?" Alex took another sip of wine.

Tess looked at Alex's eyes, steady and clear, not at all concerned with what might be coming. "Did you and Steve ever sleep together? It sounded like you were headed in that direction. Then, he turned up dead."

"Are you really back on that?"

"I'm not talking about the unbelievable circumstances of his death, I'm asking if you and I had the same guy."

Alex smirked and lifted her eyebrows slightly. "Who knows?"

"What does that mean?"

"I don't know the details of your sex life. And you don't know mine. You're my boss, remember?"

"But I also consider us friends." Where was her resolve to be more aloof, to make sure there were boundaries between her and Alex? She let out a small puff of air, hoping Alex didn't make too much of it.

"Do you? That's a little unbalanced. Have you ever thought about that? You get to decide we're friends, but I have no choice because I have to make sure I'm keeping my boss happy."

Tess winced. She thought the involuntary reaction was inside her body, but it must have flitted across her face because Alex put her hand on Tess's knee.

"We're friends." Alex smiled. "I just wanted to be sure you get that — the imbalance."

Tess shrugged. She took a sip of wine and put down her glass. She took another scoop of cheese and pastry, popping the whole thing in her mouth in one bite. Eating it in several bites would just leave cheese running down her chin. "So did you?"

"No."

"It occurred to me you seem to have a thing for older men. Steve. John. No wonder you were so fascinated by stargazing."

"That's not it. Not at all. I am fascinated by the planets. Truly and honestly fascinated."

Tess nodded. At times, it was hard to tell whether Alex was mocking or lying or being blunt. Sometimes it all sounded the same. "You didn't seem shocked that he was dead."

"I'm rarely shocked. And if I am, I don't think I show it much."

Tess sipped her wine. She'd thought they did have a friendship. She really liked Alex, but she wondered occasionally whether the feeling was mutual. Alex had accepted this job, and after the initial rough spots, she seemed content to be living in the same house, spending most of their waking hours together.

Last night, Tess had crept out of her room at twelve-thirty. She'd gone downstairs and poured a glass of white wine. She'd gone into what was now the de facto male office and retrieved the disk that provided bio feedback functionality for their app. She'd posed the question on which she'd gone back and forth a hundred times in the past few weeks — *Should I let go of trying to disprove the bullshit explanation of Steve's death?*

She'd sipped wine and answered the questions posed by the app.

The answer wasn't really surprising. That was a good thing, in that she was pleased that she knew her own mind. It was not so good in terms of the value of the app, but she'd worry about that later.

Back in bed, the remainder of the post midnight hours had moved at an agonizing pace, each minute seeming to last for ten. The clock stared at her wide-open eyes. It seemed to freeze as she turned the answer around in her mind, trying to find a way through to where she knew she needed to go.

Cathryn Grant

She shifted slightly on the couch, turning to face Alex directly. "I'm flying to San Francisco Thursday."

"Why?"

"I'm going to see about getting Damien shipped here. Sean said he's welcome."

Alex smiled. "Won't he give you trouble, seeing all his bros outside, flying free, calling out to each other? He'll be desperate to escape."

Tess smiled. "He'll be fine. He knows how good he has it."

"Does he?"

Tess nodded.

"Why do you have to fly all that way? Can't Jen or Isaiah take care of it?"

"I want to do it myself. And there are a few other things…"

Alex laughed. "This isn't about Damien. You're going to keep prying into the Steve situation."

"Yes, I'm planning to ask the detective to meet with me. I'll have lunch with Ted."

"Come on, Tess. Let. It. Go."

"No. It's not right."

"You don't owe him anything."

"I'm fully aware of that. But I need to do this."

Alex took several sips of wine. "Is it really going to be any different in person?"

"I don't know. But Steve was a big believer in the value of face-to-face, so this makes sense."

"What if it gets you nowhere? And you've wasted a week of your life, not to mention thousands of dollars?"

"It's not a waste. Besides, I'll get to see Damien, and

make sure he's prepared for the trip. I'll have the vet check him out and all of that."

Alex raised her glass and tapped it against Tess's. "Well, good luck to you. And I'm looking forward to seeing that crazy bird again." She smiled.

Tess felt the smile wasn't quite genuine.

# 71

John's body had been discovered five days after I killed him.

His housekeeper found him on his bed, just as Steve's housekeeper had found his body. Unlike Steve, John was clothed and said to have died from suffocation. It made me think about these poor women, mostly women, finding corpses. For people living alone, or staying alone in a hotel room, it would be a housekeeper who was the first to stumble upon the body. What a sudden change in the day you were anticipating, coming into someone's home expecting to scrub toilets and mop floors and be faced with that.

Sean's pep talk had been two days after that. I tried not to smile as I watched him paint the vision of his utopian start-up company. He had no idea one of the horrors in his peaceful, well-appointed, exclusive neighborhood was caused by someone sitting right in front of him. He didn't know someone within the heart of his company had killed his neighbor.

I smiled when he said we needed to move forward. Now that Lisa's torture had been avenged, I was definitely ready to move forward. I wasn't so sure about Tess, racing into the past by heading back to San Francisco, but I was still confident the detective wouldn't give an inch and she'd be back, finally forced to let go.

That night, after my brie cheese and wine with Tess, after our group dinner and four games of pool, I sent a text message to Gavin, holed up in his room once again. I invited him to visit mine. A few minutes later, he knocked on the door. He led me quickly to the bed and began removing my clothes without speaking, of course. He kissed me as he went, a long kiss after each article of clothing. When he was naked and I was down to a thong and bra, I put my hand on his chest. "Can we talk for a second?"

"Are you kidding?" He kissed my neck. His teeth nipped at my earlobe.

"While I have your attention."

He propped his head on his elbow and looked at me.

"Did you watch the recording of me in your room?"

"That's how I knew."

"Did you watch the whole thing?"

His eyes widened and his pupils seemed to shrink ever so slightly. "Uh, not yet. I saw that you came in. I saw you touching my collectibles and looking at my books."

"I also looked under your bed."

He rolled onto his back and put his hand over his eyes. "And you're disgusted."

"A little, but also curious."

He put both palms to his face, talking in a low, muffled voice. "When I was in high school, on one of our family camping trips, my sister was bitten by a very aggressive, badly-trained German Shepherd."

I swallowed.

"He took half of her index finger right off."

"But why…"

"My mum and dad were trying to stop the blood, getting her settled into the car to take her to urgent care. There was so much blood, they didn't see right away…"

I shivered.

"When they realized it was missing, my dad told me to go back to the area and find it. He said if I ran, if we moved as fast as we could, they might be able to re-attach it."

I imagined the rest before he continued the gruesome story.

"I told them I couldn't find it. The time seemed right for payback."

"So it's like a little souvenir?"

"If you want to call it that. I'm sorry, I can't bring myself to get rid of it. I swiped the jar from my biology lab. It had an eyeball preserved in it. I flushed the eyeball and put the finger in."

I shivered again. I felt slightly ill, but tried to give him a reassuring smile. I'm not the type to take souvenirs. I know a lot of killers do, but they're a different type of killer — the ones doing it for their own perverted pleasure.

And yet…

I reassured him it didn't change my view of him. Once I'd heard about his sister, I figured it was something like that. I sort of understood. Sort of. But even if I didn't, it wasn't as if I had to look at the thing ever again.

We stopped talking. We had sex, twice, and then he left.

Until now, I never have taken a souvenir. But after I removed the plastic bag from John's head and the scarves from his wrists, I walked back into the lounge and stood looking out at his secluded balcony. The telescope gleamed white in the moonlight.

It had been tricky removing it from the tripod, carrying the cumbersome scope down the stairs, across John's backyard, through his side gate, and into Sean's yard. I had to rest at several points to readjust the balance of the load of the scope and the tripod. Once I reached Sean's patio, I left it on the lounge chair while I drank a glass of water, staring at the clock, knowing I needed to hurry. Then it was up the stairs and into my bedroom where I placed it gently on the floor of my closet. I covered it with an extra blanket I pulled off the top shelf.

Now, I retrieved the tripod from the closet. I set it up on the balcony and returned for the telescope itself. Once it was attached to the stand, I removed the lens covers and pointed it toward the sky. It was cloudy, but there was a single star poking through — Acrux — the foot of the Southern Cross.

I moved away from the telescope and went into my room. I grabbed my cigarettes and lighter. I walked to the bedroom door and locked it, as I would have to do from now on.

Then, I went out on the balcony, settled in the chair, lit my cigarette, and returned my attention to the bright solitary star.

# A Note to Readers

Thanks for reading. I hope you liked reading about Alexandra as much as I enjoy writing her stories.

I'm passionate about fiction that explores the shadows of suburban life and the dark corners of the human mind. To me, the human psyche is, as they say in Star Trek — the final frontier — a place we'll never fully understand. I'm fascinated by characters who are damaged, neurotic, and obsessed.

I love to stay in touch with readers. Visit me at my website: CathrynGrant.com

To find out when the next Alexandra Mallory novel is available you can sign up for my new book mailing list here: CathrynGrant.com/contact/

As a thank you for signing up, you'll receive a free Alexandra short story — *Death Valley.*

CPSIA information can be obtained
at www.ICGtesting.com
Printed in the USA
BVHW080907040421
603806BV00012B/531

9 781943 142385